A NOVELLA COLLECTION

LOVE delivered

AMY R. ANGUISH
SARAH ANNE CROUCH
HEATHER GREER
RACHEL HEROD

Scrivenings PRESS
Quench your thirst for story.
www.ScriveningsPress.com

Published by Scrivenings Press LLC
15 Lucky Lane
Morrilton, Arkansas 72110
https://ScriveningsPress.com

Printed in the United States of America

Paperback ISBN 978-1-64917-272-3

eBook ISBN 978-1-64917-273-0

Editors: Elena Hill and Linda Fulkerson

Cover design by Linda Fulkerson - www.bookmarketinggraphics.com

Contents

A Novella

ROMANCE
at register five

Amy R. Anguish

For my Aunt Karan, who is like another mom to me. She's also one of the most creative people I know. And proves each day her strength as she lives with her MS. I'm so glad God blessed me with you!

Chapter 1

The strawberry blonde looked familiar.

Mack McDonald prided himself on knowing who came through his store. After all, what was the point of running a small-town grocery if he couldn't give the best customer service? And how could a person give good service without knowing the customers?

Sassafras, Arkansas, only had about twelve thousand people. And that was on the day of the annual watermelon festival. Most of the year, like now in October, the numbers hovered closer to ten thousand.

The woman paid little attention while Mack rang up her canned goods and snack items. Instead, she bent over her wallet. As he scanned a package of candy, something seemed off about her purchases. What was it?

Mack tried not to pass judgment on what people bought when they came through his register, but it was hard seeing someone in such good shape buying so much junk food. Maybe she was having a bad day.

He finally recalled the last time he'd rung her up. She'd

bought all organic veggies, gluten-free pasta, and vegan meat substitutes. Today's order was the complete opposite.

"Not in the mood for veggies today?" He started a conversation, hoping something would trigger his memory, and he could figure out if he'd heard her name before. The nametag clipped to her shirt did no good, showing only the back.

She laughed. "Oh, these aren't for me."

With a swipe of her card, she was done and pushing her groceries toward the door. So much for getting to know her. He should've said something earlier. More than "Hi. How ya doin'?"

Maybe next time. Surely he wouldn't forget her more than once. Especially if she returned to her health foods.

He wiped down the conveyor belt then straightened the candy and magazines at the end of his aisle. The first hour after opening was one of the busier times, and people often tossed last-minute discards among the periodicals. The most frustrating finds were the ones needing refrigeration. No telling how long they'd been sitting at room temperature.

"Jorge, can you come take care of these for me?" Mack held up an armful of items to be reshelved.

"Sure thing, boss." Jorge maneuvered the products into a cart and pushed it away.

Candie, Mack's assistant manager, came in. "Welcome back, boss. Good vacation?"

"It was okay. Can't complain too much about a few days off, but it's good to be back. You know I can't stand not being busy."

Candie shook her head. "More power to you. I'd love to take a vacation, but I need the money." She leaned against the counter. "Speaking of money, did I keep everything running well enough while you were gone?"

"As if I've had time to go over reports today." Mack laughed and waved her out of the way as another customer arrived. "I'll look over things this afternoon when we have more cashiers on hand."

"Let me know if you have any questions."

She sauntered off as he rang up Moses Perry's weekly supply of fruits and yogurt—ingredients for his daily smoothie. Candie's mannerisms had been fishy, but he didn't have time to think about it now. Moses liked to talk.

Moses frowned. "Couldn't find any strawberries worth buying today. All of them were bruised or moldy."

"October isn't a good month for strawberries, Mr. Moses. I do the best I can to get good ones, but you're going to have to wait until May and June before you start seeing good berries again. We have some frozen back there."

"Frozen aren't the right texture." The older man's hands trembled as he pulled out several twenties. "Can't stand when the texture is off."

"All right. I'm sorry we didn't have any berries worth buying today. I'll have Candie weed out the bad ones, okay?" Mack made change and handed Moses his receipt. "Need me to bring you a pint later?"

Moses waved him off. "I've survived worse times than a week without strawberries."

"You have a good week, Mr. Moses."

The older man shuffled out the door. He was in the store like clockwork each Wednesday, wanting to get the freshest items after the store clerks unloaded their mid-week truck the night before. And he was a good example of how well Mack usually remembered his customers. So, why couldn't he place the blonde from earlier? Was she new in town?

And why was he more intrigued with her than his other customers?

Grocery shopping for other people wasn't Kaitlyn Daniels's dream job. But it made ends meet while she waited for a full-time teaching position. That was one downside to moving during the school year. Nothing but substitute hours available. She snagged all those, too, if only to get a foot in the door for next year.

Why her mother chose the small town of Sassafras, Arkansas, Kaitlyn had no idea. Far as she could tell, it wasn't near anything but fields. It was about an hour north of Little Rock, where she grew up. Kaitlyn had settled near Fayetteville after college, while her mother downsized and relocated here. Mom claimed Sassafras had charm.

Maybe she was thinking of the quaint family-run grocery store, McDonald's. Not to be confused with the famous burger chain. The store wasn't huge, but it did stay well-stocked and clean, something Kaitlyn hadn't always found in chain grocers.

"Avocado, avocado." She scanned the dark green veggies in front of her. "Softer, riper, or something for later in the week?" To be on the safe side Kaitlyn sent a message with the hopes the customer would reply quickly.

On to the almond milk. Kaitlyn shook her head as she loaded up the carton along with several kinds of kombucha. At least this small-town store carried such items. A few years ago, she'd have had to travel to Little Rock to find the fermented drink.

Her phone buzzed. Ah. Riper. She returned to the avocados and finished her order. One more scan of the list showed she had everything. On to the register.

The same man who had rung up yesterday's order stood at the register. His hairline, or lack thereof, was deceiving. When he spoke with her yesterday, he came across much closer to her age—late-twenties. Would he comment again? This order was opposite of the junk food. She set the veggies and fruits on the belt.

"Hello, again." His eyes crinkled at the edges when he flashed her a smile.

She couldn't help but grin in return. "Hi."

"Doin' okay today?"

"Pretty good." Not a riveting conversation, but what else could she say? He hadn't asked for her life history, and she wouldn't have shared it anyway.

He weighed the butternut squash. "Going healthy again today, huh?"

"This isn't for me, either."

A frown crossed his face, and she schooled her smirk. Didn't he know his store participated in Grocerease, the new-to-this-area grocery shopping and delivery service?

"You're awfully nice to shop for so many other people." He scanned the last bottle of kombucha and pointed to the screen. "Fifty-four, sixty-seven."

She slipped her company card through the reader. "Thanks. But it's not so much about being nice. I get paid to do it."

"You get paid to grocery shop?"

She quickly tapped the app on her phone to show the logo. "I work for Grocerease."

The red creeping up his neck and over his stubbly face darkened his already dark tan. His flush showed brighter on his shaved head. Was he angry at her? Why?

He jerked the receipt off the register and thrust it at her, offering no other words. Instead, he stormed toward the door marked *office*. Weird.

"I'm home, Mom!" Kaitlyn pushed through her garage door and into the kitchen.

"In here."

The temperature in the house sent shivers up Kaitlyn's arms, but the cool air kept Mom more comfortable, so Kaitlyn stashed cardigans throughout the house for when she needed to warm up. She drew the sleeves over her arm as she walked into the living room.

"Whatcha up to?"

"Not much. Trying to work on some props Barb can use in Bible class on Sunday. She's sharing the story of the apostles fishing, so I'm trying to rig a net of sorts."

Yarn was laid out in a crisscross pattern over half the living room floor. Mom was knotting the intersections one piece at a time, but it resembled a fishing net to a point. And since Mom's health wasn't reliable, this activity enabled her to help with the Sunday school program.

"Looks good."

"Something's wrong." Mom pointed a finger. "You look worried."

"Not worried. Just had a weird experience."

"Oh?"

Kaitlyn eased down into a wingback chair. "I was checking out with that last order for Grocerease and the checker mentioned how I purchased health food today instead of the junk I bought yesterday. I commented that I wasn't shopping for myself, but that I worked for Grocerease. He barely finished handing me the receipt before he stormed off."

"Which store?" Mom narrowed her eyes. "Mack's or Foodland?"

Kaitlyn shook her head. "I was at McDonald's."

"Was it Mack who rang you up?"

She hadn't even paid attention to the ID tag on his shirt. "I don't know."

"Around your age, smooth head, friendly smile?" One of mom's eyebrows lifted.

"Sounds right. Why?"

"That store has been in Mack's family for ages. His great-grandfather opened it around the turn of the century. And Mack was raised to keep everything exactly as it always has been. He doesn't do change well."

"But Grocerease isn't changing anything for him. Except that he'll see me quite a bit." Kaitlyn shrugged. "What's the big deal?"

"I don't know, but I'd almost bet it has something to do with this app you work for. Don't take it personally."

"I'd better get our dinner started." Kaitlyn pushed back to her feet and wandered into the kitchen, her mind awhirl.

Was he that upset over her buying groceries for other people? Why?

Chapter 2

"What did you do?" Mack pushed the office door closed before he said anything else. No need to let the whole store know he was considering firing his assistant manager.

Candie glanced up from some inventory sheets. "What?"

He jabbed a finger back toward the front of the store. "Why was someone in here shopping for that Groceries app or whatever it's called?"

"Because someone ordered from here?" A flash of guilt or fear or a similar emotion zipped across her face.

"Since when are we signed up to allow that?" He worked to keep his voice low instead of shouting.

Candie scooted the chair a bit farther away from him, motioning toward the paperwork in front of her. "I thought you wanted to and had just forgotten. I found the papers on your desk while you were gone, and the due date would have passed before you got back. So, I filled them out and turned them in."

He pressed his knuckles into his furrowed brow, wishing it

could ease the headache coming on. "If I'd planned to participate, I would've turned the application in."

"Why wouldn't you?" Candie shot to her feet, hands on hips. "The shopping app is a great idea."

"No, it's not. It keeps people from coming in the store. That means fewer sales, which means I won't be able to afford an assistant manager." The last threat escaped before he could stifle it.

Candie flinched. "How do you figure it will bring in less sales? People will still be buying from us. They'll just do it through the shoppers instead of themselves."

"But if they don't come in, they won't see other things. Impulse buys. Forgotten needs. Clearance items." He counted out options on his fingers for emphasis. "Don't forget the seasonal merch. Is *that* on those apps? And what if they order something we're out of? They won't be here to see if there's anything that replaces it."

Her mouth formed an *O* as if she hadn't thought of that.

"This is why I shouldn't take vacations. It's not worth the hassle." He pointed to the messy desk. "Any hope we can back out of it now that you've signed us up?"

"The app is running a sixty-day trial period in Sassafras to see if they'll have enough interest to keep it in the area. We're obligated that whole time." Candie shuffled a few pages and came up with the contract. "But I know for a fact Foodland is participating too."

"What does Foodland have to do with us?" The chain store was on the other side of town. Most of Mack's customers were loyal even if some of his items were a few cents higher.

"Because ... if you're not an option, but Foodland is, people using the app for sure won't shop here." Candie thrust the papers at him.

Much as it hurt to admit, she had a point. He skimmed the

legalese, but didn't see any way out of the mess she'd put them in. "My grandfather would roll over in his grave. How are we supposed to offer customer service to people when they don't even come in the store?"

"It's not going to be as bad as you assume." Candie shook her head. "Last week's numbers are actually up."

Mack rubbed his temple. "I'll look at those later. I'd better get back out to the front in case a *real* customer comes in."

"Mack." Candie's soft tone implored him to face her once more. "I'm sorry I didn't ask before I registered us. But I'm not sorry to be signed up. I think it'll turn out to be a good thing."

"When I hired you on as assistant manager two years ago, your optimism was one of the reasons. But I'm not sure it'll hold up this time, Candie."

Candie's slumped shoulders almost had him reneging, but not quite. This store had been left to him, and he couldn't let his family or the town down. McDonald's was a big part of Sassafras. Without the personal service and customer relationships, how could the legacy continue?

Despite his irritation, he caught himself watching for a particular strawberry-blonde. Would she be back? Considering her reason for being there, would seeing her again be a good thing? The next day, as he stocked an endcap full of pumpkin-flavored goodies, he spied her.

She was so focused on the list in her hands, she didn't even see him as she walked past. Her basket held normal purchases. A few fruits and veggies. Pasta, eggs, milk, juice, and bread. She even had a few packs of fresh meat. Who was she shopping for today? All these customers he knew nothing about.

Swallowing his disappointment, he set the last few bags of pumpkin bagels on the shelf and gathered the empty boxes. Almost time for peppermint and gingerbread, though he hated skipping over Thanksgiving to sell Christmas.

Would any of the Grocerease customers buy such things? How would they know about them? What was listed on that app, anyway? Everything in their inventory? How did it work?

He needed to do more research. Later. His Grocerease shopper was ready to check out, and the other two lines were packed.

As he stepped up to the register, she paused. A look of caution crossed her face. Guilt cut through his middle. He hadn't handled the news well yesterday. And even though she wasn't a real customer, he needed to be friendly—especially considering the sales were still valid. Maybe she could pass the customer service vibe on to the people she delivered the groceries to.

"I'm sorry I ... ended our transaction the way I did yesterday." He scanned her potatoes and set them in her cart. Not the most graceful apology he'd ever offered, but maybe it was enough to thaw things out.

Kaitlyn nibbled her lip. Today, she took time to glance at his nametag and confirm this was the Mack her mom mentioned. So, he was the owner? Manager? How did he miss that his store was participating in the trial run of Grocerease?

"Apology accepted."

"Thank you." He rang up her grapes and bananas. "I guess we'll be seeing quite a bit of each other, huh?"

"More than likely. I live on this side of town, so I tend to grab these orders instead of the ones at Foodland. Besides, your store is usually better stocked, which makes my life easier."

"I'm glad to know I'm better stocked than the chain store."

He chuckled as he scanned her wheat bread. "Maybe I'm doing something right."

She simply nodded. What else could she say?

"This customer seems to be between the other two extremes I've seen you buy for lately." He set her milk in the cart and tapped the screen where the total was.

"I'm shopping for me today." She inserted her debit card in the reader.

"Oh. I guess I just assumed ..."

"That I only shop when someone pays me to?" She lifted a brow as she slid her card back into her wallet. "I need groceries, too, you know?"

"I apologize again."

"Hopefully, our future exchanges won't require so many apologies."

She barely controlled the grin trying to escape the corners of her lips. It had been a long day, and the look on his face was somewhere between chagrin and annoyance. Almost like some of the second-grade boys in the class she'd subbed for earlier.

"Thanks so much, Mack." She accepted the receipt he held out.

He kept a grip on the small slip of paper. "You know my name, but I don't know yours."

"Kaitlyn. Kaitlyn Daniels." With that, she pulled the receipt free and pushed her cart away.

"See you soon, Kaitlyn Daniels." Mack called after her. This time, her smile escaped.

Such strange interactions.

She loaded the groceries into her little car and pointed it toward home. Much as she enjoyed being back in school, she'd much rather be a full-time teacher. Having the same students every day and using lesson plans she'd written were easier than filling in for someone else. But subbing helped pay the bills. As did Grocerease.

And with the increase in her mother's medical bills lately, they needed every penny she could bring in. So, whether Mack McDonald liked the program or not, she'd continue to work it. After being a shopper for the app all through college, she understood how the program could thrive in a town even as small as Sassafras. That's why she'd petitioned to get Grocerease in this area.

She needed the income and knew quite a few people who found the service indispensable. Not just people like her, who could use the extra money, but customers who couldn't get out and about as well, like her mother.

If Mack decided to sabotage the trial, he was in for a fight. She wasn't going to let these sixty days end in failure. Even if a shopping app wasn't the way McDonald's Grocery Store had always operated.

Chapter 3

Running a business didn't always allow Mack to make it to Sunday worship services. But this week, he attended without worrying. Everything would be taken care of. Though he was still at odds with Candie, he trusted her with the general management of the store.

He even arrived early enough to snag his favorite spot in the auditorium. Most people sat in the back corner to avoid others, but he chose this place because it allowed him to greet members as they left. Customer service wasn't only for during work hours, after all.

His mom turned and waved from her front corner. She'd said she never understood why Mack liked sitting so far from the stage but was always glad to see him there. His dad was probably off teaching another class. Or doing deacon duties. Mack would catch up with them another time, when there weren't so many others around.

James Stewart, the minister, patted Mack's shoulder. "Haven't seen you in a few weeks."

"I know. I was on vacation then had to play catch up. But I missed being here."

"I'm glad you're back." James moved on down the aisle, greeting others as he went. He had his own customer service going on, as it were.

Mack had just tucked his bulletin away and settled in for Sunday school, when a particular shade of strawberry-blonde caught his eye. Toward the front, on the other section of pews, next to a window. Was it? Yes. Kaitlyn Daniels. Interesting. Had he seen her here before?

"Good morning." The Bible class teacher started before Mack could ponder any further.

"We're at the end of Matthew 25 this morning. Talking about Judgment Day. Always a good way to start a week, right?"

Mack snickered as he flipped his Bible open.

"Let's start around verse 34."

Mack silently read along in the passage. *Then the King will say to those on his right, "Come, you who are blessed by my Father, inherit the kingdom prepared for you from the foundation of the world. For I was hungry and you gave me food, I was thirsty and you gave me drink, I was a stranger and you welcomed me, I was naked and you clothed me, I was sick and you visited me, I was in prison and you came to me."*

The teacher perused the room. "Wow. These people had done quite a bit for God, hadn't they? But let's keep reading."

Mack continued following along. *Then the righteous will answer him, saying, "Lord, when did we see you hungry and feed you, or thirsty and give you drink? And when did we see you a stranger and welcome you, or naked and clothe you? And when did we see you sick or in prison and visit you?" And the King will answer them, "Truly, I say to you, as you did it to one of the least of these my brothers, you did it to me."*

This. This right here was part of why Mack was so adamant about giving good customer service. It wasn't just about bringing in business. It was shining God's light to the world around him.

"Sounds like maybe serving others is a little important, huh?" The teacher patted his Bible. "So, let's talk service for a minute."

Mack relaxed and crossed his ankle over his knee. No need to lean forward. He was certain he would agree with the rest of the lesson. He could probably teach it himself.

"Obviously, there are some great starting points here. Giving people food and clothing and shelter. That's why we offer things like the food pantry and coat closet, right?"

Several nods agreed with the teacher.

"Okay, well, it might be a little more awkward to visit people in prison. And no one likes hospitals." The teacher scrunched his face up. "But I guess if we really had to ..."

Mack shifted a bit against the hard pew. When was the last time he'd visited someone who was sick? Or done those other things?

"Of course, visiting the sick and stuff is really just what the preacher's supposed to do, right? Isn't that part of his job description?"

This lesson wasn't going where Mack had expected.

"Keep reading. Because the next few verses might make you think again. It says anyone who didn't do these things, didn't do them to Jesus. And 'these will go away into everlasting punishment.' Yikes. Not the retirement plan I'm hoping for."

Mack either.

"So, let's talk. What are we doing, and what can we do better?"

Several people threw out ideas. Keeping snack foods in the car to hand to the hungry. Building the coat closet up more. Starting a prison ministry. The usual.

"Do you think there are other ways to serve? Or ways to simply make people's lives easier so they don't have to worry? How can we live in such a way that people see Jesus in us?"

A few more ideas came. Looking beyond the clothes people wore. Helping unemployed find jobs. Comfort boxes for those grieving.

"What about families with health issues who might need a little extra love? I know at least one family here who has an autistic child and can't get out as much as they'd like." He pointed to the right side where a teen rocked side to side, headphones covering his ears.

The DeWitts. When was the last time Mack had seen them?

"Does anyone go visit? Or people who aren't housebound all the time, but have days harder than others? How can we help those?"

Kaitlyn turned and shot a glower right at Mack, searing him with its intensity. She lifted a brow and then turned back toward the front. What had run through her head? Was she trying to tell him something telepathically? Mack shifted. He wasn't a mind reader.

Mom nudged Kaitlyn every time the preacher made a point about judging as if she thought Kaitlyn needed to make note of it. Was she still eight or something?

Kaitlyn didn't consider herself judgmental. She tried to give everyone a fair chance and not assume she knew their whole backstory before making assumptions. But Mom had caught that look Kaitlyn sent Mack's way during class. Now she hammered home her own looks. If karma were a biblical idea, this morning fit the definition. Of course, the Bible would never include something like that.

"I'm not a complete heathen, you know." Kaitlyn hissed at her mother as the conversations around them grew loud enough to cover her statement.

"I never said you were."

"No. You just treated me like the sermon was addressed to me personally."

Mom patted her already perfect hair into place. "I'm sure I don't know what you're talking about."

"Mm-hmm." Kaitlyn gathered their things and then followed Mom into the crowd.

"Lovely to see you ladies today." The preacher offered his hand to shake. "I don't think I've had a chance to meet you."

"Kaitlyn Daniels. I'm May's daughter."

"James Stewart." He smiled and winked. "The preacher, not the actor."

Mom chuckled. "That joke never gets old. Kaitlyn moved here a few weeks ago to help take care of me. She's substitute teaching at the elementary school and working for Grocerease."

"Well, then I'm sure you've met our esteemed grocer, Mack McDonald." James waved over the last man Kaitlyn wanted to speak to.

"Kaitlyn." Mack nodded at her. "Ms. May."

"How are you today, Mack?"

"Doing just fine. How about yourself? I don't think I'd made the connection between you and Kaitlyn before now."

"She's the best daughter I could ask for. Things are so much less stressful since she's moved in with me." May patted Kaitlyn's arm.

Kaitlyn shook her head. "I'm not doing anything more than any other daughter would do."

"I don't know about that." Mr. Stewart wagged his finger.

"Seems like you're doing a great job of living up to that Bible lesson we had this morning."

Mack grimaced. What was that about? Had he understood the look she shot his way in hopes of getting it through his thick skull that an app like Grocerease could ease people's burdens? Or was it something else?

"I'm just doing my best." Kaitlyn shrugged. "It was lovely to meet you, Mr. Stewart."

As she and Mom walked toward the car, Mack fell in step on her other side.

"I think maybe we got off on the wrong foot." He didn't meet her eyes.

A corner of her lip lifted. "I believe that's why there were so many apologies the other day."

"Oh, I need to talk to Barb for a minute." Mom pointed and scurried off toward her friend.

"Seriously, though. I never wanted things to be awkward between us. Especially since we'll be seeing so much of each other due to our jobs." Mack shoved his hands in the pockets of his dark jeans. "And it's even more important now that I know we're brother and sister in Christ. Think we can call a truce?"

"Depends." Kaitlyn shifted her weight.

"Depends on what?" Mack raised a brow.

"When you say truce, does it mean just agreeing to not fight? Or does it mean attempting to see each other's perspective?"

His lips bunched up and a *V* formed between his brows. "I guess if we're really going to live out today's lessons, we need to aim more for the second option. Don't we?"

She nodded.

"Willing to give it a try?" He extended his hand.

Hesitating only a second, she reached out and shook on it. "Let's try."

"What are we trying?" Mom reappeared at her side.

"To get along." Kaitlyn smirked at Mack, and he chuckled.

"I think the lessons this morning were about more than that, but I'm glad you're heading in the right direction." Mom considered the two of them. "Want to join us for lunch, Mack?"

"Can't today, Ms. May, but thank you. Maybe another time."

As Kaitlyn and Mom made their way home, Kaitlyn pondered over the whole incident. She would hold to their truce. But she'd also make sure he stuck to his end of the deal. Each time she went shopping at McDonald's, she'd prove what a great asset Grocerease was. And show him what a tragedy it would be to discontinue it.

It was only fair. He'd agreed to try and see things her way.

Chapter 4

"Shopping healthy again today, huh?" Mack set a box of lunch meat down on the edge of the cooler and glanced in Kaitlyn's cart.

"Hey, Mack." Kaitlyn didn't even look his way, but kept her focus on the phone in her hands. "Do you have any more of this juice?"

He leaned over and studied the picture. "Might. Let me check in the back."

She nodded and moved over a few feet, grabbing a carton of sour cream.

Okay, then. Either she was a very focused shopper, or she was avoiding him. Until he discovered more, he'd guess the first option. It hurt less. Though why her avoidance should bother him, he didn't know. It wasn't like they were anything more than acquaintances.

Toward the back of a storage cooler, he found what she'd requested and grabbed the box, hefting it onto his shoulder. A scan of the area showed no strawberry-blonde hair, so he opened the cooler and restocked the juice. Hopefully, she'd return and grab a bottle before checking out.

"Thanks, Mack." Kaitlyn's gratitude pulled him from rearranging various shredded cheeses that had been mixed together. "This is your only brand without red dyes. My customer's son is allergic. I know she'll appreciate you keeping it stocked."

"See?" He broke down an empty box. "That's something I would normally know about my customers, but with you doing their shopping for them, I can't keep up with facts like that. If I'd known it sooner, it would've been in the cooler before you even had to ask."

"You can't know that." Kaitlyn's grin tilted up on one side. "Someone could've come through and bought several bottles for a party or a wedding shower or something and emptied the slot right before I reached it. It's not a big deal. You found some in the back, and the problem was solved."

"But now that I know it is needed by customers, I can make sure we always have some in back." He pointed at the bottle. "Without that knowledge, I might not've prioritized it."

"Great. It worked out then." Kaitlyn tapped a few things on her phone. "And I think this order is now complete."

"Great."

"Great." She started pushing her cart toward the front.

Something inside him wasn't ready to let her leave. "Any other details I need to know about this customer?"

Kaitlyn paused and glanced over her shoulder. "She needs these delivered in the next half hour."

"Right. See you later, then."

"See ya, Mack."

Mack added the cardboard to a pile and turned to finish what he'd been doing. He needed to make a note to always have that juice on hand. And get his mind off a certain shopper so he could focus on the real customers in his store.

KAITLYN MUST NOT BE SUBBING this week. This was the fifth time he'd seen her in the store in three days. Today, though, she'd passed the same aisle three times, brow furrowed. Was she lost?

"You okay?" He stepped up next to her as she studied the spice section.

"Do you have any smoked salt? Or celery seeds?"

He blinked a few times. "Celery seeds?"

"Mm-hmm."

"Like, to plant in a garden?"

She finally turned her attention from the spices to him. "No, silly. To cook with. They're like a seasoning. A spice."

"Huh." He quickly skimmed the spices in front of them but didn't notice anything of the sort. "Hang on."

Pulling his phone out, he opened the inventory app and typed in her request. And got nothing.

"I don't have any. Is there something else that would be similar and work the same?"

"I'm not sure. I don't even know what she's using it for. I'd assume a dip or something." Kaitlyn scrolled down her own screen. "What about the smoked salt?"

Another search left him disappointed. "I guess we're not supplying items for fancy cooks. We only have regular salt and sea salt."

"Okay. I'll see if she wants me to try substituting anything else. Thanks."

"Is there a way the app can connect with my inventory so people know what I do and don't have? Because I'm not sure I've ever had those two items. Do other stores?"

Kaitlyn frowned, her mouth to one side. "I don't know. I've never actually used the app to order—only to fulfill orders.

Might be an idea to submit to the designers and see if it's possible. As to whether or not other stores carry those items, I couldn't answer that, either. This is the first time I've looked."

"Hmm. Seems strange."

"Holiday season. People are getting together for meals. Thanksgiving is just a few weeks away and then Christmas." She shrugged. "She's probably trying out some new recipes."

He nodded. "Anything else?"

"I think I found the rest. Thanks, Mack. See ya later."

"See ya."

He shook his head and headed for the office. If people were going to insist on using apps like this, surely there was a way to make it work better for not only the customers but the stores too. He needed to contemplate that more.

"Uh-oh. I know that look."

Kaitlyn grinned. She had to admit she hoped she'd bump into Mack after seeing him almost every day the last few weeks. Though they still didn't quite see eye-to-eye.

"What can't you find now?" Mack leaned over to see her screen.

"This sauce mix. I've searched this aisle about a dozen times and can't spot it."

He grabbed her cart and pushed it away. "Follow me."

No time to even squeak a protest. He turned the corner. She unplanted her feet and took off after him.

"Check here." He pointed to a whole section of sauce and gravy mixes two aisles over.

"Why is it on this aisle?"

"Hmm?" Mack glanced around like he didn't understand the question.

"Mack, why are the sauce mixes on the aisle with bread and peanut butter and coffee and cereal? They would make much more sense over where I was with the soups and seasonings."

"But they've always been on this aisle." He rubbed the top of his head.

Kaitlyn grabbed the packets she needed and shook her head. "It's not logical. Sauces have nothing to do with breakfast or peanut butter sandwiches."

"I can't rearrange the whole store just because one little section throws you off. Everyone who shops here knows this is where these are because this is where they've always been." Mack shrugged. "Anything else you need help with?"

Kaitlyn paused a moment, wondering if it would do any good to push her point. Probably not. Moving on. "Sun-dried tomatoes?"

"This way."

At least this ingredient's placement made more sense. Between the cans of tomatoes and chili. Though she might move the chili over near the soup, if it were her. One glance at Mack's face told her to not even try.

She set the jar in her basket and marked the last item off her list. "That's it for this trip. Thanks. I was afraid I wasn't going to be able to finish the order when I couldn't find the sauces."

"Now you know where they are." One side of his grin tilted up. "Come on. I'll check you out."

She shook her head but meandered behind him up to the register. "You know, I'm probably not the only one who can't find things like that. Think how many more you'd sell if they were in a logical spot."

"It's logical to me." He scanned her fruits and veggies as she placed them on the belt.

"But why?"

"What?"

"Why is that logical?"

"They've been there my whole life. Like an automatic response, I know exactly where to go." He waved the sauce packets at her before running their barcodes over the scanner.

"Now, if you had to go shopping somewhere else—"

He started to protest, but she held up a hand and stopped him.

"I said *if*."

His curt nod gave her courage to continue.

"*If* you had to shop somewhere else, how would you know where to look for items?"

"I imagine they'd have signs above each aisle just like we do, Kaitlyn. Grocery stores aren't that hard to figure out."

"They shouldn't be. Unless one item is placed in a completely different spot from where you're used to looking. How long do you think you'd search for it before giving up and either living without it or taking your business elsewhere?"

"You going to start shopping somewhere else?" One of his brows rose, sending a wave of wrinkles up his forehead.

"Not me. But I bet some people would."

"You and Candie." Mack shook his head. "Both telling me I'm going to lose business if I don't change things around. This store has had the same layout for almost seventy years now, and no one has complained. It's this app that's causing all the ruckus."

"You still hate it, huh?"

His mouth twitched.

She widened her eyes. "Mack?"

"Let's just say you've helped me notice a few things I didn't know before and wouldn't have learned about without your stupid app."

"Whew!" She slid her card back in her wallet and blinked. "You didn't even grow spots or anything when you said that. Did it hurt?"

"I'm not saying I like the app." He ripped her receipt off with extra gusto. "I'm just saying I'm grateful to know about things like the special juice. Or the rare items we haven't been able to find for you. It's good to know people are looking for those."

"Well, it's not much, but I guess I'll take it. More than I expected after only a month."

"Mm-hmm." He waved at her cart full of groceries. "Better get these delivered before your tip gets cut."

"That would be a big shame after working so hard to make sure I got everything she ordered." Kaitlyn smirked. "See ya around."

"See ya." Mack started ringing up the next customer in line even before Kaitlyn made it out the exit.

His words played in her mind. He was a puzzle, for sure. Friendly and wanting to be the best at customer service. But stubborn when it came to change, even if the changes could bring more opportunities to his customers.

Would they ever find a way to see eye to eye?

Chapter 5

"Candie, have you seen Mack?" Kaitlyn stepped up to the open register where the perky brunette worked.

"Um, I think he was in the office a bit ago. Did you need to ask him something?" Candie scanned the kombucha Kaitlyn's customer loved.

"Oh, no. Just curious. I guess I'm used to seeing him." Kaitlyn pushed against the wave of disappointment. It was silly. Why should she be disappointed to not see someone who always disagreed with her?

"Mm-hmm." Candie raised an eyebrow but didn't say anything else except the total owed.

"Is he …" Swiping her card, Kaitlyn paused a moment before saying more. "Is he relenting at all in regard to the app?"

Candie sighed before handing her the receipt. "Not that I can tell. He was grumbling earlier about numbers being down. I don't know."

"I wish I could find a way to help him see the good in it. But nothing I do seems to help. It's like his mind is so made up there's no crack big enough to sneak a new idea in."

"Trust me. I know." Candie shook her head. "But I can't say I'm sorry I signed us up."

"Wait. You signed McDonald's up for the program? Not Mack?"

"Ye-ah." Candie shot her a sheepish glance.

The office door on the back wall opened, and the man himself walked out. Candie put a finger to her lips and handed Kaitlyn her last two bags. Obviously, this conversation would have to wait for later.

Mack hadn't glanced her way yet but headed across the store, straightening items and greeting customers. He really did have a good head for remembering people. As a teacher, it was a skill Kaitlyn envied. The first few weeks of a year were always brutal while she learned students' names—and who needed to not sit next to whom. Subbing was worse, because her students constantly changed.

At the end of one of the other registers, two little boys each greeted Mack with fist bumps and big gap-toothed grins. They appeared to be about six, identical down to the blond cowlicks on their foreheads. Mack teased them for a few moments, distracting them while their mother finished paying. Then, they waved and were off, jumping on each side of the cart as their mom pushed it toward the door.

Mack glanced in Kaitlyn's direction. Something zinged through her, making ripples in the warm gooiness that had formed watching his interactions with the children. He really was a good guy. Why did he drive her so crazy?

"How's my favorite personal shopper?" Mack's smile stirred up her insides even more.

What was going on? "Not too bad."

"No trouble finding anything today?" He motioned toward her purchases.

"Nope. This is a pretty standard order."

"So, the customer orders almost the same thing every week?"

"Pretty much." Kaitlyn frowned. "Why?"

"Curious."

She crossed her arms. "There's more to it than that. What is it?"

Mack shook his head. Rubbed a hand over the top of it. Blew out a deep breath.

"Mack, what's wrong?" Kaitlyn pushed her cart out of the way so others wouldn't have to move around them and motioned for him to follow. "There must be a reason you asked about this order."

"It's not necessarily this order in particular. It's ..." He motioned toward a couple of end caps on the other side of the registers. "Did you get anything from that section?"

Kaitlyn studied the offerings. Mostly holiday goodies and seasonal items. Nothing her customer would want.

"No. This customer is fairly health conscious. Avocados, organic eggs, multi-grain bread, organic fruits, stuff like that. She hardly ever wants anything pre-packaged. I'm not saying she won't want a can of pumpkin before the end of the year, but it would surprise me."

"Are seasonal items even offered on the app?" Mack pinched his lips together for a second. "Because we haven't sold nearly as many holiday items as I expected."

"It could be a slow year. The economy isn't great. Maybe people are cutting back."

Mack shook his head. "Not this much. People don't cut back this much all at once."

"You're blaming your seasonal items not selling on the app, aren't you?" Kaitlyn crossed her arms and barely kept herself from stamping a foot. The goo was freezing fast.

"What else could it be? I mean, I've never seen my numbers

drop like this. Ever." He shook his head. "That app is hurting my business."

The stubbornness of this man knew no bounds. But she could be stubborn too.

"You're being ridiculous. It's still a few weeks until Thanksgiving. There will probably be a run of last-minute holiday shoppers next week, everyone grabbing their stuffing mixes and pumpkin pie fillings and cranberry sauce. You're worrying for nothing."

"You're assuming they'll come to the store where those items are an option."

"How do you know those items *aren't* an option on the app?" Kaitlyn pulled her phone out and grimaced when she noticed the time. She needed to get these groceries to her customer in the next fifteen minutes.

"I don't. I don't know how the stupid thing works."

She pushed a button and pulled it up for him to see. "There are all the categories they can shop in. It should pull from your inventory to know what you have to offer."

"And yet, you've found items we've *never* carried, like that spice last week. If it's pulling my inventory, wouldn't it *know* we didn't have that?"

"I'm not sure all the logistics of it, Mack. I recommend making a list of questions to take to the owners and programmers when they have their meeting next month to see if it's worth keeping the app in the area. Because the only way they can improve things is by getting feedback about what works and what doesn't."

"I'm not sure they could make that many improvements. My numbers are down quite a bit."

"Do you even hear yourself, Ebeneezer?"

"Ebeneezer?"

"Scrooge! The one who only worries about how much

money he makes and how things affect him and his business. Who cares if it helps a ton of other people if it's not good for him."

"You'd worry too, if your business might have to make cuts due to losing money. How am I supposed to pay my employees if I don't bring in as much? Or if we're not selling as much and don't need as many stockers, what if I have to cut their hours?"

"Oh, for crying out loud. All this over a few cans of pumpkin and cranberry?" Kaitlyn stuffed her phone back in her purse and grabbed the handle of her cart. "No, Mack McDonald. Your store is not going to die because of one little app. You're still getting business, even if it isn't the way it's always been done. And if you don't sell all the stupid pumpkin by Thanksgiving, I'll buy it myself."

She pushed through the doors before he had a chance to protest. Was anything as impossible as getting through his thick skull? Even his hair couldn't do it, as evidenced by his bald head.

Okay, that was a bit mean. But really. There came a point where he needed to weigh the pros along with the cons and see that things couldn't be nearly as bad as he projected them. Could they? Couldn't he see any good in it at all?

A niggle of contrition wiggled down her spine as she set the groceries on her customer's porch, barely in the time limit for a good tip. With a quick rap at the door, she climbed back in her car and headed to Mom's house.

"She's right, you know." Candie didn't even look at him as she said it, but Mack could tell she spoke to him.

"I don't see how." He turned toward the office even though he'd accomplished his earlier list of tasks in there.

"That's because you can't see anything much past your nose." Candie exchanged a glance with Mr. Moses as she rang up his order.

The older gentleman's lips twitched, but he didn't join the conversation.

"Do you agree, Mr. Moses?" Mack folded his arms over his chest. "Am I missing something?"

Mr. Moses meticulously pulled out several bills from his wallet and handed them to Candie. "You know, in my day, we didn't have cell phones. Nothing but a landline, and those were rather pricey."

Mack shifted his weight, wondering if the customer had misunderstood the question.

"Every time something new came out, everyone would get all up in arms about it. It was either the best thing since sliced bread or was leading us straight to the devil." He nodded while accepting his receipt. "After a while, everyone calmed down again and just got used to it. And then it would happen again with the next big thing.

"I figure this app-do-whatsit is one of those things. Until people figure out how to use it best, it's going to stir up trouble. But once things calm down, you'll find not much has changed after all."

With that, the older gentleman pushed his cart toward the door and waved over his shoulder.

"It is still a few weeks to Thanksgiving." Candie motioned to the end cap full of seasonal favorites. "I bet we're not as bad off as you think. You're just looking for signs that the app is causing problems and seeing them where they aren't."

"Believe it or not, I'm not searching for signs." Mack swallowed a groan of frustration. "They're written in the numbers."

Candie shook her head. "Don't count your holiday sales

before the actual holiday. And don't make an enemy of Kaitlyn. She might prove to be even more than expected, just like this app."

"What's that supposed to mean?" Mack frowned, not in the mood for double-talk.

"Let's just say she looked disappointed that you weren't working Register Five today." Candie walked away before he could react.

Mack blinked a few times. Deep inside, he admitted he often scanned the store for the strawberry-blonde hair of the personal shopper. Couldn't stop the smile that stretched across his face when he spotted her looking for another ingredient. Relished the few extra minutes to be close to her when she needed assistance.

But there couldn't be more, could there? Not when they could never be nice to each other longer than it took to solve her problem and move to a new subject. Not when she always criticized something about his shop.

Besides, she didn't act any different around him than she always had. Did she?

Chapter 6

"Still not talking to me, I see."

Kaitlyn's lips twitched fighting a smile. "Terribly sorry, Mack. What should I say?"

"I've always been told the weather is a safe topic. Or your health."

"Mm. My health is fine." Despite the exhaustion threatening to take over her body, she wasn't sick.

"Fine." He nodded as he scanned a bag of potatoes. "I'm glad to hear it. And the weather is lovely today."

"If you like rain."

"Okay, so lovely might be a stretch. Still, better than the drought we had in July."

"True. But not fun when subbing in a room full of fifth graders who have been cooped up for three days."

Mack grimaced. "No. I imagine not."

They were quiet a few more minutes while he finished ringing up the purchases. Awkwardness settled between them despite the light-hearted banter. Because that's all it was—banter. Sure, he'd tried to be friendly, but she had a feeling if they went deeper, they'd end up fighting again. And that was the last thing she needed today.

"If you subbed today, why are you working this job too? I imagine you're dead on your feet."

"You aren't wrong, either. But this is a regular customer, so I wanted to grab it. They're always so grateful, and I know what to expect. I figured I could get it really fast on my way home and brighten their day. Especially since it sat unclaimed for an hour."

"Does that happen much? No one claiming orders?"

"Not terribly often. But this is still a fairly new market, and there aren't a ton of us working for the company yet. That means if a lot of the regular shoppers are also working other jobs, they may not be able to snag an order as soon as they'd like to."

Mack handed her the receipt. "Good thing they have loyal shoppers like you to step up and pick up the slack. I've only spotted a couple of others working for the app, and none seem to be in here as often as you."

"I'm not anything special. Just wanting to make sure those I know who truly need the help get it. That's why I want this app to work out here in Sassafras. For the families it really benefits."

Mack glanced to make sure no one else needed his help at the moment. "And what makes this family so special?"

Kaitlyn opened her mouth to reply, but Mom's ringtone sounded. She frowned and held up a finger. Mom didn't normally call unless she needed something.

"Mom?"

"Kaitlyn, can you meet me at the hospital?"

Her heart skipped a beat. "What? The hospital? What happened? What's wrong?"

"Calm down, honey. I fell refilling the bird feeders, but it's just a bad bump."

The beeps of monitors sounded in the background along with people saying all sorts of medical terminology.

"Are you there now?" Kaitlyn glanced at the groceries in her cart, trying to figure out how long it would take her to drop them off before she could head that way.

"On my way. I'm in the ambulance with some very nice gentlemen. Just come when you can."

"I'll be there as soon as possible, Mom."

"Don't you get in an accident. I'll be here when you get here."

That was all fine and dandy for her mom to say. But Kaitlyn's heart disagreed big time. She wanted to be there now. Or even before the accident to keep it from happening in the first place.

Filling the bird feeder. Of all the tasks that could have waited … but no. Her mom had to do it on the wettest day they'd had in weeks.

"How can I help?" Mack touched her arm.

"I don't know. I need to get these groceries dropped off and then get to the hospital. My mom fell. She's headed there by ambulance now."

"Let me drop off the groceries for you?"

Kaitlyn's mouth opened and closed, but she had no words.

"Is that against Grocerease policy? I don't want to get you in trouble with the company, but I know you'd much rather head straight to the hospital."

"I don't think it's against policy. I mean, all I have to do is set the bags on the porch and give a little knock. Don't ring the bell. Their son is autistic and the loud sounds bother him." Her hands flapped over the bags as if trying to decide where to roost.

Mack caught her hands in his. "Kaitlyn, can you drive safely?"

"I—yes. I can drive."

"Give me the address for these and go check on your mom."

She paused for only another moment before pulling her phone out and showing him the information. He quickly tapped it into a map app on his phone and shooed her toward the door. "Go."

"Mack, are you sure?"

"Go. You can thank me later."

Spontaneously, she wrapped her arms around him and hugged. He stiffened for a second and then returned the hug, his large hand gently rubbing her back.

"Thanks, Mack." Kaitlyn dashed a tear from her cheek and headed out into the soggy afternoon.

The whole way to the hospital, her mind dashed back and forth between how bad her mom really was—she never made a big deal over any health issues—and how Mack would handle dropping the groceries at the DeWitts' house. Would he remember to knock instead of ringing the bell? Would it make him hate the app even more?

At the hospital, she found a parking space and headed for the Emergency entrance. After giving her information and assuring them she was next-of-kin, she was admitted back to the curtained area her mom occupied. A large knot swelled on Mom's forehead, but other than that, she didn't look too worse for wear.

"Mom."

"Kaitlyn. You got here fast."

"Mack took the groceries so I could head straight here."

"He did?" Her mom's eyebrows shot up in surprise, causing her to wince as it wrinkled her bruise.

"How are you?"

Mom batted the question away. "*Pshaw.* It's just a bump. I'll be fine."

"Is that what the doctor says?"

"Not when I first saw her, but she'll run a few scans just to be on the safe side."

A woman not much older than Kaitlyn stepped through the curtain and offered her hand. "I'm Dr. Pearce."

"Kaitlyn, the daughter."

"Don't worry. We'll take good care of your mom, and as long as I don't find anything on the scans, you'll probably get to take her home tonight."

"Tonight sounds good." Kaitlyn released a long breath.

"See? Nothing to worry about." Mom winked before they wheeled her through the curtain toward radiology.

Nothing indeed. Kaitlyn settled into the uncomfortable plastic chair to worry anyway. No. To pray. Praying was a much better use of her time than worrying. And she'd pray that Mack's delivery went well too.

MACK RECOGNIZED the address as he pulled up. He'd been out here a time or two with different church groups. The family had three kids, two in the youth group. Sometimes, they needed help getting the teens to various activities so the church van would pick them up. And Mack was one of the drivers when he was available.

What else did he know about the family? Kaitlyn mentioned an autistic child. That's right. He couldn't handle loud noises or anything that might startle him. He was the one who wore noise-canceling headphones during the worship service when his family was able to come.

Mack set the bags on the porch and gave a light knock.

The light flicked on and the door opened almost immediately. Patti DeWitt stuck her head out.

"Oh! I expected Kaitlyn."

Mack grimaced. "So sorry. Her mom had to go to the hospital. I think she fell and bumped something. So, I sent Kaitlyn to her and offered to bring these myself."

"That's so sweet of you, Mack. We appreciate you offering the services of Grocerease at your store. It makes my life so much simpler to not have to get Patrick out in all the noise and overstimulation. And I've always thought you had the best produce in town."

Mack ducked his head. "Thanks, Patti. But it's nothing, really."

"It's something to me." She reached out and squeezed his shoulder. "And to several others I know too. Thank you. And I'll be praying for Ms. May."

He shook his head, but she was already picking up her bags and heading back inside. Guilt niggled at the edges of his belly. This was a family who actually needed a service like Grocerease. For the first time, he recognized a case where the benefits outweighed the negative.

And Kaitlyn wasn't even here to gloat.

Not that she would. She was better than that. He cranked his truck and pointed it back to the store. A few more hours before closing. He should be there despite his heart being somewhere else.

Namely, wondering how Kaitlyn was holding up at the hospital. She'd been exhausted before she headed that way. Was anyone taking care of her?

At the next light, he turned and drove the other way. Even if someone else was taking care of her, it didn't mean he couldn't check on her too. Or take her something to eat. Or at least let her know the groceries were dropped off successfully.

Though he might not admit what Patti had told him quite yet.

It took some doing, but he finally found a nurse who helped him locate Kaitlyn. Nowadays, visiting someone in the hospital was almost like trying to break into a prison. And while he understood, it also made it hard to help out a friend.

"Mack!" Kaitlyn stood from a chair in a small cubicle. "What are you doing here?"

"Thought you might need some sustenance." He held out a bag with some chicken and fries. "Wasn't sure what you liked, so I guessed."

"Thank you." She accepted the bag with a frown. "You didn't have to do that."

He shrugged.

"Did the groceries get to the DeWitts okay?"

"Patti sent her thanks. And promises of prayers for your mom."

Kaitlyn nodded. "I forgot you probably knew them from church."

It was his turn to nod. "Listen—"

"I—"

They both stood there awkwardly for a minute.

"You first." She set the food down and turned to face him.

"I know we haven't seen eye to eye on everything since you moved to town." Mack rubbed the back of his neck. "But trying to talk things through at the store isn't working either. We never have time, and there's always an audience."

Kaitlyn raised a brow but didn't say anything.

"What if we go grab a bite to eat sometime and really talk? I ... well, I think after today that I might understand things better. And maybe you could give me a chance to tell my side of the story too?"

She blinked a few times. "Oh. Um, I don't know. Dinner?"

"You do eat dinner, right? I didn't just waste my time buying you chicken?"

Her lips quirked up at the corners. "I do eat dinner."

"So, eat dinner with me one evening. I get off early on Tuesdays and Fridays. And I promise not to bite."

For a moment he thought she might refuse. But then, she gave a single nod. "Okay. Friday. That will give my mom a few days to recover."

"Why do I need to recover?" Ms. May was wheeled into the small space, forcing Mack to step closer to Kaitlyn. Reminding him of that hug earlier—the one that had felt like Christmas came early.

"I'm taking your daughter to dinner Friday."

"This day is just full of miracles." Ms. May smirked. "If I'd known my falling would start all this, I would've done it sooner."

"Mom!"

Mack turned his head to hide his laugh, though his shoulders shook with it. If nothing else, dinner with the Grocerease girl should be interesting.

Chapter 7

Even when they'd been in the middle of a fight, Kaitlyn had never felt awkward around Mack. Until now. Fifteen minutes in, and this dinner was full of inane comments and heavy silences.

Why had he suggested meeting to talk if he wasn't going to say anything that mattered?

"I don't handle change well."

Kaitlyn jerked her head up. Mack grimaced and shrugged before slicing another bite of steak.

"My grandfather opened McDonald's back in the fifties. It was the first grocery store in Sassafras. Before that, people had to drive to Little Rock. Or over to Searcy or Conway to buy more than just the staples."

She ripped off a piece of roll and sat back. "So, your family is pretty big in town."

"I don't know about that. But I wanted you to understand why I don't want anything to happen to the store. It's my heritage. My history. And a lot of people rely on things to be the same each time they come in."

"Has the app changed things so much?"

Mack shook his head. "Not as much as I thought it would. But every time you come in and suggest I move an item—or that we don't have what we need—it's hard to hear. Because we've been doing just fine the way things were since my grandpa opened."

Kaitlyn shook her head. "I wasn't asking you to change that much. And I thought you appreciated knowing what items people were wanting but couldn't find on your shelves."

"I do appreciate it. Because it means I can serve them better. But that doesn't make it easy to hear." He sighed. "I don't think I'm explaining this very well."

"I understand not wanting to change. Trust me." She played with a pile of uneaten carrots and broccoli. "When my mom moved down here, I couldn't understand it. It wasn't where I'd grown up or closer to me. But now that I've lived here a few months, I can see the charm. And it's closer to her doctor without having to be in a more expensive area. But just because it was hard for me to uproot and move down here doesn't mean it wasn't something I could adapt to."

She took a sip of water. "The same should go for you. Just because it's not easy doesn't mean some good can't come from it."

"I agree."

She barely kept herself from dropping her fork. Of everything he could've said, those were the last words she expected. "What?"

"You're right. The app isn't all bad."

Pinching her arm, she confirmed she wasn't dreaming.

"I saw that." He lifted a brow, sending ripples up that side of his forehead. "I know what I said. And no, I'm not on any kind of drugs or anything."

"So, what brought all this on?"

"The DeWitts." He pushed his plate back, empty except for

a few potato skins. "I've been around them for years, helping where I could. But I never realized it was so hard for her to do normal tasks, like buy groceries."

"Patrick is a sweetheart, but the stimulation makes him hard to handle in social situations."

Mack nodded. "I'm so used to the noise in my store, it doesn't even cross my radar. But it would be overwhelming to someone like him. And that got me wondering if others who use the app have similar problems. Do you know?"

Kaitlyn brushed a strand of hair behind her ear. "I don't know for sure about all of them, of course. Some of the people never interact with me except to maybe answer a question through the app when I need to substitute one item for another or get clarification."

"But the ones you've met?"

"Of the ones I've actually spoken to, I know there are at least two unique situations like the DeWitts. One guy works nights and needs to sleep during the day—his hours make it hard for him to get to the store very much before closing. My mom has MS, obviously, and is prone to falls, so I don't like her getting out more than she has to, especially when the weather is hot."

"Why in the hot weather?"

"Heat makes the symptoms worse. Our house is like an ice box most of the time because it helps keep her pain manageable."

Mack nodded.

"I know there's one mom who has three kids under three. She could come, but it stresses her out because having three in the basket doesn't leave much room for groceries. And she'd have to deal with them asking for items not on her list or possibly getting in a fight. Not to mention one of them is potty training, which adds a whole other challenge."

"I get that."

"So, maybe you're understanding more that there is a great need for something like this?"

Mack tapped his fork against the table. "For those situations, yes. But it doesn't take away all the frustration. I'm still losing the ability to reach out and connect with those customers. And my numbers continue looking worse than before."

"I just don't understand the numbers thing. Seems to me you should actually be getting more business instead of less."

"It's strange, for sure."

"I wonder if Foodland is having similar issues."

Mack rolled his eyes. "Foodland."

"Yes. You know. The other grocery store in town."

"I know what Foodland is. I just prefer to pretend like they don't exist."

Kaitlyn snickered. "Because I'm sure that makes them less likely to steal business."

"I'm not really worried about them." Mack raised a shoulder. "Most people know I have better produce and meat because I have a lot of local suppliers. And for the most part, a bigger majority of the population live on this side of town."

"Except for those new townhouses and apartments on the Foodland side."

"You just can't leave it alone, can you?"

"I simply want to make sure you give them enough credit. Because they do exist, whether you like it or not."

"Kaitlyn Daniels, are you worried about me?"

"I don't know if I'd go that far." She smirked. "Just don't want your head to get any bigger. You need someone to keep you humble."

"You applying for the job?"

Despite the flirtation lacing his voice, her heart skipped a beat. Because the question held undertones of a much more serious subject. One not nearly as aversive as it had been several weeks before.

"I already have a job."

"Right. Working for Grocerease."

"And subbing."

"Why not teach full-time?"

She wrinkled her nose. "I hadn't planned to move when I did. Mom got her diagnosis a few years back, but she'd been handling everything well. Then, she had some flare ups and scares over the summer, and I decided I wanted to be closer than several hours away. Just in case she needed me."

His large hand covered hers where she fiddled with the napkin. Warmth and something else worked its way up through her arm. She cleared her throat.

"She has MS, right?"

Kaitlyn nodded.

"Remind me again what that means."

"Basically, it's a disease of her nerves. They don't always fire right, and that means she has some pain, but also can have some numbness in her limbs. And it affects her eyes sometimes, so she can't see as well. She can have dizzy spells. It works differently in different people. A lot of MS patients end up in a wheelchair, but she doesn't need one of those. Yet."

Mack nodded, his thumb rubbing the back of her hand gently.

"Anyway, by the time I got everything tied up in Fayetteville and moved down here, the school year had already started. They didn't have any positions to offer me except as a sub. I grabbed it just to get a foot in the door for when something opens up down the road. And to bring in enough to help pay the extra medical bills."

MACK UNDERSTOOD Kaitlyn had moved here for her mom, but he hadn't had the whole picture until now. She'd given up whatever life she had back in Fayetteville and accepted two or three part-time positions just to be nearby. He wasn't sure he could do the same if his parents needed him to move somewhere else. Thankfully, they still lived in town.

"So, that's why you do Grocerease too. To help make ends meet while you don't have a full-time position."

"I worked for the app while I was in college. Learned it was a good way to make a little extra. And I knew it would be helpful for people like Mom. It's why I suggested they do a trial run here when they were looking for new places to offer their services."

She was one of the people who had gotten the app here? Anger jumped in his chest, pounding to escape, but he pushed it back down. He'd just agreed a few minutes before that she was right about some families in town needing an app like this. He couldn't get mad now, even if he wanted to.

"I thought Candie told you." Kaitlyn drew her fingers out from under his.

Apparently, he hadn't hidden his anger as well as he thought.

"I realized she signed us up without permission, but not that you were one of the ones behind getting it here in the first place."

"I started the process before I decided to move here. Because I wanted Mom to be able to get groceries even on the days she couldn't get out."

He nodded.

"I'd only visited Sassafras a few times—had never even

been in a grocery store here. And I didn't know until the other day that Candie signed you up without you knowing."

"It's like we were doomed to start off on the wrong foot." He offered a slight grin to soften his words.

"That doesn't mean we have to stay there, though. I mean, haven't we talked and interacted enough now to be friends, at least?"

Swallowing a lump in his throat. "I never have enough friends."

But the "at least" part of her question had him wondering if there might be potential for more. Could they go from starting out as near-enemies to something more than friends? Sure, he'd been attracted to her from the beginning, with that gorgeous strawberry-blonde hair and those deep blue eyes. And he had to admit, he searched for her in the aisles almost every day.

But was that enough?

"You look deep in thought."

Her statement pulled him back to the moment. No need to daydream about what-ifs when he should be soaking up the here-and-now.

"Not as deep as you might think." He winked.

The waitress brought their check and he paid for both their meals before Kaitlyn could object. Though she sighed. Not a good sign if he wanted to head toward more-than-friends.

"So, how many cans of pumpkin will I have to buy?" Kaitlyn bumped his arm with hers as they walked out into the cool November evening.

"None."

"You sold them all?"

He shook his head. "Not yet, but I won't hold you to that promise. It was made in a moment of anger. Besides, it's not Thanksgiving yet."

"Can I at least buy one? I promised Mom a pie."

"Sure. Want me to set one back for you?"

"Only if you think you're going to have a sudden run on canned pumpkin before I can get there again—tomorrow."

He grinned. "You're probably safe, then. There were at least ten cans left this afternoon."

She nodded, stopping at a tiny blue car. "Thanks for dinner, Mack."

"You're more than welcome. Thanks for coming. Maybe now we both understand where the other is coming from a little better."

Tilting her head, she studied him for a moment. "Maybe."

Her phone chimed and she glanced at the screen before a chuckle burst from her. "Mom wants to know how things are going on my *date*."

His lips twitched. "Tell her it went great."

Part of him wanted to lean over and kiss her cheek, but the other part held him back. They hadn't even talked about moving in that direction. Were just now admitting to friendship. But maybe ... down the road.

"See you tomorrow." He reached over and squeezed her hand, then waited while she got in her car before he headed to his truck.

Something told him Grocerease was changing more than just the way his store worked. And he was having an awful lot of trouble getting upset about that.

Chapter 8

"That's the biggest smile I've seen on your face in ... well, maybe ever." Mack grinned as Kaitlyn unloaded groceries at register five.

"I probably shouldn't be this happy about it, but I just can't help myself."

"Oh? What's that?"

"One of the third-grade teachers has been put on bed rest and wasn't planning to finish the spring semester after her baby is born in February anyway. So, I will be the full-time sub for the rest of the year and possibly get a full-time position next fall."

"You'll be teaching again." Mack pointed to her total. "That's great. I know you want to get back into the classroom."

She nodded. "It is great. A lot of craziness thrown at me all at once, but at least I'll have next week off for Thanksgiving to sort of map out a plan and get my feet under me. Just a couple days of chaos and uncertainty this week. And let's be honest. It would've been crazy this week, anyway, with the kids excited about their upcoming break."

"I remember how it was. Not wanting to do much work because there were only a few days until you didn't have to."

"You remember that, huh?" She smirked as he handed her the receipt.

"I'm not *that* old."

"You sure? Don't ask a third grader your age. They always guess too high."

He loved how she made him laugh. Not that she always had, but the more playful interactions had definitely increased over the last few weeks.

"I'll try to remember not to ask any kids how old they think I am. Pretty sure I learned that lesson with my nephew a few years ago."

"I didn't know you had a nephew." Kaitlyn paused in grabbing the bags of groceries.

"There are a lot of things you don't know about me. Maybe we should do dinner again and chat about something besides Grocerease."

She pulled her bottom lip through her teeth.Had he pushed too fast?

"Maybe we should." She looped the bags over her arms. "Next week while I'm off?"

"Tuesday?"

She nodded. "Just let me know when and where."

"Can I pick you up?"

Another pause. "Sure."

He mentally fist pumped. Did she realize she'd basically agreed to a date? Or was he reading too much into this?

"See ya later, Mack."

"Bye, Kaitlyn."

He turned and winked at Mr. Moses as he rang up his weekly supply of fruits. "You're off schedule. Today isn't Wednesday."

"And a good thing too. Otherwise, I would've missed that little show."

Mack feigned offense, but then chuckled. "Made a bit of a fool of myself, huh?"

"Nope. But I'm glad to see you two have made up and more. Last time I saw you talking, your voices were much louder. I take it you took my advice and decided to embrace this new-fangled app thing?"

"I don't know if I'd go so far as to say 'embrace.'" Mack grimaced. "But I decided to at least give it a fair chance. And definitely not let it get between me and a friendship worth much more than a bit of technology."

"You might rather be embracing *her*." Mr. Moses chuckled at his own joke.

Mack joined in, even as heat rose through his cheeks. No denying the thought had run through his head a time or two lately. But something told him he had a lot further to go before any embracing happened between him and Kaitlyn.

Still, with her teaching full-time, she wouldn't have to work for the stupid app anymore. And while that meant he wouldn't see her as often, at least that bit of contention wouldn't stay between them. No need. That should help things move a little faster.

"I DIDN'T EXPECT to see you in here this week." Mack grinned from his perch behind the register. "Figured I wouldn't see you until I picked you up this evening."

Kaitlyn shook her head and placed another item on the conveyor belt. "Groceries are needed even on school holidays, you know."

"Did you forget your mom's pumpkin?" Mack glanced over the items left to scan. "I know you said you still needed a can."

"No. I got it the other day." Kaitlyn put the last few things out and then pushed her cart to the end. "This is for the DeWitts."

Mack's head jerked up. "The DeWitts?"

"We've talked about this. It's hard for her to come in—"

"I know who you're talking about." Mack shoved a sack of potatoes her way. "I guess I didn't realize you'd still be working for Grocerease now that you'll be teaching full time. Especially since you said you'd be swamped working on lesson plans and figuring out the rest of the year."

Seriously? No wonder he was so excited for her to get the position.

"Even a teacher needs to get out every now and then. And I probably won't be working for the app as much, but I can grab an order here and there just to stay active in it. Besides, I love helping the DeWitts."

He didn't reply.

She huffed out some of her frustration. "I thought we'd moved past this."

"This?" He handed her the receipt. "This what?"

"This prejudice you have against Grocerease."

"Prejudice?"

"Yes. Prejudice. That thing where you 'pre-judge' something or someone and then hold it against them forever more because you're too big-headed to learn better." That was harsher than she meant it to be, but she was too angry to take the words back.

"Big-headed, huh?"

"Obviously. Your head's so big, it's outgrown your hair!" She motioned toward his shaved head.

A sound somewhere between a laugh and a protest shot

from his lips. "Wow. Talk about small-minded. I shave my head because it's easier to take care of. This is a choice." He circled his pate with a pointer finger.

"So is working for Grocerease." Kaitlyn pushed the cart away. "But apparently it's a choice you can't accept."

"Kaitlyn, wait." Mack leaped down from his stool, but she kept going. "Kaitlyn!"

"No, Mack. I can't do this right now. Just ... sorry, but let's cancel tonight for now."

He blinked a few times, his broad shoulders folding in on themselves. "Seriously?"

"What's the point of going? We can't talk five minutes without arguing. That doesn't sound like much fun to me." She shook her head. "I'll see you around."

She didn't stay to hear how he might reply. Her disappointment was too bitter. She'd really been looking forward to this evening.

The drizzly morning matched her mood perfectly. She ducked under her low hatch and loaded the groceries. Maybe Patti would have time for a quick visit. That would cheer her up.

No such luck. The house stayed silent while Kaitlyn unloaded the groceries on the porch. They were either all in the back where they hadn't spotted her, or busy with something else. She gave a quick rap on the door and then walked back to her car and slid in. After waiting one more minute with no sign of Patti or her smile, Kaitlyn sent a notice through the app that the groceries were there and then drove home.

The smell of baking pumpkin would normally lift Kaitlyn's spirits like nothing else, but it did nothing this afternoon. Her mom paused in scooping batter into a leaf-shaped muffin pan. Kaitlyn dropped her purse on the table by the door and then slid into Mom's side-hug.

"What's wrong?"

"I really thought Mack was changing. Maybe we'd moved past his whole aversion to Grocerease. But the way he talked today, it was like he was surprised I was still working for the app now that I have the full-time position. Like he was disappointed I was still filling orders."

"You know people don't change overnight, Kait."

"I know. But it's been more than one night." She gave her mom a sheepish grin. "I mean, we're almost to the end of the trial period. A few weeks ago, I thought he was starting to see the benefits and how they outweighed whatever downside he keeps thinking exists, but today …" Kaitlyn pressed her palms to her eyes. "Why does he have to be so stubborn?"

"Maybe you should ask him that tonight at dinner?"

Kaitlyn stepped away and shook her head. "I canceled."

"What? Why?"

"I just told you, Mom. He can't get past this. So, there's no potential for us for anything more than fellow Christians who sometimes talk at the store."

"You're seriously going to let an app come between you and the possibility of friendship—or more?" Mom clasped her shoulder. "I see the way you guys smile when you see each other. There's some definite attraction there."

"A relationship can't be built on attraction alone. You need so much more. And as long as that mountain of an app hangs between us, I don't think we could dig a strong enough foundation for anything else."

"Don't give up on him yet."

"I don't see how I have any other choice." Kaitlyn turned her head. "Especially considering some of the things I said earlier."

"Do I even want to know?"

"Probably not. I'm not particularly proud of it, myself. But he just aggravates me."

Mom squeezed her once more. "Pray about it. If for no other reason than you're both Christians. You need to find a way to get along even if nothing more comes from it."

Kaitlyn nodded and escaped to her room. When she closed her eyes, Mack's face was before her, disappointment and frustration of his own reflected there. Good thing she didn't plan to work for Grocerease anymore this week. They both needed time to cool off.

Chapter 9

"How's my store?" Mack's dad popped a bite of roll in his mouth on Thanksgiving.

"Can't you wait until later to talk business?" Mom passed a bowl of mashed potatoes. "There's more to life than groceries, you know."

"Says the woman who used groceries to make this meal." Dad winked before forking out a big serving of sliced turkey.

Mack hid a smirk behind his napkin. Some things never changed, and that included holiday meals at his parents' house. His sister-in-law, Shanna, and his brother, Micah, sat on either side of his nephew, Joey, making sure he got more than meat and bread. Grandma occupied the head of the table, but obviously had her hearing aid turned off because she wasn't paying attention to anything but her food.

"I'm not saying we don't use groceries." Mom waved the slotted spoon Dad's way as she paused in scooping out green beans. "I'm simply saying we can talk about other things than the store for a while."

"If it wasn't for that store, none of us would be here today. McDonald's Groceries has provided for this family for almost seven decades now. And I'm thankful for it." Dad gave a quick nod. "Which makes it a perfectly legitimate topic for conversation on Thanksgiving."

That did it. Mack could no longer hold in his laughter. How could Mom argue with logic like that? Though part of him wished she'd been able to change the subject. He wasn't sure he wanted to talk shop with his dad after the way things had gone the last few months.

"Uh-oh. What's that face about?" Micah tossed a roll at him. "Please tell me I'm not going to have to save the store."

"Micah!" Shanna swatted him over Joey. "Be nice."

"The store is doing okay." Mack barely refrained from sticking his tongue out at Micah. "No little brothers necessary."

"Hmm." Micah sat back and scratched his hair which was quickly going the way of Mack's—a hereditary gift from their father and his before him—not that Mack would take back what he'd told Kaitlyn. "Not sure I believe you. Rumor has it you've had some run-ins with some new app that had you all in a knot. Or was it the girl working for the app?"

Shanna shot Mack a look of apology, but she had very little control over his ornery brother. Mack still couldn't figure out why she'd married him.

"Every new piece of technology takes time for adjustments." Mack focused on his cranberry sauce. "We're getting there."

"You mean you really have had problems with some new app?" Dad leaned forward in his seat, not noticing his shirt swiping through a dollop of gravy.

Mack sent a glare his brother's way before facing his dad. "The app is one that lets people shop for other people so they don't have to come in the store themselves. It just took us a bit to get used to how it worked."

Dad sat back again, shaking his head. "People are too lazy nowadays. Can't even bother to go buy their own groceries."

"Actually, some of the customers using it can't get out to buy their own groceries. Kaitlyn's mom has MS and is prone to falling or has days where she just doesn't have the energy to get out. The DeWitts have an autistic child who can't handle the extra noise and stimulation that comes with a trip to the store. Mrs. Felder broke her hip a few weeks ago and has been using the app to get her weekly supplies too."

"I heard you hated the app and were going to quit using it after the trial period is up." Micah reached for another roll.

"Where are you hearing all this gossip?" Mack set his fork aside, only a few pieces of celery left on his plate. "You don't even live here."

"Not gossip if it's true."

"Yes, it is." Mom flicked Micah in the ear. "And you know better. I'm sorry, Shanna. I tried to raise my boys to be good."

"You did an excellent job, Mama M." Shanna wiped some cranberry sauce from Joey's cheek, despite the scowl he sent her way.

"I'd still like to know your source." Mack folded his arms over his chest.

"I may not live here anymore, but I still have friends in town. Word has it you've been fighting with the girl who shops for the app every time she comes in your store."

"I have not been fighting with Kaitlyn *every* time she comes in. She's actually raised a few suggestions and ideas I've considered implementing after the holidays." Mack didn't dare glance at Dad—he was worse than Mack about adjusting to change. "We're both Christian adults who respect each other and can be friendly even if we don't always agree."

"You definitely weren't agreeing on Tuesday." Micah finally filled in the last blank Mack needed to figure things out.

"You were in the store Tuesday?"

"Mom needed a few things. I chose Candie's register because she's nicer than you are." Micah made a face. "Just happened to overhear everything. Including her canceling dinner."

Mack cursed his skin that showed his feelings so well. As hot as his head was, he was bound to be redder than one of Mr. Moses's strawberries. How had he not spotted his own brother? Had he been so distracted?

Yes. Kaitlyn had become a huge distraction in his life.

"Has the app affected anything else in the store? Besides your love life?" Dad smirked as he sopped up the rest of his gravy with a bite of roll.

"I, for one, wouldn't mind seeing Mack love more than that store." Mom swatted Dad before getting up to carry her dishes to the kitchen. "It's amazing you spent enough time outside of work to fall in love with me all those years ago. It would do him good to settle down."

"I didn't have to spend time out of the store. You came to see me every week when you bought groceries." Dad called behind her.

"I should've gone to Foodland!" Her reply from the other room carried enough tease in it to keep tempers from rising. No one in this house would dare step foot in Foodland. And despite their picking at each other, Mack knew his parents loved one another.

"You didn't answer my question about the app affecting anything else." Dad sat back and studied Mack.

"Couldn't get a word in edgewise." Mack grinned. "Things were a bit off for a while. But I think we'll be okay."

Dad nodded. "Sounds like when everyone stopped using checks and cash and went to cards. Then they went to those newer chip-reader machines. And when we changed from carrying milk from one local company to another who had better prices. People rebelled for a while that year too."

"Have you ever rearranged products?" The question slipped out before Mack could stop.

The room fell silent. Everyone looked at him like he'd lost his mind. Maybe he had. But Kaitlyn's suggestions of putting things on aisles that made more sense wouldn't leave him alone. Mom brought in a pumpkin and pecan pies and set them in the middle of the table.

"If you're wanting to move the sauces over near the soups, I think it's a great idea." She sliced through the pumpkin pie without looking at him. How did she know what he'd been thinking?

"Why would he need to move anything?" Dad gestured wide and almost got a handful of pie for the trouble. "Everyone who shops at McDonald's knows where everything is. It's always been in the same place since it opened."

"But it doesn't make sense there. I've never understood why your dad put some things where he did." Mom thrust a dessert plate in his hands. "And the first time I shopped there, I couldn't find half my list. If you hadn't been so cute, I might not've come back."

Dad blinked. "What?"

"Mack is the manager now, and I say he gets to arrange the store however he thinks it makes sense. And if that means moving the sauces to a more logical spot, then he can do that."

"No one will be able to find anything."

"Sure they will. Because most people know sauces and soups go together." She sat down, having served everyone dessert. "Eat your pie."

Mack quickly stuffed a bite of pumpkin pie in his own mouth before anyone else could ask him another question.

Would rearranging the sauce mixes help him get back into Kaitlyn's good graces?

"T‍HIS LOOKS like Mr. Moses's order." Candie scanned the strawberries Kaitlyn laid on the conveyor belt the next Wednesday.

Kaitlyn had avoided the store as much as she could since calling off dinner with Mack the week before. But when she'd seen Mr. Moses's name on the app notifications this afternoon, she had to grab it. He ranked right up there with the DeWitts.

"It is."

"What?" Mack's voice came from behind her.

Kaitlyn's heart skittered a second. She hadn't seen him as she walked through the store and stupidly hoped maybe he was off. He came into view and grabbed some items to bag.

"It is Mr. Moses's order. He evidently caught something from his family who visited over the holidays. One of his grandsons was still in town, so Mr. Moses got him to teach him how to use the 'newfangled app thingy,' as he calls it." Kaitlyn ran her card through the reader. "I called him before coming to the store just to make sure it really was him."

"But Mr. Moses never lets anyone else pick out his groceries for him." Candie handed her the receipt.

"I guess he decided it was worth it to get his smoothies." Kaitlyn gave a slight shrug. "And he didn't order anything less than he normally buys. So, you didn't lose any money by him shopping this way."

Mack grimaced at her words, but Kaitlyn couldn't take them back now. There was something about him that had her hackles raising, even when he hadn't said anything. Yet another reason why it was good she'd canceled their dinner last week.

"Kaitlyn." Mack touched her arm before she could push past him.

She paused but didn't dare meet his eyes.

"Can we talk?"

"I'm not sure it's a good idea. We can't seem to be nice when we talk."

"I promise to be nice."

Her lips twitched as she spied him holding a hand over his heart.

"I'm sorry you thought I'd worry about losing money when it came to Mr. Moses. I was more worried about him, honestly." Mack touched her shoulder and the heat from his hand reached her heart. "And more worried about you."

"Me?" Her gaze moved his way of its own volition.

"And the fact that you seem to think I'm callus and grouchy. The exact opposite of how I want you to think of me."

She pinched her lips between her teeth. "You're not *always* grouchy."

"It's a start anyway." He gave a squeeze before moving his hand away. "Will you tell Mr. Moses I said to feel better?"

"I will."

Mack nodded and stepped back. "Thanks."

She blinked and took the groceries out to her car. What just happened? Where had her decision to stay away from Mack McDonald gone? And why could she still feel the imprint of his hand on her shoulder?

She gave herself a mental shake. No need to get any closer right now. Not with the meeting scheduled for next week to determine if Grocerease would stay in the area or not. Not to mention stay at McDonald's Grocery. She'd have to wait until after that before deciding what to do about the manager.

Chapter 10

City Hall wasn't packed, matching Kaitlyn's expectations. Grocerease wasn't that big a deal, even in a small town like Sassafras. It was just a big deal to *her*.

She scanned the crowd gathered on old metal folding chairs. Mack sat near the front left. She veered toward the right. Maybe it was the coward's way out, but just like the other day at church, she couldn't face him yet. Not before this meeting was over. Too much at stake.

Fred Malone, the Foodland manager, wore a bowtie two shades off from his baggy suit coat. No one else attempted to dress up, not even the Grocerease representatives seated at the table in front of the room. Kaitlyn slid into a seat three rows back. Near enough to overhear Fred, but nowhere close to Mack.

"We'll start in ten minutes." Mayor Grimsby tapped the end of the microphone, sending a squawk through the small space.

Mack glanced back her way, moved slightly her direction, but then faced front again. Kaitlyn gathered her notes into a neat pile in her lap. Who knew if she'd be called on to give her feedback? But being one of the main shoppers who worked for the app, she came prepared.

However this meeting went, she couldn't let Mack distract her.

"Okay, people. Thanks to everyone for coming this evening." The mayor was in rare form, nodding and waving as if up for reelection. "We're going to try and keep this meeting short and to the point. Here's the order we'll go in.

"The Grocerease Reps, Garik Miles and Isaac Smith, are here to get feedback from our trial run. We'll let the shoppers go first. Then, the store managers. Then, anyone who has used the app and wants to put in their two cents."

Kaitlyn wasn't sure why the shoppers would go before the managers, but she wouldn't argue with it. This was her last chance to convince Mack the app was a good thing. Besides, she'd taught all day and was exhausted, so better to take her turn early before her brain completely shut down.

"How many shoppers do we have present tonight?"

Three or four other hands went up, along with Kaitlyn's.

"Okay, let's work from this side of the room." Garik pointed to Mack's side.

So much for going first.

A guy with a man-bun and beard stood, hands shoved in his pockets. "I'm Tyler. I started working for Grocerease about a week after it came to our area. Did probably six or seven orders a week."

"Tyler, tell us about your experience with the app. Was it easy to use? Is this something you think you'd like to continue doing here?" Isaac scribbled notes on a legal pad.

"It worked okay. Shopping for Grocerease was the first time I'd ever done this kind of work, so I didn't really have any expectations going into it. For the most part, I was able to find all the items customers ordered. And it's not a hard way to make a little extra money every week."

"Any suggestions for how we can improve the app?"

Tyler shrugged. "Not really."

"Okay, thanks. Who's next?"

If that was the way everyone replied, this meeting would be fast. And useless. Had Tyler given them anything they didn't already know? Kaitlyn squirmed—three more people before her turn.

Mack's gaze collided with hers across the room, and she quickly turned her attention back to a woman named Melinda. She wasn't ready to attempt reading Mack's thoughts on all of this.

Melinda giggled. "It was such a great way to make some extra money without having to find someone to keep my baby. He could just ride in the cart while I worked. I appreciate you bringing this opportunity to our area. Such a help for moms like me."

At least that was a bit more helpful than Tyler's testimony. Though from the expressions on Isaac and Garik's faces, maybe not what they'd expected to hear.

"Okay, Melinda. We're glad it worked out so well for you. Any suggestions on how to make things better?"

Melinda tapped a finger to her chin. "Hm. I guess ... well, I don't even know if this is a possibility, actually. But if it is ... if you could have a way to update the inventory on the app to match the store a little better, that would be helpful."

"What do you mean?" Garik frowned.

"It's just super frustrating to have to send a message and ask about substitutions then wait for the customer to reply. I couldn't always wait around, so the customer didn't get that item or a substitute. And sometimes, they took away from my tip because of that when it wasn't my fault."

Had the woman been shopping in Foodland or McDonald's more? Kaitlyn didn't remember her, but that didn't necessarily mean she hadn't shopped at the same place. Just that their paths hadn't crossed.

"I'm not sure how much we can improve the inventory issues. That's partly the store's responsibility, too, because we're linked with the program they send us. We get our information right from their servers. But it's definitely something to look into. Thanks."

The next two shoppers were even quicker than Tyler had been. One had done something like this before with another app and said Grocerease worked better. The other shopper acted like she couldn't use more than fifty words.

"Okay, thank you." Garik scanned the crowd. "And did I see one more shopper?"

Kaitlyn rose. "Hi. I'm Kaitlyn Daniels."

"Hi, Kaitlyn. Can you tell us a bit about your experience?"

"This is actually the second time I've worked for Grocerease. I was a shopper back in college in Fayetteville and petitioned for it to move to this area. I know quite a few families who have benefited from having an app like this— like my mom because of health problems, or other issues that make it hard for people to get out. The app has improved since the last time I used it. I never had any problems getting ahold of my customers when I needed to substitute things."

She started to glance Mack's direction but caught herself. "And the grocery store managers were willing to help me with making sure everything was found or in stock."

"Great." Isaac smiled. "We're glad to have you on the team. Is there anything you can recommend we do to improve the app?"

"I can't think of anything in particular."

"Okay. If you do down the road, just let us know through our customer support contacts."

Kaitlyn nodded and sat down. She'd done her best.

"Okay, moving on to the managers now. We'll go right to left this time."

Fred bounced out of his seat as if there were springs under him. "I'm Fred Malone, manager at Foodland."

"Hello, Fred. What can you tell us about your Grocerease experience?"

"Nothing but good. I know apps like this are exactly what our customers were wanting in this area, and we're thrilled to be a part of this trial. Everything went as well as possible, and we're hoping you decide to stick around so our customers can continue to have access to such a great app."

Could he be more schmoozy? Had he really had no problems whatsoever with the app? Or was he just trying to be the store that won more customers?

Kaitlyn leaned back and crossed her arms while the representatives asked Fred a few more questions and received answers that really didn't answer anything. Isaac and Garik exchanged a look, whispered a few things among themselves, and then nodded.

"Okay, thanks Fred. We're glad your experience went so well."

"Sure, sure." Fred nodded, but still stood.

"Did you have anything else to add?" Garik asked.

"Nope."

"Okay, we're going to move on to the other manager, then."

Fred slowly sank down while Mack stood. Kaitlyn's chest constricted. Part of her wanted to flee, to not hear what might come from his mouth. Would he be the complete opposite of Fred? She wrapped her arms more tightly around her torso and held her breath.

"I'm Mack McDonald, owner and manager of McDonald's Grocery."

"Hello, Mack. Tell us about your experience."

"Honestly, I wasn't sure about this app when we first started using it. I thought it would take away the personal customer service I liked to offer to each of our customers." Mack cleared his throat. "How was I supposed to get to know people if they never came in the store?"

Kaitlyn swallowed a groan and squeezed her eyes shut. Would only one store in town be enough to keep the app in the area? Maybe the dollar store would want to sign on to use it. How had she thought he'd changed?

Before he could continue, Kaitlyn's phone buzzed in her pocket. She pulled it out, frowning at the message.

Mom needed her.

She woodenly gathered her purse and slipped out the side. No idea if the rest of the meeting would go better or worse. It took all her willpower to drive back to the house instead of staying to hear what else Mack had to say.

"THAT BEING SAID, the longer the trial ran, the more I realized I got to know some of the customers through the shoppers who came in for them. And it turned out to be helpful to know when we weren't ordering enough of a product some customers needed for health issues. Or that certain items were listed on our inventory but not actually in stock."

Mack refused to look back and see what Kaitlyn was thinking. He focused on staying positive.

"I'm still not completely satisfied with some of the ways this app works, but I don't hate it as much as I thought I would." Mack shifted his weight.

Isaac tapped a pencil against the table. "We appreciate your insight. Could you give us a few more details?"

"Right." Mack skimmed his notes. "Store managers could benefit from a way to see what things look like without having to log in as a customer. And a way to include items that aren't in our normal inventory, like seasonal products. I am gathering, simply from sales data, that some of our seasonal items weren't listed on the app."

"Can you give me an example?" Garik scribbled furiously.

"Cans of pumpkin pie filling around Thanksgiving. Right now, it's mint and gingerbread items for Christmas. Things that we might have one or two on hand through the year, but people look for more around the holidays."

"Okay. I thought we had it set where anything you had in inventory would pull to the app, but we might need to tweak something. This is very helpful." Isaac nodded. "Can you stick around afterward so we can go over a few things with you?"

Mack glanced over his shoulder and his stomach plummeted. Where was Kaitlyn? When had she disappeared?

"Mr. McDonald?"

He turned his attention back to the front. "Sure. I can stay."

Numbly, he sat once more to wait until the rest of the people had taken their turns. Had Kaitlyn left because of something he said? He'd tried to be positive about everything, but he wanted to be honest too. Wasn't that more important than saying only what people wanted to hear? He didn't want to be like Fred—that was for sure.

The meeting stretched on longer than it should have, with most of the customers repeating the same things. And while there were only a handful of them, going through each person was monotonous. The mayor glanced at his watch. Mack avoided looking around to see if Kaitlyn might just be standing in the back now.

Finally, they made it through everyone. Mack answered a few more questions from Isaac and Garik before he left. No decision was given tonight on the status of Grocerease, but he had a feeling it would stick around. Would that make things better or worse between him and Kaitlyn?

That was another decision yet to be determined.

Chapter 11

Kaitlyn hadn't been in McDonald's in over a week. Honestly? She'd even used Grocerease a few days before to have someone else do her and Mom's shopping. But all she needed was a gallon of milk, eggs, and some bread today. Not enough to warrant an order through the app.

She took a deep breath and stepped out of her car. She could do this. She and Mack were both adults and Christians. Even if he was upset about the app still being in Sassafras, maybe he wouldn't hold it against her.

She waved at Candie then headed to the back of the store with her basket. In and out. No big deal. Just a quick grocery run.

"There you are."

Her feet halted only a yard from the refrigerated section. Mack stood, a box of shredded cheese under his arm. Her heart raced as if it wanted to skip over and greet him, but she urged it to slow down. While he didn't sound upset, it was better to get the lay of the land before rushing into anything.

"Was I missing?" Kaitlyn hugged the basket to her front.

"Yes, actually." He set down the dairy products and stepped closer. "I went from seeing you almost every day, and sometimes more than once a day, to not seeing you at all for ten days. I wondered if you'd caught whatever Mr. Moses had."

Kaitlyn ducked her head. "No. Nothing like that. Just busy with, you know, lesson plans."

"And that's all that's kept you away?" He inched nearer.

She swallowed and brushed back a strand of hair. "I mean, it's been a big part."

"Got a minute now?" He reached across the narrow space left between them and touched her arm. "I want to show you something."

"Um ..." Any and all thoughts that normally made sense scattered. "I guess."

He called another worker to finish stocking cheese and wove his fingers through hers before tugging her toward another part of the store. What in the world? What could he possibly need to show her in the ... soup aisle?

Motioning to the section in front of them, he turned with raised brows and a grin. "What do you think?"

What was she supposed to be noticing? Her eyes skimmed over the various pouches of sauce mixes, but they all looked pretty standard. At the edge of her mish-mashed thoughts, something sparked, but she couldn't quite grasp onto it.

"You honestly don't remember?" Mack leaned his head and studied her. "It was your idea to move these here."

Oh! The conversation from weeks ago came into focus. Wait. He'd moved something in his store which had been in the same spot forever? Mack McDonald? The guy who never wanted anything to change?

Kaitlyn turned to him, narrowing her eyes. "Who are you, and what did you do with Mack?"

His laughter burst forth and drew her lips up at the edges. "Come here."

Once again, she found herself being tugged through the store, this time to the front and into the manager's office. She'd never been in here before, but the piles all over the desk didn't surprise her. Everything was haphazard to her, but Mack probably had a system.

"I owe you an apology." He leaned back against the desk and pulled her to stand in front of him. "Did you leave the meeting last week because of something I said?"

"No!" Kaitlyn set the basket down in an extra chair. "No. Mom needed me. She was having trouble finding her monthly shot and needed it within a certain timeframe. She's just been taking them the last few months, and we'd rearranged some things due to the holiday leftovers so the medicine slipped down where she couldn't find it. I had to go help hunt."

"But she's okay? She got it in time?"

She studied their fingers still twined together and nodded. "Yes. She's fine. Though it just about killed me to walk out while you were still up. I wasn't sure what you might say. How things would go."

"I pointed out both the good and the bad. Made some suggestions of ways they might improve things. Even agreed to another trial as they test some of the suggestions."

"Is that why peppermint chips and gingerbread house kits were front and center when I opened the app the other day?"

"You used the app? To order groceries for *you*?"

"I—"

"Was avoiding me." His fingers loosened for a second, and his lips pinched together.

A sigh deflated her. "Yes. I just wasn't sure where we stood. How you were handling the app still being around. And where we'd left things a few weeks ago ..."

"I really messed it all up." He tugged her just a bit closer. "I'm sorry."

She shook her head. "I came in here trying to force my opinions and wishes on you and not taking into consideration how it might affect you or the store. I know things don't work the same way in different situations. I see it every day with my third graders. But for some reason, I didn't want to apply it to this."

"And it can work here. But it will work easier with a few tweaks." He let go long enough to reach up and lift her chin. "You helped me see that sometimes just because we've done something the same way forever doesn't mean it's the best way. I mean, if Mr. Moses can figure out how to use this 'newfangled app thingy,' surely I can, right?"

A giggle escaped. "I don't know. He might be more open-minded than you."

"Mm. I'm not sure about that. I'm thinking more and more about possibilities that had never occurred to me before." With one more tug, he had her where his arms could wrap around her waist.

She gasped and pressed her hands to his chest. "Possibilities?"

"Sure. I mean, one day I move the sauce mixes over near the soups. The next, who knows? I might switch the meat department with the produce, just to keep people on their toes."

"Let's not get crazy here." Kaitlyn patted his shoulder. "I mean, we still need to be able to find the ground chuck."

He dropped his voice where she had to lean in to hear him. "Know what I want to find?"

Unable to speak, she simply shook her head.

"Your forgiveness. And maybe another chance at dinner. And then ... maybe even more after that."

"Yeah? Sounds like a pretty big order. Might require a big tip."

"I've got an idea about that too." And he pressed his lips to hers.

She froze and then melted. Best tip ever. Though she wouldn't want it from anyone else.

"Mack?" Candie burst through the door. "Oh! Sorry. Never mind."

Kaitlyn smiled and pressed her lips together as she turned and retrieved her basket.

"Sounds like duty calls." Mack straightened and tucked a flyaway strand behind her ear.

"Yes. And I better get the milk and stuff Mom wanted."

"Think we can grab dinner tomorrow night?" He opened the door for her and Candie shot her a wink.

"Dinner sounds great."

"Let me know when you're ready to check out, and I'll be waiting up front."

"You've been *checking her out* for months." Candie poked him as he walked by. "About time you two did something about it."

Kaitlyn giggled. Who knew she could find romance at register five, of all places?

About Amy R. Anguish

Amy R Anguish grew up a preacher's kid, and in spite of having lived in seven different states that are all south of the Mason Dixon line, she is not a football fan. Currently, she resides in Tennessee with her husband, daughter, and son, and usually a bossy cat or two. Amy has an English degree from Freed-Hardeman University that she intends to use to glorify God, and she wants her stories to show that while Christians face real struggles, it can still work out for good.

Also by Amy R. Anguish

Roadtrip for ~~One~~ Two

Roadtrip Romance—Book Two

Recovering from heartbreak is hard when

the ex-fiancé tags along ...

Dallas wasn't in the plans when Bree Henley set out to use the nonrefundable honeymoon tickets from her canceled wedding. Nor was running into ex-fiancé Nathan Hart. But their mutual friends and the weather have other ideas. A hurricane cancels their cruise and Bree decides to turn the disaster into a roadtrip for one, never imagining Nathan would object.

Nathan is furious when he uncovers the plot to get him back with Bree. But he can't just let her go roaming around the big city of Dallas alone. Though he knows calling off their wedding was the right thing to do, he still cares for Bree. And before he knows what hits him, he's volunteered to tag along. Suddenly, it's a trip for two.

Spending the week together might remind them of why they fell in love. But is it enough to overcome the obstacles standing in the way of "til death do us part"?

Get your copy here:

https://scrivenings.link/roadtripfortwo

Destination: ~~Fun~~ Romance

Roadtrip Romance—Book Two

It's not every day you bring a boyfriend back as a souvenir.

Katie Wilhite is ready to settle into her new job as a librarian now that college is through, but friends Bree and Skye want one more girls' trip, and when Bree insists this is her bachelorette fling, Katie agrees. What she didn't agree to was allowing fun and flighty Skye to dictate the itinerary or for her anxiety to kick in harder than ever ... right in front of a cute guy.

Camden Malone had no idea when he agreed to be the voice of reason on his cousin Ryan's vacation that the trip wouldn't stay in New Orleans as planned. But when Ryan plots with Skye so that the guys can tag along with the girls all week, he isn't nearly as upset as he should be. Not with Katie's fiery temper and flashing eyes intriguing him more by the minute.

Can Katie relax enough to trust Camden and a possible future, or will she continue to push him away as only a vacation fling? And can Camden move past a rocky history of his own to be able to jump into a better future? For a trip that was supposed to be all about fun, there's a lot of romance going around.

Get your copy here:

https://scrivenings.link/destinationromance

No Place Like Home

Can love secure Adrian's wandering heart?

Roots are overrated, at least to someone like Adrian Stewart, preacher's kid, who has never lived anywhere longer than six years.

That's why her job with MidUSLogIn Inc., is so perfect for her—lots of travel, and staying nowhere long enough to have it feel like home. But when work takes her to Memphis, closer to her family for the first time in years and in the same small office as Grayson Roberts, she starts to question her job, her lack of home, and even her memories of her rocky past with the church.

Gray is intrigued by Adrian from the moment he sees her, and he's determined to get to the bottom of why this girl, who loves old movies and hums when she works, won't go to church with him. As they grow closer, he wants more too, but how can he convince her to stay in Memphis when she doesn't believe in home—or God? Can he use his own broken past to break through hers?

Get your copy here:

https://scrivenings.link/noplacelikehome

Saving Grace

Michelle Wilson's one goal in life was to become a top journalist at the local paper back in her hometown of Cedar Springs, AR. But on the way to bringing that dream to reality, a life-changing wreck interrupts Michelle's plans and adds an orphaned baby into the mix. Now, she has tough decisions ahead—did God put her in that accident to save baby Grace? And if so, why is it so hard to convince everyone else she should be the baby's new mommy?

Greg Marshall has been Michelle's best friend his whole life. He's thrilled she's moving back home, but not so sure about her sudden desire to be a single mom. His feelings for her have grown through the years, but she's never seemed to notice. Can he help Michelle with the adoption and grow their relationship at the same time?

Get your copy here:

https://scrivenings.link/savinggrace

Faith and Hope

Get your copy here:

https://scrivenings.link/faithandhope

An Unexpected Legacy

Get your copy here:

https://scrivenings.link/anunexpectedlegacy

A Novella

where LOVE *is planted*

SARAH ANNE CROUCH

To Michael, Elizabeth, Lily, and Peter.
I choose you.

Chapter 1

How many flower shops could there possibly be in a town the size of Trammel, Texas?

More than one would think, apparently. Grant Keller drummed his fingers on his desk as the search engine results finished loading on his phone. He didn't have time to waste ordering a bouquet for his mother, but ten minutes calling a florist was better than an hour apologizing to his mom. Or—even worse—making a trip out west to Trammel.

Grant selected the first business to materialize on his screen and pressed call.

"Aaronson Flowers and Gifts, this is Ivy. How may I help you?" The voice on the other end sounded a little raspy, but not old. He guessed she was in her twenties or thirties.

"Hi, Ivy, I'd like to order a bouquet."

"Of course. What's the occasion?"

"A birthday."

"Sure, we have plenty of selections appropriate for a birthday."

Grant immediately realized his mistake. "Sorry, it's not actually for a birthday." He ran his fingers through his hair. He was wasting precious time. Why could he not accomplish such a simple task?

"Oh, okay." She was understandably confused.

"It's my birthday. The flowers are for my mom."

"Ahh." She dragged the word out, and he sensed they were finally getting somewhere. "Kind of a 'thanks for giving birth to me' present?"

"Yes. Something like that." More like a *please don't be mad at me present*, but she didn't need to know that.

"Well, does your mom have any favorite flowers?"

Grant racked his brain. He should've figured out what he wanted to buy before he called. He was about to tell her to pick something when he remembered. "Sunflowers. She always decorates with sunflowers."

"Hmm." Grant deflated a bit at the tone of her voice, but she continued. "We don't get many of those big yellow sunflowers in March, but I can order some. It'll only take a few days."

"Oh, no. I can't wait that long." He should've called sooner, but he just came up with the idea of an apology bouquet.

"Okay. I think I can come up with something just as sunny and vibrant. We've got some gorgeous gerbera daisies in the shop right now. They're *my* favorites."

"That sounds great." He'd never heard of a gerbera whatsit, but he'd agree to pretty much anything she suggested at this point.

"What size bouquet would you like?"

Grant poked his head out of his office. No sign of his boss. He ducked back inside. "How about a dozen?" A dozen flowers sounded like a generous amount.

"And a vase? We typically include those in our arrangements, unless told otherwise."

His mother must have a vase somewhere in the house, but

he hated to make her go on the hunt for the perfect container when the flower shop could just provide one for her. "Yes, please."

"What name should I put on the order?"

"My name is Grant, but my mom's name is Lisa."

"Okay, Grant. And will you be picking it up in the shop?"

"No, I need it delivered."

"Sure thing. When would you like the bouquet sent?"

"Today?"

Ivy paused on the other end. He winced and waited for her to tell him she couldn't make the delivery.

"I'll make sure she gets it."

Grant breathed a sigh of relief. "Oh, thank you so much, Ivy."

"Sure thing. But next time, give me at least a day's notice."

"I will." Although no one was around to see it, Grant smiled.

"What would you like on the card?"

He hadn't thought through that part either, but Grant was an excellent extemporaneous speaker. "Mom, I'm sorry I can't give these to you in person. Thank you for twenty-seven years of putting up with me. I love you to the moon and back. Grant."

Ivy's pen stopped scratching on the other end. "That's lovely."

Grant's cheeks warmed. "Thank you."

He'd finished giving his credit card information right as a knock sounded on his door. Grant held up his finger and motioned to the phone. "Thanks for your help, Ivy. I appreciate it."

"Thank you for your business, Grant. I hope you think of us again when your mom's birthday rolls around. Maybe we'll have some sunflowers for her."

"That'd be great. Thanks."

"Have a blessed day."

Her statement caught Grant by surprise. Not many business owners in the metroplex offered benedictions. "Oh, um, you too. Thanks." He punched the screen to end the call.

"You get that email from Hughes?" Marcus Thacker, Grant's coworker and fellow associate at Packer, Hughes, and Price, stood in the doorway.

Grant sat in his desk chair and swiveled to face his computer. In bold letters at the top of his inbox "Darby Hearing Date." He skimmed the body of the message.

He groaned. "The hearing's been moved back."

"What's the problem? Now you've got more time."

"I know, but I've been putting off my parents about a visit home, and now it's too late. I couldn't possibly make it there and back in time for work tomorrow."

"So go over the weekend. Your parents are in-state, right?"

Grant leveled his gaze at his friend. "Did you know that if you left Dallas for Los Angeles today, when you'd arrived at the halfway point you'd still be in Texas?" He'd made the drive many times while shuttling back and forth to see his college girlfriend. She'd attended a more prestigious—and much more expensive—law school, while he'd opted to stay in-state and closer to home. Funny, that decision hadn't translated to more time with his family.

"What's your point?" Marcus raised an eyebrow.

"My point is, Texas is a massive state. And my parents live three hours away, plus it's nearly rush hour. While it is technically possible for me to drive all the way to middle-of-nowhere West Texas, I can't make the trip and catch up on the briefs I have to finish for Jenna."

Marcus shrugged and pushed off the doorway. "Suit yourself."

A reminder pinged on Grant's digital calendar as Marcus walked away. He had five minutes to read over his files before meeting Jenna in her office.

As Grant reached for the papers he needed, a framed photo caught his eye. The last family vacation he'd taken with his parents and siblings was at least four years ago. Will and Hailey hadn't had any children. And his sister, Addison, was going through her platinum blonde phase. Grant missed spending time with his parents, he really did. But everything he did—working long hours, spending nights and weekends reviewing cases, and barely surfacing to see fellow humans at church services once a week—was all for the greater good.

He was making his father proud by dedicating himself to his career. And he was providing for another family, a future wife and potential children. He just hoped all the effort was worth it someday. And he prayed that his mom would be satisfied with some flowers while he climbed the corporate ladder.

For the sake of family.

Chapter 2

Twenty-seven-year-olds went out and partied on their birthdays, right? What young man called a local florist to have a beautiful bouquet delivered to his mother on his own birthday? Grant Keller. He was a special man.

"Luke? You got time for one more delivery today?" Ivy Aaronson twirled her fingers around the telephone cord. Her parents probably should've shelled out twenty bucks at some point in the last few decades to buy a cordless phone for their flower shop. Fiddling with the coiled line while making calls was something Ivy had been doing as long as she was old enough to answer the phone and take notes.

"I've got a mandatory training tonight. And I don't think anyone else is scheduled for deliveries—Victor will be there with me." A rustling sound came from the other end. "It's getting late, Ivy. I'm dropping my last arrangement then I'm heading straight to the station."

Ivy trailed her finger down the pink and yellow ribbons wrapped around Lisa Keller's vase. She couldn't let these flowers wait until tomorrow. A devoted son was counting on her.

"Never mind, I'll make the delivery myself."

"Thanks, sis. Talk to you later."

Her brother, like most Aaronson Flowers and Gifts deliverymen, was a firefighter. Ivy's mom liked that they could navigate the city and were able to work on weekdays. Luke and his buddies liked making easy cash on their days off.

But tonight, firefighter duties called, so the job of delivering Grant's birthday bouquet was left to Ivy.

Ivy's responsibilities included keeping the store, taking calls and helping her mom with the arrangements, but pitching in was part of working for a small family-owned business, and she was no stranger to performing random tasks for the sake of the flower shop.

Once, a particularly difficult bride had Ivy tying bows around dozens of candy canes and gluing heart charms to the middle of each tiny bow for her December wedding. She'd burned her fingers four times on the hot glue gun. It had been a long night of preparations, but she and her family were in it together. And that made everything she did here worthwhile.

The shop was quiet, so Ivy risked a visit to the studio in the back—the ringing bell of the front door would alert her to any new customers. Past a glass door and through a short hallway was her mom's domain. A long table ran down one side of the room. On either end stood spools of ribbon, cans full of scissors, and rolls of floral tape.

Cool air laden with the scent of baby's breath and roses filled the space. Along the back of the wall stood shelves lined with containers—glass vases, tinted bottles, painted tin buckets, and baskets. In a large refrigerated unit sat dozens and dozens of flowers and plants. The front of the store always held a few arrangements, simple bouquets for customers to grab, but the back was filled with the colors and smells of a garden.

Ivy's mother, Daphne Aaronson, stood in the middle of it all. Frizzy brunette curls, which sometimes hovered around her head like a halo, were swept into a pink scarf. A green apron wrapped her short, stout frame.

Mom glanced up as Ivy walked toward her. "Hi, sweetie." She smiled but still wore a far-off expression. Sometimes it was as if her mother traveled to another world when she worked.

"Do you mind if I take off early? There's one more delivery, but Luke couldn't make it."

"Let me finish this last arrangement, and then I'll step in." She flipped her wrist to check the time on her watch. "Your father should be here soon."

"What's he up to today?"

"Oh, making the rounds at the hospital. And probably swinging by the church office." Dad was a minister. He'd tried to retire years ago but ended up preaching at a smaller congregation and working even more. When he wasn't writing sermons or visiting church members, he came to the flower shop.

He was great with customers and familiar with every funeral parlor and hospital corridor. He'd lived in and around Trammel most of his life, so Mom hadn't had much trouble drumming up business when she first opened the shop almost thirty years ago. Or so Ivy had been told. Aaronson Flowers and Gifts had been around longer than she had.

Back at the front of the store, Ivy helped a customer find a houseplant for her friend while her mom carried the newest arrangement to the front display. She closed the refrigerator doors and helped ring up the pothos plant at the register.

"So, why the last-minute delivery?" Mom asked after the jingle of the door bid the customer farewell.

Ivy grabbed her purse from under the counter and pulled her car keys out. "A son called in a flower arrangement for his mom on *his* birthday. Isn't that sweet?"

"Yes, but we get lots of gentlemen who send flowers to their mothers."

"Not twenty-seven-year-olds." Ivy raised her eyebrows and waited.

Mom grinned and wagged a finger at her. "See? I told you there were still some good guys out there."

"Oh, my goodness!" Lisa Keller clasped her hands to her heart. "These are gorgeous."

Ivy's cheeks lifted in a smile. She loved this part of the job —when customers appreciated the beauty of God's creation as much as she did. "Thank you. Would you sign here, please?"

Lisa signed the delivery slip, then her hazel eyes met Ivy's. "Who are they from?"

"Your son, Grant." Ivy beamed, but Lisa's smile slipped a fraction.

"Oh." Lisa turned her face down to the bouquet, but Ivy wasn't fooled. Lisa had been happier about the flowers when she didn't know they were from her son.

Had Ivy been wrong about Grant? She normally wouldn't pry. But she just had to know why Lisa was disappointed. Something about this mother-son relationship was not what she'd assumed.

"I thought it was such a kind gesture. We don't get many customers his age ordering flowers for their mothers on their *own* birthdays."

Lisa bit her lip, hesitating, but only for a moment. "It's just that … I was hoping *he'd* be here instead of the flowers."

Okay, so maybe he couldn't get away as often as she liked. But at least he was generous and remembered his mother.

"He kept promising he'd come visit," Lisa went on. "It's been months since we last saw him, and I thought surely he'd take off for his birthday."

"Does he live far?" If visiting her parents required taking time off work, she'd see them a lot less often too.

Lisa shook her head. "Dallas. And we'd be happy to drive there, but we still wouldn't get to see him. He's always—" Lisa clapped her hand over her mouth. "I'm so sorry. I don't know why I'm blabbing on and on." She took the vase in both hands and held it to her chest. "Thank you so much …"

"Ivy. Ivy Aaronson."

"Thank you, Ivy. These flowers really brightened my day."

"I'm so happy to hear that. You have a blessed day."

Lisa smiled again at that. "You, too, sweetheart."

So, Grant Keller was not all she'd thought he was. In fact, he was about as lousy at family time as every other guy she'd ever known. With the possible exception of her brother.

No, she'd never find a man who cared as much about family as she did.

Chapter 3

The phone gave a shrill jangle. Must be Mr. Richardson. Somehow, when he phoned the flower shop, even the ringtone sounded more urgent and annoying.

"Aaronson Flowers and Gifts, this is Ivy. How may I help you?"

"Hello, sweetheart."

Ivy cringed. She wouldn't usually mind if an older man called her sweetheart, but something about Mr. Richardson's tone rubbed her the wrong way. Perhaps it was because he was about to ask her to do something impossible.

"I need flowers for Joe Pengdergrast's funeral. He lived in Portland, Oregon, but his family is down in Memphis."

"Memphis, Texas?" Ivy scribbled away on her notepad. She'd get precious little information out of Mr. Richardson before he hung up.

"Tennessee. Unless his family decides not to have a funeral. You know, people do that sometimes. They just skip the service altogether. Cryin' shame, if you ask me."

"And you'd like the flowers sent to Memphis, Tennessee?"

"Just wherever the service is held. Assuming they have one."

"Do you know the name of the funeral home?"

"Well, no. But he worked for Frisco Electric until he retired. And he worshiped at the 42nd Street church up in Oregon."

"Okay, Mr. Richardson." If she got him back on track, maybe he'd provide some useful details. "Do you know the name of his children?"

"No idea. But his wife's name was Verna."

She added that to her notes. "And his wife already passed away?"

"No. She's still alive. Maybe you can ask her where the services will be."

"Do you—"

"Thank you, sweetheart. Put it on my bill."

The line went dead.

Ivy let out a breath as she read the paltry notes she'd taken. Joe Pendergrast. Oregon. Memphis, Tennessee. Frisco Electric. Verna. Now she just had to piece together enough information to figure out where to send these flowers.

Every time Ivy complained to her mother about Mr. Richardson, her mom reminded her that he was one of their best customers. The shop only made a small commission off the funeral arrangements they ordered for him sent to all corners of the country. But he also bought flowers anytime his law firm hosted a dinner, seasonally for his office, for Rotary Club functions, and anytime he wanted to treat his wife to something special.

The problem was, he was a well-connected old man with an aging group of friends and colleagues. He'd stepped back from most leadership roles around the community. Now he almost exclusively called to send flowers for funerals. If only he could provide useful information for these cross-country deliveries.

Ivy sighed. Time to do some sleuthing on the Internet.

The phone rang again. Ivy prayed it was Mr. Richardson with the name of a funeral home.

"Aaronson Flowers and Gifts, this is Ivy. How may I help you?"

"Hi, Ivy."

The voice sounded so familiar. Male, not too old, with only a hint of a Texas drawl.

"This is Grant Keller."

Her heart skipped a beat, and Ivy couldn't tell if she was anxious or disappointed to hear his voice. "Oh, hi, Grant." She hoped her response was upbeat and friendly.

"I'd like to order flowers again, but this time I made sure to give you more than twenty-four hours' notice."

"Technically, you gave me about two hours' notice."

"Sorry about that."

"No problem." Why did she feel the need to chastise him? She mentally kicked herself. So far today, she wasn't doing a great job of winning customer loyalty. "What can I do for you, Mr. Keller?"

"Grant, please." He paused. "Do you have something for Easter? With bunnies or eggs or something?"

"Of course." Ivy tapped her pen as she visually checked the shelves. "We've got a couple in stock now or we could make something fresh if you'd like it ready closer to Easter next weekend."

"Anytime this week is fine." The sound of a clicking keyboard echoed in the background. He must be working on something while they talked.

"How would you feel about a basket of flowers? We have different sizes, but my favorite has daffodils, tulips, and hyacinths. It's really lovely." She wasn't lying when she said that arrangement was her favorite, but she also didn't bother telling him it was the most expensive.

"I'll take your word for it. Do you still have my card from last time?"

"No, Mr Kel—Grant." Ivy corrected herself. "Would you like to add an account at the store?" She paused. The typing on the other end had stopped. "It would expedite future purchases. That is, if you plan to make any future purchases." Was she being too pushy? She didn't want to assume anything, but with his silence she worried she'd made things awkward.

"Um, yes. I think so. Thank you." His voice was friendly. Good, not offended.

She breathed a sigh of relief, although she was careful to turn away from the phone. It always picked up any heavy breathing or loud consonants. "I'll just copy some information here." A few more clicks and keystrokes. "Could I have your email address?"

Ivy finished typing his information. "I'll get that arrangement out to your mother within the next two days."

"Thank you, Ivy. I appreciate it."

Her heart warmed a little when he said her name. "You're welcome. Have a blessed day." She hung up the phone. She was being ridiculous. Since when did she get flustered like that with a customer?

Why did this always happen? She'd know in her head that a man was all wrong for her, but she'd fall for him anyway. After her conversation with Lisa Keller, Ivy had been disappointed. She'd never expected to hear from Grant again.

Chapter 4

"Cancel your plans."

If Grant had a nickel for every time Jenna said that, he wouldn't need to work ever again. That wasn't technically true, but it didn't change his frustration as she pulled up a chair at his desk. "We've hit a snag and I'm going to need you up here with me tonight and tomorrow. I've already ordered pizza."

Of course, she meant that her administrative assistant had placed an order for pizza.

"Jenna, Sunday is Mother's Day."

She stared blankly at him.

"I'd planned to see my mom in Trammel this weekend. I've been putting her off for ages."

Jenna sighed and rubbed her fingers over her chin. "Listen, Grant. I'm going to tell it to you straight. You've been here two years, right? Give or take?"

"It'll be two years in July, yes."

"Just wait a while longer. Once you've put in your time at the firm, five years or so, then you can take random trips to see your mama. Until then, you've got to bust your tail end just like the rest of us did when we were fresh out of law school."

What kind of person considered Mother's Day a random trip? His boss, that's who.

"Aaronson Flowers and Gifts, How may I help you?"

"Hi, Ivy. This is Grant Keller."

Ivy paused in her twirling of the phone cord. Grant's voice sounded off—sad and resigned.

"Hi, Grant. How're you doing today?"

He sighed on the other end. "I really tried to come see my family this time, and it just didn't work out."

"I'm sorry to hear that. I know your parents would enjoy a visit from you. It must be hard living so far away from home."

"Trammel was never home," he said. "My parents moved there from Amarillo after I graduated from high school. But it's where my family lives, so I guess it's where my heart is, you know?"

"I do. I lived in New York City once. Hardest year of my life."

"What were you doing in New York?"

"I interned for a fashion designer, an old friend of my mother. I was lucky to get the opportunity."

"But it didn't work out?"

"I loved the work and learned a lot. But, no, turns out living nearly two thousand miles away from home was not the life for me." Ivy cleared her throat. "I'm sorry. Here I am rambling about myself—"

"No, it's okay," Grant interrupted. "I don't mind. It's been a rough day. I've got a situation at work, and Mother's Day is Sunday."

"And you hoped to be here?"

"I really did. Is it too late to order something for Mom? Something that might prevent her from coming up to Dallas to wring my neck?"

"I think I can put an arrangement together for you." Ivy smiled. She glanced up as the shop door opened. Waving at the customer, she pantomimed that she'd be off the phone in a minute.

"Thank you, Ivy. You're a lifesaver."

"Sure thing, Grant. Happy to help."

Ivy contemplated Grant as she assisted the visitor in selecting a bouquet. A new side of him came out in that conversation on the phone. Maybe she'd misjudged him. Again. He sounded genuine in his regret. But that also meant that maybe he hadn't actually wanted to come to Trammel the other times he'd sent flowers.

Thinking about Grant led to thinking about that year in New York. And the fallout that came as a result. Her boyfriend broke up with her, she'd floundered while she settled into a new career, and all her friends went off to big and exciting careers while she stayed in west Texas.

"Would you like to purchase a card as well?"

"No, thank you."

Ivy rang up the order and said goodbye. Mom had two appointments with brides in the schedule book for this afternoon. And they had a wedding coming up Saturday.

"Hi there, Ivy."

In waltzed a girl she hadn't seen in about four years.

"Francine!" She walked around the counter to give her friend a hug. "It's been so long. How are you?"

"Well ..." Francine waved her left hand where a giant diamond sparkled. "Jack finally proposed."

"That's wonderful." Ivy had never met Francine's

boyfriend—fiancé, now—because he lived in San Antonio, where Francine worked. But she'd seen plenty of pictures on social media of Francine and Jack eating at fancy restaurants, going on weekend getaways, and dressing up for formal events. "Are you here visiting family?"

"I'm actually planning a wedding in Trammel. Mom and Dad thought a small wedding at home would be nice."

Francine's childhood home was not small by any stretch of the imagination, but it certainly was nice. The sprawling, three-story ranch boasted a beautifully manicured desert prairie garden and saltwater pool.

"I set up an appointment with your mom for this afternoon, but I didn't realize you were still here."

Ivy bit her cheek to keep from responding right away. Still here. There was no mistaking the implication. Ivy hadn't left Trammel like all her friends. Like she'd planned to do. She was *still here.*

"How about I go see if Mom's ready for you?" She gave what she hoped was a genuine-looking smile before stepping out the door.

"Your next appointment is here." Ivy found her mother wrapping ribbon around mason jars on the long table. "I'll pull the bridal binders for you."

"Thanks, sweetie. Do you want to run this one?" Mom wiped her hands on her apron before untying the back ties and hanging it up on a peg on the wall. "I think she's a friend of yours from school."

Since Ivy came back from New York, Mom had been encouraging her to try different aspects of leading the company. "I'd better not this time. Maybe the next one."

No way could she endure an hour of pitying glances from Francine while selecting which color of lily would best coordinate with the bridesmaids' dresses. She couldn't avoid involvement in the wedding altogether—they all had to pitch in on large orders—but she could allow herself to sulk in the front of the store for a little while today.

"Mom's all ready for you in the back." Ivy used her sweetest Southern-charm-laced voice. She gestured for Francine to follow her.

"So cold back here." Francine rubbed her arms as they walked to the back. Her floaty silk top was perfect for the warm weather outside but offered little protection against the air conditioning of the studio.

"Do you need to borrow a sweater?" There was always a random sweatshirt or cardigan lying around in the office.

"No, it's fine." Francine waved to Mom and gave her a hug before turning back to Ivy.

"Let's get lunch together sometime."

"Of course. That sounds great." Ivy assumed Francine was offering a lunch date out of pity or false kindness. She grinned, then ducked her head and walked quickly out of sight.

Still here. Francine's words echoed in Ivy's head. The choice to stay in her hometown had been intentional. This was exactly what she needed—to live close to family and in a community that valued relationships over accomplishments. She didn't want a life in the fast-paced fashion industry of New York.

But a tiny voice whispered inside of her. *Your life is too small.*

Ivy busied herself with checking the plants in the display window. She trimmed a few dead leaves and turned each pot to the left to prevent them from all growing in one direction.

What am I doing here?

Her brother saved lives for a living, and her father saved souls. Her mother grew a thriving business from the ground up, but Ivy just existed within their worlds. She helped customers and volunteered at church and supported the fire department in whatever small ways she could. None of it was her own.

Could God really be pleased with my small and insignificant existence?

Mercifully, the phone rang, saving Ivy from her own thoughts.

"Aaronson Flowers and Gifts, how may I help you?"

Chapter 5

Grant sighed as he fell into his swivel chair. The image he'd had of lawyers as a child was far from his reality. In the books and movies, attorneys waxed eloquent in packed courthouses. They fought for civil rights and human decency. Atticus Finch would never work for someone like Turbocorp.

From the very beginning, the lawsuit had been an uphill battle. The prosecutors possessed an overwhelming amount of evidence against Turbocorp. They were a shady corporation, there was no way around it. But Grant worked for Packer, Hughes, and Price, and with that came certain expectations. And if he didn't meet those expectations ...well, Grant needed a win if he wanted to keep his position at the firm.

But Atticus Finch was a fictional character, and everyone had the right to an attorney. Even corporations that he didn't personally support. Grant never did anything illegal—far from it. His job was to make sure everyone abided by the letter of the law, feelings and opinions aside.

Grant hit a button on his keyboard to wake up his monitor. An alert popped up from his calendar. Mom's birthday. Thank goodness for technology that could keep track of details his brain simply did not have any room for. His family might disagree that birthdays were mere details, but those dates were a lot more likely to be remembered by a computer than by his feeble human mind.

He clicked on the alert, and his calendar filled the screen. Mom's birthday fell on a Wednesday this year. Not the most convenient time for a trip, but he honestly needed to take some vacation days soon. He'd run the dates by Jenna. Surely he could leave town for a couple days, even if the cell service in Trammel was spotty at best.

After two hours of reading, Grant was back in Jenna's office for a debrief. "I've found supporting cases in Oklahoma and Arkansas. It might be worth my time to search farther outside of the region."

Jenna scowled and tapped her fingers on her knee while gazing at the ceiling. It was her typical thinking posture. "Have you talked to Reiter?"

The oldest and most obnoxious partner at the firm? Grant avoided the man as much as possible. "Not about the Turbocorp case, no."

"He's practiced so long, he's seen just about everything." Jenna scribbled something on a notepad beside her. "Set up a meeting with Reiter, take him out to lunch. Pick his brain and see if he can think of something that might help."

Grant nodded even though his innards squirmed as he contemplated a meal with Reiter. The last time he'd been at a work dinner with that man, he'd witnessed him objectify or catcall every waitress in the restaurant.

"We've got a new case on the docket I'll need your input on soon, but for now I want your full attention with Turbocorp." Jenna stood, signifying the end of the meeting. "This close to the trial date, we need all hands on deck."

Grant swallowed hard. He'd have to make a real effort to spin his trip to Trammel. "Of course." With as nonchalant a tone as he could muster, he continued. "By the way, it's come to my attention that I need to take some vacation."

Nope, that wasn't the right approach. "Did you not hear what I just said?"

"Of course, I'm sorry." Grant cleared his throat. "You ever have family pester you to come visit?"

"Not in a long time." The scowl returned, but this time it was directed at him.

"I was thinking after the trial has passed, perhaps I could use some of those days."

Her face cleared. "After Turbocorp is finalized, we could all use a vacation."

With a swift motion, Jenna pulled open the door. "Check in with me after your meeting with Reiter. Then we can discuss next steps."

Grant nodded, but her office door was already shut. He made his way down the hall to Reiter's office.

Kelly, Reiter's admin assistant, glanced up as he approached.

"I was wondering if Tim might have an opening for a lunch sometime this week."

"Of course." Kelly smiled at him before clicking her mouse a few times. Her eyes flitted back and forth as they scanned the computer screen. "He's out of town for meetings the rest of the week. But there's an opening next Wednesday."

Mom's birthday. "That's a little late for me. I was hoping to meet sooner."

"I can see if he's free Saturday. If it's urgent."

Was the universe set against this trip to Trammel? Now he couldn't possibly travel next weekend. He still had the weekend after Mom's birthday.

"Happy Birthday Mrs. Keller."

"Thank you, Ivy. And please call me Lisa. Come on in."

For the fourth time in as many months, Ivy found herself at the Keller home with a beautiful arrangement of flowers. She followed Lisa inside and walked through a hallway lined with family photos. The hall connected to a front sitting room and a formal dining room, but Lisa led her back to a kitchen, airy and open with late afternoon sun pouring in from the windows to the west.

"Cookie?"

"Oh, uh—" Ivy glanced up from arranging the vase on the kitchen island.

A blue porcelain plate of sugar cookies, chocolate chip cookies, and strawberry cookies sat in Lisa's outstretched hand.

"Are these for your birthday? I couldn't—"

"Please, take one. I insist." Lisa pushed the plate closer.

Ivy selected a sugar cookie, thinking it wasn't likely to be anyone's favorite, and took a delicate bite. Buttery crumbs melted in her mouth. Ivy rescinded her initial thought that the cookie wouldn't be missed. It was delicious.

"Thank you." Ivy accepted a napkin from Lisa and wiped her fingers.

"Would you like to have a seat?"

"I can't stay long." She had two more deliveries to make before five o'clock. "I just wanted to make sure these sunflowers got to you before your birthday tomorrow."

"Sunflowers are my favorite." Lisa smiled as she traced a finger over a bright yellow petal.

"That's what Grant said." Looking around, Ivy could see that it was true. On the table were crocheted sunflower placemats. Vases and plates covered in the plant dotted the china cabinet and open shelving. And a stained-glass sunflower hung over the sink window.

"I'm surprised he remembered." Lisa smiled wistfully.

The house was quiet and empty, just like every other time she came by. She assumed Mr. Keller would come home from work soon. And there would be gatherings with the grandchildren pictured in all the family portraits on the walls. But maybe Lisa was lonely.

"It's none of my business," Ivy said. "But Grant seemed very sad he couldn't make it for your birthday or for Mother's Day."

"I know." Lisa sighed. "He called last night to apologize."

"He said there was a wrinkle in the case that needed working out but that it might actually be a good thing. For the case."

Sighing, Lisa sat on a black metal barstool next to the kitchen island. "He told me the same. I know I just need to be patient. Supposedly, in a few more years he'll be able to choose his own cases and take more vacation days." She grabbed a chocolate chip cookie off the plate. "I just miss my son."

Not sure what else to do, Ivy patted Lisa's hand resting on the countertop. "He misses you too."

Lisa smiled at Ivy. "I'd better not keep you from your other deliveries. I appreciate you stopping by."

"Thank you for the cookie. I hope you have a happy birthday!"

"HELLO, IVY."

"Hi, there, Grant."

She'd finally convinced Mom and Dad to splurge on a

cordless phone with caller ID after Mom nearly clotheslined a customer. Thanks to the new phone, they'd already noted a difference in the clarity of their calls, and the convenience of knowing who was on the other end of the line.

Despite the fact the new phone was Ivy's idea, she missed having the cord to fiddle with. Her fingers tapped a beat on the counter and her foot twisted while she stood behind the register.

"How can I help you today?"

"Did you know July Fourth is just around the corner?"

"Oh, is that what all those fireworks stands are for?"

"Aren't you glad I called?"

"I am." And she was. She'd come to enjoy their monthly phone calls and her visits with Lisa. Grant cared about his family a lot, just not enough to drive the three hours to Trammel. But he was a nice guy, and she hoped he could get his act together someday. "You should know we've updated the website. There's a way to order online now."

He paused before responding. "I read that. I get the emails."

"Oh, okay. I just thought ..." Ivy hoped she hadn't come off as rude. She'd been telling all the customers, since some people liked the convenience of online orders. The contribution had been all her doing, and she hoped the effort paid off soon in increased sales.

"Is it okay if I call anyway? I like to talk to a person."

Ivy's stomach fluttered. What if he didn't call just to order flowers? What if he called because he wanted to talk to *her*? She shook her head. What a ridiculous thought.

"Well, that's perfectly fine. I'd be happy to take your order today."

"Do you have anything red, white, and blue?"

"How about a couple white and red arrangements in some

blue buckets? They've got glitter stars in them, and they're very cute."

"I'd love that."

What did Grant's smile look like in person? What might it be like to watch his face transform, his eyes light up, his grin flash? She'd probably never find out.

Chapter 6

Grant rolled back his shoulders and stretched his neck as he drove another mile of straight interstate over flat terrain. Reason number fifty-two he rarely came out west to Trammel: the endlessly boring drive down I-20. Once he left the suburbs of Fort Worth, empty plains dominated the landscape until Abilene. And after Abilene —nothing.

Nothing until the tiny town of Trammel, in between Abilene and Lubbock. Grant took the exit to downtown, noting a new restaurant since his last visit. Lampposts decked out in seasonal flags lined Main Street. Some read "Thanks" and others read "Fall." Many of the storefronts were painted with red, orange, and brown leaves.

Now that the Turbocorp case was behind him, he'd been able to take off a half day—still answering calls from his car—so he could make it to town before five o'clock. He wanted to be at Mom and Dad's for dinner, but the biggest reason sat right in front of him. Aaronson Flowers and Gifts.

Grant pulled his car into a spot right in front of the door. He pushed the park button before wiping his hands on his pants. When he'd made the plan to stop by the flower shop, it seemed like a great idea. He'd get to meet Ivy in person and thank her for everything she'd done to placate his mother over the past several months.

But now that he was here, nervousness fizzled in his belly in a way he hadn't anticipated. Why was his heart racing? *Stop being ridiculous. She might not even be here.* But that thought made him even more anxious. What if this whole visit was for nothing? Grant shook his head quickly and blew out a breath. Might as well get out of the car.

The light brown brick of the storefront matched the rest of downtown. And a number in cement above showed the building had been around since 1923. But the inside didn't look a hundred years old. As Grant pulled open the door, exposed brick and ductwork drew his eye. Wood shelves hung on brackets along the walls holding plants of every kind. The front windows filled the shop with light. Tables and shelves laden with gift items like fancy towels, books, and candles sat in the center of the floor. The black and white tile under his feet might be original to the building, but he wasn't an expert on those things. Someone had put a lot of time and effort into making the flower shop nice, and their work had paid off.

Grant poked his head around the shelves. He figured he could visit the shop on the premise that he needed to pick up a table centerpiece for his mother. Out of the corner of his eye, Grant spotted some yellow, orange, and red flowers in the windows. He walked closer to get a better look, but a voice called out behind him.

"Can I help you find anything in particular?"

Ivy. He'd recognize that voice anywhere.

Grant turned and came face-to-face with a woman even more beautiful than he'd imagined. Curly brown hair framed a heart-shaped face. Large green eyes blinked back at him, and her lips curved into a smile. He realized that she'd asked him a question.

"Um, I'm trying to find for a centerpiece for my mom."

She tilted her head to the right, narrowing her eyes. "Have we met?"

"Grant Keller." He stuck out his hand, and she laughed as she took it.

"It's nice to meet you in person, Grant." Her emerald eyes lit up. Grant found it hard not to stare.

"I couldn't stay away forever." He shrugged, then put his hands in his pockets. The warmth of her skin lingered on his fingers, and he was unsure of himself—something that *never* happened. "But I figured Mom might still appreciate some flowers." And he'd wanted to meet Ivy. Something in his heart tugged toward her.

On the phone, they'd shared a comfortable banter. Their conversations were never longer than a few minutes, but each time Grant found himself opening up to her more. Now that he was here, he couldn't deny the sparks between them. At least, he hoped the attraction wasn't one-sided.

"A Thanksgiving centerpiece, you say?" Ivy's mouth twisted in a conspiratorial smirk. She turned on her toes and beckoned with a finger for Grant to follow.

"I'd thought I could just buy one of those plants in the window." They passed the tables of candles and trinkets, then she led him past the checkout counter to a door. "Where are you taking me?"

"The mums are nice, but I've got just the thing for you here in the back." She pulled open the door.

It was as though he'd walked into Santa's workshop. A jolly-looking woman stood before a long wooden table, cutting red and green ribbon. The curly hair escaping from her white bandana reminded him of Ivy's. A slender man wearing wire-rimmed glasses bent over a stack of papers and a calculator on a round table. Two muscular men jostled each other jokingly as they carried boxes of … Christmas ornaments?

Except it couldn't be the North Pole because all around them were green flowers and plants. The air carried a thick floral perfume. Grant smiled as he took it all in.

Ivy grinned back at him, waving her arm in a sweeping gesture. "Welcome to the studio."

"I love it. Is this place secret?"

"Not at all." She laughed. "We meet with clients back here all the time."

"Oh, it just feels special, I guess."

Her expression was still happy, but her smile faded, and she stared at him intensely, as though she were measuring him up. "It *is* special."

Then her excitement returned as she walked to a tall refrigerator unit. "Look, we still have a few sunflowers left."

She grabbed a vase from inside and walked back to him. "What do you think? We could put them in an arrangement with some other orange and yellow flowers." She turned to her right. "Mom?"

The curly-haired woman glanced up. Her eyes widened at the sight of Ivy and Grant standing right in front of her. "Hi, there." Her wide grin made her cheeks even fuller than before.

"Mom, this is Grant Keller."

Wiping her hands on her apron first, the woman reached for a handshake.

"Daphne Aaronson." She turned to her daughter. "Are you using up the last of the sunflowers?"

"I thought maybe a low centerpiece in one of those wooden trays."

It was like the two were speaking a language with only eye contact. They stared at each other, both obviously thinking hard. Then Daphne nodded. "Right, we have those yellow roses."

"And the mums."

"I'll grab some of the fall leaves and cranberries."

Ivy and Daphne dashed separate ways, then came back together, arms filled with supplies. Daphne placed some green foam in a long wooden rectangular tray. Ivy trimmed the flowers they'd brought to the worktable. Daphne watered the foam and then began stabbing flowers and greenery into it. Finally, both women stepped back.

"Ribbon for the bottom?"

"Yes," Ivy said. "And something else." She held up a finger and began searching the shelves. She brandished her find, and her gaze landed on Grant. His heart skipped a beat when she smiled at him.

"The oranges. Perfect."

Ivy added several dried orange slices to the centerpiece. Grant never would've thought to do something like that, but the effect was great. "Mom's going to love this."

"I hope so."

Grant said his goodbyes to Daphne as Ivy led him back to the front of the store, carrying the centerpiece.

"Nice to meet you Mrs. Aaronson."

"The pleasure was all mine. And, please, call me Daphne."

Back at the counter, Ivy rang him up. He barely registered the price before signing the receipt. "I'm going to win some serious brownie points today."

Ivy cocked her head as she stared at him. "I mean, you're here *and* you bought flowers."

"My brother and sister will never be able to catch up." He was only joking, of course. Will and Addie were miles ahead of him in the race for Mom and Dad's approval.

Instead of taking the arrangement, Grant shoved his hands

in his pockets. He couldn't just leave the store. He needed to know he'd be able to see her again. "Hey."

Ivy's eyebrows raised, and she bit her lip. She waited while he mustered his courage.

"Do you—would you like to get coffee? This weekend?"

Her expression transformed from patient to surprised. He waited until the sound of the front door interrupted Ivy's thoughts. She blinked three times quickly, then said, "Yes. I'd love to."

Relief washed over him. "Great. Okay." He didn't have her phone number. "Should I call you here or …"

Breaking her gaze from the other customer in the store, Ivy glanced at Grant's phone held out in hand. She recited her number while Grant typed it in his contacts. "Thanks. So, I'll text later to set up a time?"

"Okay." A slow smile crept over her face, and his heart swelled.

Why had he waited so long to come back to Trammel?

Chapter 7

Ivy breathed in the scents of cinnamon and ginger when she walked into the coffee shop. The smell almost tempted her to stray from her typical coffee order to something called Christmas Cinnamon Stick or Gingerbread Cream.

Paper snowflakes hung from the ceiling and silver garland graced the counters. She admired how quickly the staff had put up their decorations. She and her family had just started transforming the flower shop for the season.

As the novelty of her surroundings wore off, Ivy scanned the crowd at the restaurant. There. Grant spotted her from a table in the corner. He stood up and smiled, and her heart flipped.

She'd seen Grant in a picture or two at the Keller residence but hadn't realized how handsome he'd be in person. His dark hair was thick and just long enough to hang down a little in the front. Her fingers itched to touch those silky locks.

"Hi," Grant said. "Can I get you a drink?"

She nodded and stepped up to the cash register. "Medium caramel latte, please."

"And I'll take a cortado."

The barista copied down their orders and took Grant's card. Ivy couldn't help but notice the generous tip he gave.

When Grant had asked her out the day before, the teenage girl inside had jumped for joy. The man was charming, loved his mama, and was as cute as they came. But she'd hesitated before answering.

What if Ivy fell for Grant? He had a terrible track record of never coming to Trammel for visits. If his own family couldn't bring him out west, how could she?

But their chemistry on the phone, and now in person, was undeniable. Didn't she owe it to Grant to hear his side of the story? He'd acted genuinely remorseful that he couldn't come home the last few months. Surely, his work life would slow down soon and he'd be able to travel more often. Maybe she should give him—and whatever this relationship was—a chance.

"Grant?" The barista set two cups on the counter. Ivy grabbed hers carefully. A delicate leaf pattern adorned the foam of her drink. It threatened to slosh over the side of the wide mug.

Grant's drink was in a short glass.

"What is a cortado? I've never seen one before."

Grant pulled out a chair at their table and smiled at her. Ivy couldn't remember the last time someone had done that for her.

"I only discovered them within the past couple years. It's two shots of espresso with steamed milk." He joined her at the table and took a sip from his glass. "Nice. I never know what to expect at new coffee joints. This one is good."

"Unless you want to go to the diner or the gas station, Trammel Coffee Co is pretty much your only option around here. Thank goodness they make a good cup of coffee." She sipped her own drink. Still a little hot, but plenty tasty.

They fell into an uncomfortable silence. *What do I say now?*

Ivy cleared her throat at the same time Grant started to talk. "Have you—"

They both laughed, but Ivy's came out more like a weird giggle.

"Sorry," she said. "You were saying?"

"I was just wondering how long you've worked at the flower shop."

"About as long as I can remember. Mom's had the place since before I was born."

"So, it's the family business?" He took another drink, then leaned back in his chair.

"Pretty much. My dad is a semi-retired preacher and my brother is a firefighter, but we all pitch in. Mom and I are the only ones there full-time."

"Did you grow up wanting to step in for your mom someday?"

Ivy shook her head slowly. "No, I majored in fashion merchandising and design. I've always loved to sew and draw and craft. Everyone figured I'd go off to become a fashion designer."

"That's when you went to New York?"

Ivy was surprised he remembered their phone conversation from a few months ago. "Yes. I spent a whole year there." She'd known a few months in that she could never be happy so far from home but stayed to fulfill the year-long commitment. "My mom scored me the internship of a lifetime. And I could've used that job to launch a great career."

"What happened?"

Ivy grimaced. She'd expected a surprised or irritated response from Grant. He was so focused on his career. But when she glanced up at his expression, he waited with an inquisitive look on his face. It was as if he was just interested in hearing her story—no judgment, no words of advice.

"My boss—my mom's friend from college—was very successful and good at her job. But the more time I spent with her, the more I realized I didn't want her life. The only people I worked with who ever visited their families were from New York. Everyone else went home for major holidays, but they usually treated it like a burden.

"I loved working there—I really did. My boss was amazing, and I met so many incredible people. But I couldn't handle living so far from home. No matter how far I advanced in my career, I'd never be happy."

Grant's expression turned thoughtful. She loved how a little crease formed between his eyebrows.

"Couldn't you work in a bigger city, like Dallas?"

"I could." She took another drink before replying. "That's what Jeremy wanted me to do."

Grant's eyebrows raised.

"Ex-boyfriend. We broke up after I came back to Texas."

Grant tried to hide his relief, but Ivy could tell he'd been jealous for half a second. The thought made her smile.

"He was so disappointed when I decided to work at the flower shop. He thought I'd wasted my one chance to have a fulfilling career."

Grant scoffed. "You're young. Who's to say what will happen down the road?"

"He thought he could, apparently. And so ..." Ivy twisted the cardboard wrapper around her cup. She shrugged.

"I'm sorry. He sounds like a jerk." Grant laid his hand on top of hers.

Ivy gazed into his eyes and melted, just a little. He had the dreamiest dark brown eyes she'd ever seen. When he looked at her with such concern, for *her* well-being no less, she got all swoony. Thank goodness for that seat underneath her.

"If it makes you feel any better, I've been wondering about my own career choices."

"Oh?" Ivy took a sip, both grateful to have the attention off her, but disappointed that Grant's hand no longer rested on hers. "You don't like being a lawyer?" Over time, Lisa Keller had told her all about Grant and his job at the big law firm in Dallas.

"I like being a lawyer. I just hate where I work."

"Aren't they supposed to be the best firm in the metroplex?"

He nodded. "Probably in the state." He sighed then gave her a rueful look. "I don't know if you've noticed, but I don't have a ton of free time."

"I thought you just loved sending me with a vase of flowers as a stand-in for family functions."

"Maybe I do a little." He laughed. "But it would be a lot cheaper to come in person. And I don't really love the *type* of law that I practice."

"What do you want to do instead?" Not that she'd be able to give advice on the ins and outs of legal careers.

"Not sure, but I'm thinking about it."

Ivy drained the last of her latte. "Just make sure you still send flowers occasionally. I'd miss your mother terribly if you stopped."

Now Grant gave a giant belly laugh. "I'll keep that in mind."

"Plus, who else will order Labor Day or Halloween flowers?"

"Both highly underrated holidays." *Ooof.* That smile of his sure was handsome.

Later, as Grant walked her out to her car, a warmth filled

her belly that couldn't have come from the latte. Her drink had run out over an hour ago. No, the happiness must have been caused by the man standing beside her.

"Thanks for the coffee." She held her keys but waited to open the door. "I had a nice time."

"Me too." Grant leaned forward slightly, then pulled himself back. "Could I call you?"

A grin spread across her lips. "I'd like that."

Ivy was not the type of girl to kiss on a first date, so she had a hard time explaining the urge to pull that man into her arms. She couldn't just say goodbye. On impulse, Ivy tugged on his hand and gave him a quick peck on the cheek.

Her heart beating wildly, she climbed in her car and proceeded to drive in the opposite direction of her apartment for three miles before realizing her mistake and turning around.

Chapter 8

The offices of Packer, Hughes, and Price were closed for a whole week from Christmas Eve to New Year's. Grant was free to enjoy a trip to Trammel. Not only was he out of the office, but his boss was as well. He could leave, and no one would call him on his vacation. Pure bliss.

Of course, email was another matter. Even with his automatic out-of-office message, he could expect to receive more than one notice about upcoming meetings and deadlines.

But Grant pushed those thoughts from his head. He was at his parents' house, and he could smell bacon. Hopping out of bed, Grant pulled on a T-shirt and padded down the hall. He inhaled deeply. Beyond the overwhelming scent of bacon, he could detect eggs and blueberry muffins. Knowing his mother, there would be fresh fruit and juice as well.

"Morning, Mom." Grant bent to hug his mother. Reaching up, she patted him on the cheek.

"Merry Christmas Eve."

Classical arrangements of holiday carols piped through the kitchen speaker. Grant had pitched in with his brother and sister to buy smart assistants all around the house for Christmas last year. His parents had resisted at first, but Will and Addie reported that they'd grown to depend on the convenience of the little devices.

"This looks delicious. Are Will and Hailey coming soon?" His sister was already upstairs, having driven from Amarillo the night before. His brother's family lived in nearby Lubbock but had to split time with in-laws, and he couldn't remember their schedule this year.

"They'll be here for brunch, so don't eat too much. I want to make sure we have plenty for the kids."

Grant suspected that even if he ate multiple helpings, he wouldn't make a dent in the spread of food on the kitchen island. But he rarely ate breakfast anyway, so he didn't mind restricting himself to a slice of bacon and a banana. All he truly required in the morning was a strong cup of coffee.

"So ..." His mother gave him a mischievous smile as she trailed off. She grinned down at the sausage she was flipping in a pan. Grant had a sinking feeling she was about to pry into his love life. "I hear you and Ivy Aaronson have been talking."

He'd told her about their coffee date at Thanksgiving, but only because she still insisted on knowing where he was at all times. Grant's parents could track his phone—they claimed it was because they liked knowing he was safe. But how did Mom find out he'd been talking to Ivy so much? Maybe it was a lucky guess.

"We have."

"And?" Spatula in hand, Mom turned to him with a pointed stare.

"And I think we've really hit it off." Grant couldn't help but return her smile. The last few weeks of texts had gotten him through another month of soul-sucking work at Packer,

Hughes, and Price. Somehow, her funny and kind nature motivated him to find the bright spots in his job.

"Are we going to get to see her?"

"You see her all the time." From talking to Ivy, it sounded like the two had become friends in the past several months.

"Not since you started hand-delivering your flowers." She pointed to the potted poinsettias on a bench by the back door.

"I haven't asked yet, but I was planning to get together whenever she's free."

"You should bring her by to meet everyone."

Grant paused mid-banana-bite to check his mother's expression for any hints of sarcasm. Nope, she was serious. He forced himself to swallow. "Don't you think it's a bit too soon? I don't want to scare her off."

Mom waved an oven mitt at him dismissively. "Not at all. We'll be good. I'll make sure of it."

"What time is it?"

The speaker in the corner chimed. "The time is eight thirty-one a.m."

"I'll text her later to see when she's free."

Mom's eyes lit up. "Bring her for dinner."

"Or maybe," Grant topped himself off with another half cup of coffee. "I could take her out to a quiet restaurant and actually have a nice time." He winked to let Mom know he was joking—mostly—then left to hide somewhere while he waited for his niece and nephew to arrive.

Later that morning, after everyone had eaten their fill of brunch, Grant sat on the couch, his niece under one arm and his nephew on his lap.

"Read us another story!"

"How about you give Uncle Grant a break?" Hailey swooped in between picture books. "I think Grammy's got a movie for you to watch in the den."

"What is it?" Finley and Nate jumped up to check out their mother's claims. The din of their tiny feet grew smaller and smaller.

"I hear you've got a girlfriend." His brother, Will, carried a mug of coffee to the armchair closest to where Grant sat on the couch.

"We've only been on one date."

"That's one more than you've been on in the past two years." Addie, their younger sister, joined Grant on the couch.

Although that statement was true, it didn't keep Grant from rolling his eyes. "I've been busy."

Will held up his hand defensively. "Hey, I get it. You have to prove yourself to everyone and fight your way up the ladder. I remember."

His brother had married Hailey right out of college and quickly started a successful career in finance. By this point in his life, Will had two kids, an MBA, and a six-figure salary. He was everything Grant hoped to be, even if he was a little overbearing at times.

"You know," Grant leaned his head back to check that their parents weren't near enough to listen to their conversation. "Mom has been pestering me to settle down for *years*. I finally meet someone nice, and I get the third degree."

Will laughed and crossed his ankle over his other leg. "We're just excited. I'd almost given up hope on you and Addie ever finding someone."

"I've had plenty of boyfriends!" Addie's lip stuck out in a pout.

"Yeah, that's the problem." Will shot her a pointed look. Their sister was always dating someone new, but she'd never brought home anyone impressive.

Grant rubbed his chin. "I've always wanted to settle down, you know. The timing hasn't been right yet."

"What does that mean?" Will wouldn't know about timing problems. Everything had always worked out perfectly for him.

"You know, Dad taught us how important it is to be a leader and a provider."

Addie snorted beside him.

"I'm not saying I don't want to marry someone with a career. But I want to take my role seriously. If I'm not ready to support a family, what right do I have to start a serious relationship?"

His sister raised one perfectly manicured eyebrow at him. "What about all those stories about Mom and Dad as poor newlyweds? And Grandma and Grandpa? Didn't they live in a trailer for the first five years they were married?"

"He was in the military—that's different. And Dad started out in a lower position, but he worked his way into management quickly." Grant sighed. "I'm just saying, I wanted to wait until I was ready. In three years, I'll be able to pick my own cases and take vacation days. Maybe it's almost time for me to find someone."

"Three more years of this? Of only seeing you for the holidays?" Addie's expression was both shocked and sad.

"I thought that's the way you preferred it." He wrapped his arm around her shoulder. "Why else would you have given me so much grief all our lives?"

He got a good laugh out of Addie. They chatted for a bit before she stood up to check on Mom.

"Hey, Will?" Grant hated to humble himself in his brother's eyes, but he honestly needed some help. "Could you do me a favor?"

"Sure thing." Will's eyebrows lifted.

"I'm looking into other firms. Maybe someplace smaller. Could you ... put out some feelers for me?"

"Of course." Will patted him on the back. "I can't make any promises, but I might have a connection somewhere."

"Thanks."

Grant pulled out his phone to text Ivy. Maybe his family wasn't so intimidating after all. He'd find out soon enough if she was up to the challenge of meeting the Keller clan.

Chapter 9

Ivy paced the floor while she waited for the doorbell to ring.

"What's got you all riled up?" Her brother chuckled as he downed his third mug of Dad's hot chocolate.

"She's got that date, remember?" Mom called from the kitchen. They'd all gathered for Christmas Eve lunch—Luke had to work tomorrow—and they'd attend an evening church service later that night. She had a few hours before the service, which was enough time for dinner with Grant at his parents' house. Ivy sat in an armchair but wrung her hands.

"It's not a really formal date. Just a meal with his family."

Luke's eyebrows raised. "Sounds pretty serious to me."

"I've met his mom already, so I'm just going to meet his dad and siblings." Even to her ears, the words rang false.

They all turned at the crunch of tires on the driveway.

Ivy shot out of her seat. "All right, well, I'll see you at the church building at eight. Save me a seat."

"Not a chance." Luke grabbed her forearm. "You can't get away without us meeting this guy."

"You've seen him before. At the flower shop."

Luke scoffed. "I didn't know who he was." He stepped in front of her, effectively blocking her from the door. "If his family gets to meet you, we get to meet him."

"Hi, there!" Luke opened the front door and called out to Grant.

Ivy tried to push past her brother, but she was no match for his muscular arms. *Maybe I should've taken him up on his offer to exercise together.* But a firefighter's workout was more than a little too intense for her.

"I'm Luke." Her brother stuck his hand out. Ivy silently prayed he wasn't squeezing the life out of Grant's fingers.

A strange mixture of embarrassment and pride swelled up as Grant met her brother and greeted her parents. She loved her family but they'd love to make her squirm right now. Grant handled them all with grace. *Let's hope I stay this calm during the Keller family dinner tonight.*

At long last, they were able to say their goodbyes, and Grant led Ivy out to his car.

"Sorry about them."

"What do you mean?" Grant gave her a puzzled look while he pulled open her car door.

"They can be a lot sometimes."

"Just wait till you meet my family." He laughed and then shut the door, shaking his head all the way back to the driver's seat.

Inside the car, Ivy glanced around. She couldn't see any trash or clutter lying on the floor. And it smelled nice. Like Grant's cologne and a car air freshener. She wondered if he'd cleaned just for her or if he always kept it neat.

Grant started the car and backed out of the driveway. A fiddle tune filtered out of the car speakers. She glanced and it wasn't the radio but his phone's playlist.

"Oh, wow. You listen to Forest, River, and Road?" She'd

never known any other fans of that band. Except her friends she'd forced to listen.

"I went to school with the banjo player—"

"Mark Forrest," Ivy interrupted. "I saw them a couple times in Lubbock." She couldn't believe she'd met a fellow fan.

Ivy tilted her head back and closed her eyes. "I like this song." Peeking her left eyelid open, she looked at Grant.

He gazed back at her briefly before returning his attention to the road. "I like *you*, Ivy."

She wasn't sure why he felt the need to tell her so plainly, but she returned the compliment. "I like you too."

"I'm glad I got the time off to come down to Trammel."

"I wish you were able to come more often."

He bit his lip before responding. "I do too."

Ivy thought her brother and his friends could cause a ruckus, but they were nothing compared to Nate and Finley. Whether they were excited about cookies, angry at each other, or bored with the dinner conversation, they were yelling. Ivy didn't mind. She was having a blast meeting the special people in Grant's life.

Lisa had pulled Ivy into a hug right away and introduced her to everyone in the house. Will and Addie were nice enough. Hailey was distracted by children most of the time. And Nathan, Grant's father, was friendly but serious.

"How's the flower business?" Mr. Keller asked at the dinner table.

"It's going well. Mom and Dad take care of the books, but they're training me in different aspects of the business."

"Are you hoping to take over someday?"

"I don't know yet. But I do know that I'm happy to help take some of the burden off my mother."

Nathan peppered her with a few more questions before Grant interrupted. "Hey, Ivy. Did you know Addie designs websites?" He winked at her before squeezing her hand. It was clear to see Nathan pushed the people around him to be the best versions of themselves. Though she wondered if he might put too much pressure on his children.

After dinner, Grant offered her some respite from the noise and craziness. "Let's have our dessert and coffee on the porch." He opened the back door and motioned for her to follow. She was more than happy to join him in the cool night air.

A wooden swing hung from the porch ceiling and faced a quiet neighborhood side street. Ivy sat and gazed out over the grassy lawn and to the Christmas lights flickering all around them.

"Mom and Dad's neighbors always put up a big display for the holidays. It can make sleep a little difficult."

"I like it." Ivy kicked her feet out from underneath and smiled at Grant. Family craziness aside, she'd had a lovely evening with him. But one irritating question kept her from fully enjoying herself. "When will I get to see you again?"

"Tomorrow, I hope." He twisted his mouth in an adorable smile, full of hope and tinged with a little bit of insecurity.

She laughed. "Won't your family want to spend Christmas Day with you?"

"All day long? I think you overestimate how much they like me."

Nudging his elbow, Ivy said, "Maybe I could spare a few minutes for you."

"I'd like that."

They rocked a bit more, but anxiety bubbled up inside her

again. He hadn't really answered her question. "But after you go back to Dallas—will you visit again soon?"

Grant frowned. "I'm not sure. I took vacation days at Thanksgiving, but I still have a lot more piling up." He rocked his feet back and forth in time with hers. "We've got a new case that's picking up steam. I'll have a hearing for that within the next month."

Ivy ate a bite of her pecan pie. The sugar wasn't enough to fix her sour mood. Grant never visited Trammel. That was the whole reason they'd gotten to know each other in the first place. She'd just hoped for something different.

"So, it's going to be back to monthly flower orders at the shop?"

Grant rubbed the back of his neck. "I don't know. I hope not."

"When do you think work will slow down for you? Next year, the next?"

He shook his head. "Usually the first five years are the busiest."

"And you've been working for two?"

"Yes." Grant licked his fork, then set his empty plate on the porch beside the swing.

"So, you have three more years of nonstop working? Of essentially no vacation time?" Ivy pursed her lips. "You must really love your job." She was prodding him with her sarcasm. Maybe it wasn't the kindest way to speak to him, but she wanted him to cut to the chase and tell the truth.

Grant sighed. "I enjoy practicing law. Is it wrong to want to work hard for something? Should I feel bad that I want to make partner?"

"Not if it's what you really want." Ivy searched Grant's expression. She was already in over her head with this guy. If Grant wasn't going to be able to commit to a long-distance relationship with her, then she needed to know soon. "Is that what you really want? To make partner and spend your career at Packer, Hughes, and Price?"

"Ivy, I've been trying to find something less stressful. I really have." Grant turned to her. Reaching his fingers toward her face, he pushed a lock of hair behind her ear. Her skin tingled at his touch. "But until I find something better, I need to keep this job."

"Your family misses you a lot, you know."

He nodded. "They've made that clear."

"So why can't you make time for them? Surely your coworkers see their families and friends more often than twice a year."

"You don't understand—this is just the reality of being new at a large firm."

Ivy shook her head. "You're right. I don't understand why you have to stay in Dallas at a job you obviously hate."

"We've made different choices." Grant ran his fingers through his hair, tugging a little harder than necessary. "But it's important for me to build a career I can use to support a family someday. I take that role very seriously, and if I quit my job now, I don't know when I'll be able to settle down."

"Wait. When will you settle down? If you're not doing that now ..." Ivy gestured between the two of them. "What is this?"

Grant shrugged. "I like you. I'm not sure what it is yet, but I know that I like you."

"I like you too, Grant." Ivy blinked her eyes to keep them from stinging. "But if you're never here, how can I get to know you?"

"I'll call when I can and visit when I can."

Ivy glanced down at her lap. Could she wait three more years for Grant to reach his career goals? And what next? Would he want her to move to Dallas, away from her family?

"Choices are important. I chose to live close to my parents because I want *be* with my family. Not just send flowers to them on every holiday. And maybe that's not the biggest or most important goal to you, but it's important to me."

There it was—their fundamental difference. Ivy chose family and Grant chose career.

"But I *am* choosing my family—my future wife and kids. And my goals are important too. Think of all the good I can do in a powerful position at the firm."

But what power did someone have who simply worked at her parents' small-town flower shop? What important position did she hold?

Ivy halted the swing and stood. She grabbed both of their plates.

As she turned to leave, Grant held her arm. "Just because I'm busy with my job doesn't mean that we can't spend time together while I'm here. I want to see where this can go."

His thumb traced a path down her skin and rested inside the crook of her arm. When he pulled her closer, Ivy didn't resist. She closed her eyes as she breathed in the scent of his cologne.

"You've chosen a path that isn't as financially rewarding, and many might not see the value in what you do, but that's okay."

Ivy reeled, but Grant stepped toward her. As he reached for her face, she tore her arm away from his other hand. She wasn't going to be kissing him tonight—or ever. No value in what she did? How could he say those things after everything she'd told him about herself?

"I'm sorry. We want different things in life. And what I want right now is to leave."

Grant's mouth gaped as if she'd slapped him, but he closed it and took a step back. Nodding, he took the dessert plates from her hand and stepped to the door. "You can wait here. I'll drive you to the church building if you're ready to go."

Grant didn't raise his gaze to meet hers. Ivy hated that she'd upset him. But they needed to break off the relationship before either of them got even more hurt. Better now than three years down the road when she'd realized that falling in love with an attorney was the worst mistake of her life.

Chapter 10

"Need another drink?"

"No thanks," Grant raised the soda in his hand to show it was still full. "You go ahead." He motioned for Marcus to go to the bar without him and then searched the crowd.

When Marcus texted to ask if he wanted to hang out with some other people from work on New Year's Eve, Grant took the excuse to drive back to Dallas a couple days early. He'd lost the desire to stick around in Trammel the moment Ivy broke off their relationship.

The contrast between the people he was with tonight and the family he'd just left was striking. As loud as Finley and Nate had been, they couldn't hold a candle to the DJ at this club. All around him, people were together, but he doubted they were really connecting. He longed to go back in time and make things right with Ivy, but she'd made it clear she didn't want anything to do with him.

Jenna talked to one of the male paralegals at a table. And Marcus had found a woman to flirt with at the bar. Grant only came to not feel so lonely anymore, but it wasn't working. He and Marcus got along great, and he didn't mind spending time outside the office with most of his coworkers. But something about tonight—and the past week—left him feeling empty.

"Why so down?" Jenna was beside him. Grant glanced around—the paralegal had moved on to someone else.

"Do I look sad?" He wasn't quite sure how to begin to answer her question.

"Yes. Is it because you haven't been drinking? Unless there's some rum in your Coca-Cola ..." She leaned over to sniff it.

"No," He pulled his glass away from her face. "There isn't any. And that's not the reason." He sighed. "I got broken up with last weekend."

"I didn't know you were dating anyone."

"We'd been talking and had gone on a couple dates." If meeting his parents counted as a date.

"She must've meant a lot to you for you to look so pathetic."

Grant frowned. "When did you start dating your husband? Was it before law school?" *Am I the problem? Or is it just impossible to make time for a relationship while working at this firm?*

"Ex."

"What?" He wasn't sure he'd heard her correctly, the place was so loud.

"Ex-husband," she yelled. "We got a divorce last year."

"How did I not know that?"

Jenna shrugged. "I tried my best to keep it under wraps, but I assumed everyone was talking about it behind my back."

"I wouldn't do that." He took a swig of his drink.

"Maybe that's why you didn't know about it."

"Why didn't you say something?"

She raised an eyebrow at him. "Do I ever talk to you about my personal life?"

"No," Grant realized that was true. And he never talked to her about his, mostly because he assumed she wasn't interested.

"It's for the best. I'm just glad we didn't have any kids." She chuckled as she raised her glass to her lips. "And that I don't have to talk to his mother ever again."

"You didn't get along?"

Jenna swallowed her drink. "Not any worse than I do with my own mother, I suppose."

Grant grimaced. "I'm sorry." He backed away, searching for the bathrooms or someone else to talk to. He spotted Marcus across the room and gave Jenna a wave.

Nodding, Jenna moved off in the direction of the bar.

"Hey, man." Grant slapped Marcus on the back. "Did you have any luck with that girl?" The din was a bit quieter where they stood in the back of the room.

"What girl?" Marcus glanced around, as if to conjure more women with wishing.

"The one at the bar earlier."

"Oh, no," Marcus said. "She has a boyfriend."

"We don't really have time to date, anyway."

Marcus frowned. "I make time."

"Do you?" Grant's brow furrowed. He tried to think back to times Marcus had talked about dating. "When was the last time you had a girlfriend?"

"Not since last year, but that doesn't stop me from trying." Marcus tilted his head. "You okay?"

Grant gave a hollow laugh. "I'm fine. I just—" His phone buzzed in his pocket. Giving Marcus an apologetic wince, he glanced down at the screen. Mom. He pointed to the phone, and Marcus waved him away.

Now to find somewhere to take the call. He was afraid the phone would stop ringing before he was able to find a quiet place. Scanning the club, Grant finally spotted the restroom sign.

Not the perfect location, but it would work. Though the line for the ladies' room stretched down the narrow hallway, the line for the men's room was nonexistent. He tapped his phone screen and stepped inside, but he'd missed the call.

Grant frowned at the screen and waited to see if she'd send a text instead. A minute later, a voicemail notification pinged on his phone.

"Grant, this is your mother." *Yeah, I know, Mom.* She did that every time. "It's about ten o'clock." He sighed. "I want you to know that we're at the hospital."

The annoyance at his mom evaporated. His stomach dropped to his feet. "It's your father. We think he's had a heart attack. They're running some tests to make sure, but I'm fairly certain. He's stable now, but I wanted you to know." Her voice hitched at the end. "I'm sorry to tell you like this in a voice message, but I thought you might want to come as soon as possible." She took a breath. "Please call me back."

GRANT WAS STARING at a half-packed suitcase when his phone rang again. Dad's image popped up on the screen. He must be doing better if he was able to make a phone call.

"Hey, Grant." His voice sounded thin and tired. "Listen, I know your Mom asked you to come, but please don't worry about me."

"Of course, I'm worried about you, Dad." Grant ran his fingers through his hair. "You're in the hospital."

"I know, but I'm okay now. They're just going to release me in a couple days. You don't need to bother coming back."

"It's not—"

"I know how hard it is for you to get away, and we've got Will here."

That stung. He always suspected Dad loved Will more but hearing it out loud hurt.

"Are you sure? Because I can be there in a few hours."

"I'm sure. There's nothing here for you to do anyway." Muffled voices spoke in the background. "I'll talk to you later. Take care."

Take care? Grant was perfectly healthy, but his dad wanted *him* to take care? He plopped down on his bed.

What was he supposed to do? Dad was well enough to talk and really didn't want him there. So, who was he to argue?

What a strange reversal. For once, Grant really wanted to be in Trammel, and no one—not Ivy or his own family—wanted him there.

Chapter 11

"I need you to make the deliveries this morning." Mom handed the list for the day to Ivy.

"Isn't Luke working today?"

"No, he's at the station. And Victor called in sick—he broke his arm yesterday and can't drive."

Ivy pouted at her mother. "What about you or Dad?"

Mom smiled in what was probably supposed to be a cute way. Ivy groaned and grimaced back at her. Finally, she accepted the list. "All right."

She scanned the locations. Eighteen. Not their busiest day, but not the lightest either.

"You've got the phones?"

Mom gave her a thumbs up and shooed her away. "I've got everything ready to be loaded up. You just have to put it in the back and drive." She called over her shoulder as Ivy walked to the back. "It'll do you some good to get out."

She didn't usually hate deliveries, but Ivy had been in a terrible mood since Christmas. Even though she and Grant hadn't been an official couple—they'd only been on one actual date—the loss was real.

Van loaded and arrangements secured, Ivy hopped up to the driver's seat. She'd start with the closest location and work her way out to the funeral home and the hospital. She dumped her purse in the passenger seat, remembering that it was heavier because of a book Dad had loaned her.

She'd finally confessed to him her biggest fears.

"Dad? Do you think what I do has value?" Grant's words from Christmas Eve still rang in her head, days later.

Dad stared back at her questioningly, his lower lip sticking out. He patted the seat beside himself on the sofa.

Something she'd always appreciated about her father was how he knew when to stay quiet. She imagined most preachers didn't have the same skill. His gaze was gentle but steady. "What's going on, kiddle?"

He'd used her childhood nickname. Luke used to always tease her that "Lambs eat Ivy, and a kid'll eat Ivy too," from the old song. But Dad turned it around somehow and made her laugh it off. The nickname comforted her when Dad used it, as she settled in on the couch beside him.

"I watch you and Mom do such wonderful things. And Luke saves people's *lives*, for goodness' sake. But what do I do? What do I bring to the table?"

"What table?"

She leaned over, her head in her hands, too afraid to put words to her thoughts. *I know I'm going to sound stupid.* Finally, she said in a small voice, "God's table."

Dad sighed. "I'm a little biased, but I think what you do for all of us is very important. And if I may remind you, Jesus himself told us, 'Blessed are the meek, for they shall inherit the earth.'"

"I'm so frustrated." She swiped at her eyes. "I know that I don't want the lives of my friends I see on social media. But when I compare myself to them and to *you*," She glanced at him. "I feel so small and insignificant."

"Here, I have a book."

This was not unusual. Dad had literally thousands of books, so there was usually a title he could pull off the shelf for any occasion.

"It's an oldie, but a goodie." He winked at her, before handing it over. "And short, to boot."

"*The Practice of the Presence of God?*"

"It was written by a monk, Brother Lawrence. And I'll go ahead and spoil it a little for you—he finds the presence of God. Even in the small and menial tasks, he makes a spiritual connection."

Ivy flipped through a couple pages. At least this one was short, not like that time he'd handed her a complete commentary on the Gospels.

Now, in the van, Ivy turned the ignition. She tried to center her mind on God—like Brother Lawrence would do—and not on how irritable she was about making deliveries. *Maybe I should pray for all the people on the list. And all the people I pass on the road. And Grant.*

The thought surprised her. The Bible did say to pray for your enemies, although she wouldn't exactly consider Grant an enemy. Not *really*.

Her deliveries went smoothly enough. And as she prayed for each person on her list of deliveries, she found her mood lightening.

By the time Ivy pulled into the hospital parking lot, she was practically happy. *Thank you, Lord, for fixing my attitude today. Now, who's the next person on my list?*

Nathan Keller.

Her heart sank. She had no idea Grant's dad was sick. And now she'd probably have to see Grant as well as his whole family. After her very awkward early departure from their Christmas Eve dinner. Maybe she'd be able to leave their flowers at the front desk.

But the more she prayed, the more her heart tugged at her. *I should go say hello and see if they need anything. Even if it means I have to see Grant.*

"Thank you." Stacey was working the front desk. "Do you want to set that vase down with the others?"

"No," Ivy held Mr. Keller's arrangement. "I'd like to hand deliver these. Can you tell me where Nathan Keller's room is?"

Following the signs down the hall, Ivy prayed again. *Please give me courage and wisdom.* She was enjoying this newfound closer relationship with God. Although God hadn't seen fit to instantly solve all of her worries just yet.

Knock, knock.

Ivy waited a moment before stepping into the room. She stopped short. Lying in the hospital bed was a faded and thin version of the man she'd met at Christmas Eve dinner. It wasn't so much that he'd lost weight—maybe just a couple pounds—but that he'd lost all his color.

And poor Lisa. The vibrant and kind woman she'd come to care for looked so sad and tired.

"Hi," Ivy said when Lisa glanced in her direction. "I thought I'd bring these by myself."

"Oh, thank you, Ivy."

Together, they found a place for the flowers on a countertop.

"May I—um, what happened?"

Hugging her arms close, Lisa answered. "He had a heart attack a couple days ago, on New Year's Eve. It was fairly serious, but we think he'll be able to go back home soon."

"I'm so sorry, Lisa. That must've been terrifying."

"It was, but God brought us through." Lisa gave a small smile. "And Will and Addie have been so helpful."

She didn't say Grant's name. Ivy hated to pry, but something prompted her to ask. "Was Grant able to take off of work to come?"

Lisa rolled her eyes at this. "Nathan didn't want him to bother."

"There's no sense in him coming all the way down here when I'm going home soon." Mr. Keller spoke up. "He needs to be at work more than we need him here."

Lisa shrugged as if to say, *See what I have to put up with?* If the whole thing hadn't been so sad, Ivy might've laughed at the dynamic between the two of them.

"I'll let you rest, Mr. Keller. But I'll be praying for you to get well soon." Before she stepped into the hallway, she turned to Lisa. "Please let me know if you need anything."

"Thank you." Lisa waved.

All the way back to the flower shop, Ivy mulled over her visit to the hospital. Grant should've been there. Even if Mr. Keller had told him not to come, Lisa needed his support.

I have to let him know.

Parked in the back lot behind the shop, Ivy pulled out her phone. She started to type a text. Would that be too impersonal? Groaning, Ivy clicked on Grant's contact information. She'd have to call him.

Chapter 12

Grant stepped into the hospital room hesitantly, unsure of his parents' reaction to him being there, but Ivy insisted he would be wanted—needed even.

"Oh, honey. You came." His mother enveloped him in a hug. "I'm so glad you're here."

Lying in a bed in the middle of the room, looking gray and small, Dad gave him a weak smile.

"I know you said not to come." Grant winced. "But Ivy called and ... honestly, I should've come right away."

"You didn't need to bother." Though his words were harsh, Dad's expression was touched and maybe a little relieved.

Grant took a seat next to his dad. "Mom, how about you go home and get some rest? I'll stay with Dad for a few hours."

"Oh." Mom glanced around a moment, as if checking to make sure the room and all its occupants would be all right without her. "Well, I suppose I could use a shower."

"Take a nap too. I'll keep Dad company."

"Thank you, sweetheart." She leaned over to kiss Dad on the head. "I'll be back soon."

"No rush." Dad patted her face before she straightened and

backed out the door. When Mom was gone, he said, "She's hardly left me alone. And Will and Addie keep popping by."

Of course, they had. He was the only one without the good sense to show up right away when his father was in the hospital.

Around the room were cards and flower bouquets, two of which must have been from Grant's niece and nephew. The clear difference between Finley's card with glitter and flowers and Nate's card with streaks of red crayon and car stickers was amusing. Everyone but him had come to visit.

"I'm sorry. I should've been here. When Ivy called ... I felt so stupid—"

"How is Ivy?" Dad might be changing the subject to help take Grant's mind off his guilt, but the question made his stomach churn.

"Oh, um. I don't know. We haven't spoken except for that one phone call."

"What do you mean?"

"We got into a bit of an argument at Christmas." Grant scowled. "We were just getting to know each other, and she just ended things. I had no clue how to make it right, so I kept my distance."

"I don't know what's going on between you two, but don't keep your distance from a girl like her." Before Grant could stop him, Dad pushed himself up on his elbow with a grimace.

"Dad, you need to lie down and rest."

"That's all I've been doing for the last three days. It's time to get up and get going. Can't lie down forever." He grunted and shifted his body weight until he was in a semi-upright position. "Give Ivy a call."

"Maybe I will." He'd been thinking the same thing. Even if only to say thanks, he should try to reach out. "But I'm not sure she wants to talk to me."

"Worth a shot."

Grant nodded.

"What are you waiting for, anyway? Your mom and I are always wondering why you haven't settled down yet. Now you've got a great girl who likes you. What's stopping you?"

This was news to Grant. He'd thought only his mom was in a rush for him to get married. "I've got to be ready, haven't I? For family life and kids." Echoes of past conversations with his dad swam through his head. "I need to be a good provider. That's my role as husband and father."

Dad barked a laugh, wincing when he did. "But you aren't a husband *or* a father."

"No. And that's because I want to be prepared. I'm only just now getting to the place in my career where I could set my own hours and put aside enough money for kids' college and a nice retirement." Of course, that would only be true if he stuck around at Packer, Hughes, and Price.

"Is that why you broke up with Ivy? Because you think you can't support her?"

"It's complicated."

Dad waved his hands dismissively. "You don't have to tell me."

Grant stood and walked to the window. "She doesn't like that I work so much and stay in Dallas all the time. Family is important to her, and she thinks I don't care enough about mine." He picked up a card from the counter nearby. "Maybe she's right."

Setting the card back, he rounded on Dad. "But you're the one who always told me how essential my career is. As a man, I'm going to be someone's husband someday. I want to give my spouse a good life. I'm supposed to be the leader."

"You are. But good leadership is about more than one thing."

A ringtone sounded from Grant's pocket. He glanced at the screen. "It's Will, mind if I take the call?"

Dad nodded, waving him out of the room.

"I heard back from my contact at Richardson and Sons."

Weeks had passed since Grant asked Will for help searching for a new job. He'd given up on anything coming of that conversation. A bubble of hope grew inside his chest as he paced the hall.

"I wanted to give you a heads up before I connect you with Brad. They're looking for another attorney, and I think you'd be a great fit. It's less pay I'm sure, but you'd get to slow down a bit. Not work so many nights and weekends."

That sounded perfect to Grant, though he'd have to wait to hear how much the job would pay and whether it'd be a good fit. He was touched that his brother had come through for him. "Thank you, Will. I really appreciate your help."

"Of course." Will's voice lifted "I'm glad I could. You've seemed unhappy for a long time. Maybe a change of scenery will be just the thing you need."

This new job could mean more days spent in Trammel. With Dad in the hospital, he was realizing just how important family time could be. "Do you think Dad will be okay?"

"I do, but he needs to slow down. He's always lived life at a breakneck pace, pushing himself to do too much."

"He was just trying to be a good father."

"Perhaps." Will dragged out the word. "But being a father is about more than just making money."

"That's what Dad was saying earlier. He started talking about how it's time for me to settle down and have kids." Grant sighed. "I don't know where any of this is coming from."

"Maybe he's realizing some things, shifting his priorities. Health scares can do that to people."

"You're a dad. Isn't providing for your family important?

I'm building up my career so I can have something to give them someday."

"Sure, I want to give my kids a good life. But that's not all about money. The most important job I have is to be a spiritual leader for my kids. They don't care how much money I make if I'm never around and don't teach them about Jesus." Will took a breath. "I'm not saying you wouldn't ever be around ..."

"But that's what I'm like right now. I'm always working. And the people I work with don't ever spend time with their families. Except for the attorneys in senior positions." He stepped aside for a nurse walking past. She barely glanced his way as Will continued talking.

"You're a lawyer, Grant. You're never going to be struggling for cash. But even if you were, the only thing your kids would truly care about is being with you."

A memory of waiting for his dad to come home flashed through his mind. He'd always begged his dad to play with him as a boy. Maybe Will was right. "So, you don't worry about making a good life for your kids?"

"Of course, I do. But I have to remind myself that, in the end, you don't get to take it with you. The only lasting thing I can give my kids is a relationship with God."

Grant leaned against the wall. He'd never thought about it that way.

Will's phone beeped, and his lips pinched together. "That'll be Hailey. I'd better head out. I'll send that email tomorrow." He paused briefly before adding "It was good to talk."

Before going back into the room, Grant squeezed his eyes shut. Had he wasted years of his life in pursuit of the wrong goal? He'd always wanted to be a lawyer, and he honestly enjoyed aspects of his job. But was he pursuing a partnership for the sole purpose of gaining more and more wealth?

"Nice to meet you, Grant." Brad Richardson stood to shake Grant's hand.

The offices of Richardson and Sons weren't in a high rise in a big city—the building wasn't even two stories tall. And there were no interns fetching coffee. Only one middle-aged paralegal sat at a desk down the hall from Brad's office. He wasn't at Packer, Hughes, and Price anymore. And he loved it.

"I see we share an alma mater." Brad—an acquaintance of his brother and, apparently, a fellow Wildcat—nodded appreciatively. Grant's résumé sat on the desk in between them.

"Two years at Packer, Hughes, and Price. What was that like?"

"Oh. Well—"

Bzzz. Bzzz.

Brad pulled a phone from his pocket. He glanced at the screen then held up a finger to Grant. "Sorry, it's my daughter. I have an always-answer policy with my kids."

"Hi, sweetie."

Stunned, Grant sat frozen in place for a moment. Should he give Brad some privacy? He'd never had someone take a phone call during an interview before.

"Sure. I'll be there at five." Brad kept talking.

He tensed his muscles to lift himself out of the chair and made eye contact with Brad, pointing to the door. Brad shook his head and motioned for Grant to stay.

"Okay ... uh-huh. All right, I'll see you then. Love you."

Brad returned the phone to his pocket. "Where were we?"

Grant blinked. On the one hand, sitting through Brad's personal call had been extremely awkward. But on the other hand ... did that man just make time for his family *at work?*

"Is everything okay?"

"Oh, she just wanted to make sure I'll be there to pick her up from volleyball practice. She could've texted, but sometimes I think she likes to hear me say it out loud." Brad chuckled. "You leave a kid at church *one* time, and they never trust you again."

There had to be a story there, but Grant decided to let it go for now.

"You asked what Packer, Hughes, and Price was like." He gestured to Brad. "No one would have ever taken a personal call in the middle of a meeting like that. But ... maybe that's what I've been missing."

Brad smiled and shrugged. "I'm very busy—even more since Dad retired a couple years ago—but I make my family a priority." Resting his elbows on the desk, he twined his fingers together and leveled a piercing gaze at Grant. "I'm going to be straight with you. I can't offer you the salary or the lifestyle you're used to enjoying. I can't guarantee a corner office in a fancy building in a big city. But I can promise you that I will treat you like a person."

Grant slowly grinned. Atticus Finch would like this place.

Chapter 13

"Aaronson Flowers and Gifts, How may I help you?" Ivy longed for a certain phone call, one from a handsome young man. Days had passed since she told Grant about his dad, but she hadn't heard a thing from him.

Of course, he must be spending time with his family. That thought made her smile. His mom would be thrilled to have him in town. Whether or not she ever got another phone call from Grant, she was happy to know he was with the people who loved him best.

"I'd like to send a funeral arrangement."

"Sure thing." Ivy talked the customer through the different size and price options. They landed on a potted peace lily, a beautiful and hardy flower that would last long past the burial.

She plugged the information into her computer, adding the customer's credit card number. "And where would you like the lily delivered?"

"Weaver Funeral Home, for Rob Richardson."

Ivy nearly dropped the phone. She wrote down the final note on the order and managed to say goodbye before she hung up. Mr. Richardson was dead. He'd been old as long as she'd known him, but she'd never expected him to actually die. Ivy grabbed the side of the counter with one hand and covered her mouth with the other.

Behind her, the glass door opened. "Ready for your lunch break? I needed to stretch my legs anyway—" Mom stopped when she caught Ivy's gaze. "What's wrong?"

"Mr. Richardson passed away."

Mom's brows pinched together. "I'm sorry to hear that."

"I just thought—It's silly, but I didn't expect him to die."

She didn't laugh or give advice. Mom just rubbed her shoulder. "How about you grab something to eat? I'll watch the shop while you're gone."

Several more customers phoned in orders for the Richardson funeral over the rest of the week. Ivy ended up with enough arrangements to fill a van but no handy firefighters to do the delivery. Truth be told, she wanted to take the flowers herself. Maybe the act could bring her a sense of closure.

On the day of the visitation, Ivy found a woman meeting with Mr. Weaver in the front office. She shifted her weight, holding a basket of roses. Funeral homes gave a lot of people the creeps, but she'd become quite familiar with them over the years. Their floral smell reminded her of the shop, even if it was often laced with old lady perfume and something a bit more morbid. She liked to think the flowers she brought for funerals reminded people that life and death were both part of this world. Beauty and sorrow could coexist.

After waiting a moment, Ivy knocked gently on the door. "I'm so sorry to interrupt. I have some floral arrangements for the Richardson funeral, and I—"

The woman stood up and took in Ivy's name tag and armload of flowers. She wasn't tall, but she had a commanding presence. "Are you from Aaronson's?"

"Yes, ma'am. Ivy Aaronson." She gave a smile "I'll be out of your way soon, I just wanted to make sure—"

"I'm Francis Richardson. Rob was my husband."

"Oh." Ivy froze. "I'm so sorry for your loss."

"Thank you." Francis pulled Ivy's hand in both of hers. "Rob thought the world of you and your parents."

Ivy wasn't sure what to say. The skin on Francis's hands was cold and crepey, but soft. She had a surprisingly strong grip.

"You were the only ones he trusted. He always wanted to send flowers when clients or friends passed away, and now ..." Her voice broke. "Now I'm preparing for *his* funeral."

"I'm—" Ivy stopped herself from saying she was sorry again. "He was one of our best customers. We'll miss him." She hadn't known that was true until he was gone. Funny how someone so irritating could leave such a big hole.

"You're doing important work, you know. What you did for Rob meant a lot to him."

"Thank you." She squeezed Francis's hands before loosening her grip. "I appreciate that."

"You can leave the flowers in the hallway for now." Mr. Weaver spoke up. "I'll have someone come help you." He gestured for Mrs. Richardson to join him at the desk.

Ivy nodded and ducked out of the room. Her mind swirled.

All the years she'd worked at the flower shop, and especially these last few months, she'd considered Mr. Richardson a thorn in her flesh. Never in all that time had she considered the impact she'd made in his life. When he needed to send condolences, he always depended on Ivy or her mom to do the job correctly. Sure, he'd been a pain. But he'd trusted them with a task that meant a great deal to him.

Maybe Ivy wasn't a missionary or preacher. She wasn't a firefighter or even a corporate defense attorney. Her job was much more humble. Ivy was a florist who loved to brighten people's days. She was a daughter and sister who valued being close to her family.

Maybe Dad had been right. Maybe she didn't need to be someone brilliant or beautiful to get God's attention. Maybe she could have His love just by being herself.

God, I'll still fight every day to glorify you. But I want to say this out loud—I accept your love. You love me no matter what, even if I'm not the smartest or best or most important. I love you, too, God. With my whole heart.

Ivy smiled past the lump in her throat. She never would have guessed Mr. Richardson would be the one to teach her that important lesson.

Chapter 14

Valentine's Day was easily the busiest time of year for a flower shop, followed closely by Mother's Day. Ivy and her family were up to their ears in pink and red flower arrangements. And now, she had a new business venture to add to her workload. But Ivy had never been so energized.

After lots of prayerful soul-searching, She could finally appreciate her life for what it was—full of love and value. Not because she was so important or smart, but because God loved and valued her.

Ivy grinned at her brother as they passed in the studio. He stuck out his tongue and gave a hideous face that always made her laugh and roll her eyes.

Back out front, a customer held up one of her latest creations. "What's this now?"

"We're expanding our gifts line. I made that headband myself."

"Very cute." The lady smiled at her before browsing through the rest of the display, still holding the headband.

With Mom and Dad's blessing, Ivy had transitioned to a new role at the shop: Head of Marketing. She'd already made changes to their inventory, replacing lower selling items with ones that moved off the shelf faster. Customers liked buying local gifts, and Ivy enjoyed researching new products for their shop to carry.

She'd also created social media accounts for the shop, each one filled with beautiful images of flowers. Mom and Dad had insisted on a raise to go along with her new responsibilities. But honestly, just having a defined role at the company was reward enough.

And in her free time, Ivy was setting up an online clothing and crafts business to sell items like the headband. She had no idea if it would make any money, but she enjoyed the prospect of a project all her own.

"Need help loading the van, sis." Luke punched her playfully before beckoning her through the door. "Dad'll watch the shop."

Ivy cocked her head. They rarely let Dad watch the cash register unattended because he wasn't good with technology. But he loved talking to people.

"Go on. I'll be fine." Dad gave a light push toward the door.

She followed her brother to the studio where arrangements were lined up on Mom's table. Victor was working today too. Because Valentine's Day.

"Here's the list." Victor passed her the papers with his good arm. He was still nursing an injury but getting good at working one-handed. "You double-check everything, and we'll load it up."

One by one, they checked every order off their list and secured it in the vehicle. When they couldn't fit one more sprig of baby's breath inside, Luke closed the back doors and got in the driver's seat.

"What's this one here? Was it not on the list?"

"Let me see." Ivy glanced at the label on the vase in Victor's hands. It was a massive arrangement of roses, gerbera daisies, ranunculus, and snapdragons. Wait. "Someone made a mistake on this one. That must be why it wasn't loaded in the van. See?" She showed Victor the tag. "It has my name on it."

Victor winked before setting the vase on the table with a light *thud*. Before she could protest, he'd walked through the door to the front.

Frowning, she examined the tag closer.

To Ivy. With my sincerest apologies and affection—

"Hi."

Ivy's head snapped up. Grant.

"How did you …?" Words escaped her. Somehow, he'd managed to order flowers behind her back. A gigantic, extravagant bouquet of flowers. And he was here—in the studio.

Grant's smile was all the more charming because it was so shy and hesitant. "Your mom might have helped me out."

Ivy's gaze flitted back and forth between Grant and her mother. Mom gave a sheepish grin. "How about you take a break, Ivy? Maybe go for a walk?"

"But—"

"We can spare you for a few minutes." Mom practically pushed them out the back door.

Grant was glad to see Ivy had worn a coat. The air had turned downright chilly, and he rubbed his arms to keep warm.

Ivy's face was the picture of confusion. She turned from staring at the closed door to looking at him. "Grant, I—"

"I'm sorry." Interrupting, he took her hand in his. He

needed her to know how much he regretted their argument before she said anything. "I'm not sure what I said that night that made you so upset, but I'm so sorry. I never meant to hurt your feelings."

She didn't respond right away, so Grant continued.

"And I know my actions this past year haven't exactly put me in the best light. Truthfully, I should've come home more, and I could've made time for it. You were right."

Blinking hard, Ivy pressed her lips together before speaking. "So ... you don't think my job has no value?"

"Oh, Ivy. Is that what you thought?" No wonder she'd been so upset.

She winced and shrugged. "I think perhaps that's the story I was telling myself. And when you said what you did ..."

"I promise I never meant to make you feel that way. You've helped me so much this year. Those flowers might be the reason I still have a decent relationship with my mom."

"No, you would've patched things up with her." Ivy twisted her lips in a smile. "Eventually."

"Can you forgive me?" He took the other hand now.

"Only if you forgive me." Ivy stared at the ground. "I've been thinking—and praying—a lot these last few weeks. I was rude to you and didn't give you the benefit of the doubt. I know that you love your family, even when you're away."

"Well, I've got good news on that front."

"Is your dad ...?"

Grant understood what she was trying to ask and answered quickly. "Dad's doing great. He's still not one hundred percent yet, but he's much better than the last time you saw him." The heart attack had been a wakeup call for Grant and his dad both. They'd be making some changes to their habits. Healthy changes.

"What I wanted to share is that I have a new job. In Trammel."

"What?" Her face lit up with what Grant hoped was pure excitement.

"I don't start until March, but I've already turned in my notice. I'm going to take some time off. Maybe go on vacation." Dad was too sick still to travel, or he'd take his parents along. But now would be a good chance to relax a bit.

"That's amazing."

Now came the hardest part of all. She'd forgiven him, but would she take him back?

"I was wondering if … if you might like to go out again. To a real restaurant this time."

His heart skipped a beat as a slow, devastatingly beautiful grin spread over her face. "Of course."

Then she moved closer. She made him nervous like no one ever had before. But he didn't mind as long as she kept looking at him like that. When he couldn't take the knots in his stomach anymore, he slid his hand behind Ivy's head and pulled her toward him.

Her smile grew. "I like you."

"I'd like to kiss you." And he captured her lips with his.

If he'd been worried about Ivy forgiving him before, he no longer had anything to be afraid of. She kissed him back, deep and sure. He breathed in the scent of her hair, like roses.

Grant almost laughed at how far they'd come in the past year. He never thought he'd end up with the woman on the other end of the phone. But God had bigger and better plans for his life than he'd made for himself.

As they pulled apart, something cold landed on Grant's cheek. Ivy reached up to brush it away with her thumb. They both gazed up at the sky. "It's snowing."

He laughed then pulled Ivy into a hug. They enjoyed the

delightful scene for a moment more before running to bang on the back door. It was too cold to stay outside for long.

Grant thought his life was supposed to play out a certain way—a prestigious career in the big city. But his heart was here in Trammel. And who knew what would bloom where love was planted?

Acknowledgments

My undying gratitude to Amy, Rachel, and Heather. Your support and encouragement made this whole process a blast.

To Michael and our beautiful kids, thank you for your patience and forgiveness. And thank you, Michael, for giving me lots of free legal advice.

Thank you so much to Linda and everyone at Scrivenings Press. Working with you is such a blessing.

To the staff at Carren's Flowers & Gifts and my sister, Anna, thank you for your help and advice on all things floral. All mistakes are my own, of course.

Dear reader, thank you for coming along with us on this journey.

And my greatest thanks to the Creator God. May my work always and only glorify You.

About the Author

Sarah Anne Crouch lives in Arkansas with her husband, three children, and thousands of books. She always wanted to be an author, but spent some time as a teacher, earned a degree in library science, and makes feeble attempts to corral her small children as a stay-at-home mom. Sarah loves reading books, recipes, piano music, and emails from readers.

A Novella

sweet
DELIVERY

Heather Greer

If you've ever found yourself chasing a path that isn't God's best for you, know you're not alone and that we serve a God who can set us right again.

Chapter 1

"Ugh!" Will Forrester swiped his arm across the top of his desk, sending stacks of papers swirling through the air like giant snowflakes.

Movement at his office door caught Will's attention. Not bothering to school his features, he glared up at the intruder.

Madison. The mousy girl he'd hired a month earlier stared with wide eyes and a face drained of color. Did she think him a monster?

"Sorry," she squeaked before scurrying away.

The girl would never make it. Couldn't a man vent his frustration in his own office without judgment from the help? At least he hadn't resorted to swearing like some of the popular chefs. He hadn't even yelled at her or anyone else, for that matter.

He reached across his desk to return the frame he'd knocked over in his temper. His own image smiled at him from behind the glass. Flanking him on both sides Adeline Li and Taylor Prince, the *Cake That!* baking competition judges, wore similar expressions. The only difference? Their smiles were pasted on specifically for the camera. For once, his was genuine. The happiest day of his life.

Wasn't that one hundred-thousand-dollar grand prize supposed to make his dreams come true? If this was happily ever after, why was everything falling apart?

He rose from the desk and stepped over the loose papers littering the floor. After closing the door against prying eyes and listening ears, he dropped back into his chair, picked up his phone, and dialed the one person who would understand. She'd been his competition in the show until they were the only two left standing, and somewhere along the way, she became his friend.

"Hello. Thanks for calling the Sugar Cube. This is Livvy. How can I help you?"

Will smiled. His name would have flashed across the phone screen, but Livvy likely answered without checking it. Probably fully immersed in handing out cupcakes to her customers. The people in front of her always came first.

"Hey, Livvy. It's Will," he greeted her. "Do you have a minute?"

"Evan?" Her voice sounded muffled. She must have pulled the phone away from her mouth. "Can you watch things for a minute?"

Will couldn't hear the answer, but footsteps and a door opening and closing assured him Livvy was moving to a place where she could talk.

"What's up, Will? Evan and I have missed you the last month or so." Her voice wasn't accusatory—just genuinely curious.

"How do you do it?"

A light chuckle. "I'm going to need a little more to go on."

"The Sugar Cube. How do you make it work? I mean, it's a cupcake truck. Nothing special, but you and Evan enjoy success at every turn. And neither of you are even classically trained bakers."

"Thanks, Will," she said, her voice monotone. "In one breath you managed to insult me, Evan, and the dream I've worked so hard to achieve."

Will dropped his head against the back of his chair and huffed. "That's not what I meant."

"I know." Her voice was calm and patient. "But you can't put others down like that, bad day or not. You can be successful without others having to be failures."

"It was easier with Harper here," he admitted. Who knew he'd come out of the competition with a former competitor-turned-girlfriend? Considering the course of the current conversation, maybe he shouldn't have.

"I know."

"She was good for me. She'd give me *that* look every time I was toeing the line and needed to take a step back."

"I know."

"And she had great ideas. For me and for Pastry Perfect."

"I *know*."

If he rolled his eyes, would Livvy know that too? Probably. But really, had he told her anything new? Or anything requiring more than her simple acknowledgment? His current predicament would have been avoided completely, if not for Harper's inability to accept things as they were.

"Why couldn't she be happy for me *and* let me have my faith?" He reined in his voice to lessen the whiny toddler vibe. "I wasn't asking her to believe too."

Livvy sighed.

Will could imagine her toying with one of her dark curls or maybe even the teal lock of hair that always framed her face. He caught himself running his hand through his short, blond hair as he thought about it and forced his hand down on the desk.

"There was a time you didn't want to hear it either," Livvy started. "And I know you weren't pushing her, but the differences in you were undeniable. They pushed her whether your words did or not."

"But faith makes me a better person," he reasoned.

"I know Harper wanted you to be the best man you could be. At the same time, she didn't understand why your faith made you that way. It was threatening for her. Just like it was for you when we first discussed it."

"I guess," he muttered.

"Now, tell me what this call is really about."

"What do you mean?"

"We've rehashed the Harper-Will relationship devastation more times than I care to count during the first three months after she left. You know the answers, and you've done well accepting them. That is until some new stressor comes into your life. So, out with it. What's really getting to you?"

Unable to channel his nervous energy into anything productive, Will stood and paced the confines of his small office. "It's Pastry Perfect."

"Your bakery? I thought that was doing well."

The reports he'd been studying taunted him from the floor where they'd landed after being unceremoniously shoved from his desk. He glared at them. "I thought so too. When I started the bakery after winning eighteen months ago, everything was fine."

"And now?"

He shrugged, though she couldn't see it. "We're still doing decent business, but about six months ago ... one of those chain bakeries, *Cupcakes & Cookies & Cakes, Oh, My!*, opened up."

"Might as well buy a box of cookies from the grocery store," Livvy murmured.

"Yeah, well, they have delivery. As long as their minimum order of $15 is reached, they will bring it to your door."

"Does that affect you much?"

"I've lost several regulars from the local hospital and doctor's offices. Why stop before work or make a trip at lunch when they can simply have something delivered?"

"Have you considered offering the same service?"

A huff escaped before he could stop it. "No. I make quality desserts with quality ingredients. I shouldn't have to pander to the whims of lazy people looking for ways to remain blissful in their laziness."

"Will."

He adjusted the condescending tone before continuing. "Besides, Madison is only a part-time employee. And between you and me, I don't see her adding hours as a delivery driver. And we both know the disaster it would be for me to do the deliveries."

Livvy's snort signaled her agreement. Will was self-aware enough to know his personality didn't lend itself to dealing with the public. Following Harper's departure, Pastry Perfect received its first and only one-star review. After an hour venting his frustration to Livvy, he'd acquiesced to her suggestion and hired Madison to work the register during their busiest hours.

"I know you don't want to hear this," Livvy began. "But I think you should consider hiring another person and offering delivery, even if it's only limited hours each day."

"I don't know."

"Want me to get Evan? He may have a better idea."

"No, thanks," he declined as an impish idea took hold. "But do tell him he better take good care of you. Otherwise, he'll regret the delays in tying the knot, because I'll beat him to it."

"Bye, Will."

Livvy no longer responded to his baseless taunts. While he once meant every word, they'd moved beyond that early stage in their friendship. Evan did, too, for that matter. While Will wouldn't consider them close, Evan had led Will to the Lord, and they'd developed genuine respect for each other. Livvy had chosen wisely when she'd accepted Evan's proposal.

Livvy was smart, relationally and professionally. That was the reason Will couldn't dismiss her suggestion for his business even though just thinking about dealing with another employee wore him out. What she said made sense. Honestly, he'd thought about this himself.

He would spend the day in prayer, like Evan and Livvy both taught him to do before making big decisions. But come tomorrow, he had a sneaking suspicion there would be a help wanted sign in his window.

Chapter 2

"**M**r. Forrester?"

The way Madison constantly made his name sound like a question grated on Will. He glanced up with what he imagined was thinly veiled patience. The morning had not gone well, and he sequestered himself in his office trying to stave off a faint throbbing in his temples before the pounding in his head transformed into a full-blown percussion section beating out the rhythm of a samba.

Madison shifted from one foot to the other while biting her bottom lip.

"There's someone here for you." Her hands, like nervous butterflies, flitted around her as she spoke. "It's about the position."

"Send them back, and I'll speak with them."

Her chin rose and fell like a bobble-head doll before she returned in the direction she'd come from. What had possessed him to hire her when every timid action threatened to break his already strained patience?

Obedience and friendliness. Madison could deal with his customers when he could not, and she always did whatever he asked without question or hesitation. His polar opposite was what he'd sought in that hiring, which was exactly what he got. Now, he had to learn to live with his choice.

This next one would be different. He still needed someone he could count on to follow directions, but maybe not quite so far down the spectrum from his personality. Honestly, he didn't think he could take a second Madison.

"Mr. Forrester." A woman's clear voice interrupted his inner monologue.

He didn't know what he'd expected, but the woman standing before him was nowhere on his thought-radar. Her posture was impeccable. Shoulders straight, head up, standing as tall as his meager five foot five inches, if not a little above it. And, she'd said his name without that pesky question mark.

Manners drilled into him and his brothers from the time they were toddlers rushed in, prodding him from his seat, though he remained standing behind his desk. This was a place of business and a job interview.

"Yes. I'm Will Forrester." Hand extended across his desk, he introduced himself. "And you are?"

She accepted his offered hand. Must have nerves of steel. No clamminess or tell-tale trembling. That barely there hold many women often resorted to was missing as well. Like they thought their delicate little bones would break at the slightest touch. Madison had a grip like that. If it could even be called a grip. Whatever it was, off-putting defined it perfectly.

"Erica. Erica Gerard. Pleased to meet you."

An easy motion of his hand brought her attention to the chair across from his. She accepted it, sitting with the same presence she'd entered with. Unlike those whose confidence was merely bravado, Erica's proud composure suggested it was natural.

"Madison tells me you're here inquiring about the position?"

A slight nod. "Yes, sir. The advertisement in the window didn't state whether the job was full- or part-time. But I'll be up front with you—I'm not looking for less than thirty-six hours a week. I'd hate to waste time for either of us if this job doesn't fit."

Direct. Will could appreciate the quality. "This is a new position, and it is subject to change. However, what I currently require is Monday through Friday only. This is a delivery job, but when not called out, you'd be responsible for filling orders up front, cleaning, or stocking."

Pausing, he assessed whether or not she'd lost interest at the description of duties. Eyes, gray as the sky before a storm, stared intently. Full lips neither smiled, nor frowned. She was still listening. That was a good sign. Right?

"I'm offering limited delivery times. Ten in the morning until two in the afternoon. Only twenty hours a week. Far below your needed hours. I'm sorry."

Raising a slender finger, she stopped him. "While limiting hours for delivery is wise, I'm not sure you've thought through your best options relating to the times."

She had the gall to question his ability to adequately plan for his business? Meeting her gaze directly with one of his own, Will forced the tightness from his jaw before answering. "And what would you suggest, Ms. Gerard?"

"As I see it, you're missing a key opportunity with the early morning crowd." She offered him the nugget of an idea before looking to him for approval to continue.

He nodded, and she returned the gesture.

"Your menu board boasts several flavored coffee drinks, cinnamon rolls, and three Danish flavors. All geared toward breakfast."

"Yes," he conceded. "But they aren't the focus of the bakery."

"They don't have to be, but if they're going to be there, you should put them to work for you. Offer delivery Monday through Friday from eight in the morning until two in the afternoon."

"That might work. But it's still only thirty hours. Too few for your needs, Ms. Gerard. I'm afraid applying would be, as you said, a waste of both our time."

She shook her head. "Not necessarily. Let me apply. Use me for these deliveries and your special event deliveries. Weekdays. Weekends. It doesn't matter. And when deliveries and special orders aren't waiting, I can help in the front. Give your girl out there a break when needed or help during rushes."

A full-time employee would free him up considerably. Starting each morning before the sun rose and ending it after all the nine-to-fivers called it a day was exhausting. His passion was baking.

The woman made good points, and he hadn't fleshed out his plan before she arrived to inquire about the position. But still, immediate and full agreement wouldn't look good to a potential employee. He needed to keep the upper hand.

"Thirty-six hours. It's the most I'm going to offer. Delivery will begin at eight thirty, not eight, and run until two. The remaining hours will be variable depending on special deliveries and events. And some of those might take place on Saturdays."

"Then, I'd like to officially start the application process."

The hint of a smile attempted to soften the seriousness of her expression and reassure him. Her confidence won the battle. What should have evoked a sense of openness instead reminded Will of grade school picture day. While Erica Gerard was self-assured, the interpersonal nuances of conversation might be a weak point. He could understand that better than most.

Opening the drawer to his right, Will shuffled through a few manilla folders before pulling out the one he needed. He extended the stapled packet to Erica, waiting for her to accept it before repeating the action with a pen.

"You may fill this out up front and give it to Madison. If it looks like you'd be a good candidate for the position, I'll check out your references. Depending on the other applicants, we may need a formal interview time. So, be sure to indicate which method of contact is best."

He rose as Erica did and walked the few steps with her to the office door. He pointed.

"Right through there. It was nice meeting you, Ms. Gerard."

One dip of her head in acknowledgment. "And you, too, Mr. Forrester. I look forward to hearing from you."

Watching her walk without hesitation out the door leading to the dining area one word sprang to mind. Confident. At times, she even bordered on arrogant. He'd told himself hiring another Madison was out of the question. But could two Wills work in harmony without destroying Pastry Perfect and all his dreams?

Chapter 3

Will perused the application. "You worked for *Cupcakes & Cookies & Cakes, Oh, My!?*"

"Yes, sir." Erica licked her lips.

"Tell me about your time there. What did the position entail? Were you responsible to oversee anything? And why did you leave?"

Erica smiled, hoping it wasn't a grimace. It was her only job experience, so it had to be listed. But if Will knew the truth about her time at the bakery, she could kiss this opportunity good-bye.

"It was my first job. Before the local store opened, I worked in the original location." Erica offered the mundane details while debating what else was safe to tell. "I followed the company here. I only left recently. During those eight years, I filled customer orders and cleaned up after them. I also worked in the back, helping prep for the day, washing dishes, and cleaning the kitchen. My favorite task was doing deliveries."

"Why is that?"

"A couple reasons." Erica shrugged. "I enjoyed getting out and moving around. But more than that, I loved how everyone was always happy to see me. No one's cranky with the person bringing them their morning coffee and pastry or afternoon sweets. I loved being the one to make them smile, even after a trying day at work."

Will contemplated her with furrowed brows. "So, you get along well with the customers?"

"I like to think I do."

"On your application, you asked me not to contact your previous employer. Is there a reason I shouldn't?"

Erica laid a manilla folder on the desk and slid it toward him. "I've brought you a hard copy of my last performance review, signed by the HR manager. The report is less than a month old, and you can get a clear picture of my time there from it."

"That's helpful." Will flipped open the cover and scanned the review. "But it still doesn't answer why you don't want me to speak with them."

"They weren't happy when I turned in my notice." Erica squelched the urge to fidget. Stick to the basics. "My absence left them short-handed."

Will tapped a pen against his chin. "How did you feel about leaving them in a lurch? They must have treated you at least fairly well to keep you in their employ for eight years. One would think you wouldn't want to place them in that position."

"Up to that point, I'd been treated like family." It wasn't a lie, exactly. "However, during my time with the company, I finished my marketing degree. When I approached my boss about branching out into other areas of the company, it didn't go well. I understand now that there is no place for me in their business except doing what I'd always done. I don't want to settle for that."

"Yet, you came to me for a job with that exact description.

Deliveries and working front of the house." His blue eyes narrowed. "Why?"

Good question. A deep breath bought her some time. Not long enough. Still, she refused to lose her composure in front of the man who could give her the way off the hamster wheel her life had become.

"It's a steppingstone." Completely truthful. "I enjoy the business. While I want to one day use my degree, I also want to employ my skills in a bakery at that time. I'm limited to my knowledge of one chain bakery. I need a feel for how others run. As I understand it, Pastry Perfect isn't a chain. It must operate differently. Learning about those differences can only aid me in the future."

"This job is not a career choice for you, then."

It didn't sound like a question, and it didn't seem like the idea disappointed Will. Maybe he wasn't as sure of the need for this position as one might expect.

"No, sir." Erica smiled politely. "Delivery driving is not my life's goal. However, I do need to pay my bills and gain experiences outside of those I've had during last eight years. With this job, I'll accomplish both."

"One last question."

"Yes, sir."

"Will you have trouble taking orders?"

"If you're talking about filling the soccer mom's daily order for a Chocolate Obsession cupcake and large iced coffee with a spritz of hazelnut and blueberry with almond milk to get her through the afternoon with her sanity intact, then, no. I can take orders just fine."

"And if I'm not?" His brow quirked.

Erica nodded sharply. "I shouldn't have any trouble with those orders either. You seem like a more than reasonable man with realistic goals and methods of achieving them."

Without another word, Will stalked toward the door. Opening it, he held it and glanced back at her. Erica refused to let him see her disappointment. Sliding her purse strap up her arm to rest on her shoulder, she stood and faced him.

"Thank you for your time." Her voice was strong and steady, the way she intended.

"I'll see you at eight sharp tomorrow morning." Will extended his hand. "Welcome to the Pastry Perfect crew."

"I look forward to it." She shook his hand without missing a beat. "Until eight."

He got her. Not many people could say the same. She waited until she'd cleared not only the office door but the bakery door and windows, just in case her new boss was watching, before allowing a shake of her head. One thing was certain. To work for Will Forrester, she would need to stay on top of her game.

"Um, Mr. Forrester?" Madison stopped short as she came through the door separating the kitchen from the front of the bakery. "Mr. Forrester?"

The timid voice reached him both times, but it wasn't until Madison called his name the second time that Will pulled himself from his concerns. He mustered an empty smile. Feigning interest was the best he could do.

"Yes, Madison. Is there something you need?"

Madison shifted from one foot to the other. "I, uh, I thought maybe you needed something." She shrugged. "You were just standing there when I came through the door."

Was he? He shook his head. "No. Thank you. I was thinking. That's all."

"Okay." Madison scurried over to a waiting tray of Danishes, scooped it up, and hurried to the front.

At least her presence in the kitchen meant business was good that morning. Maybe hiring a delivery person wasn't necessary after all. Will returned to his desk. The reports that had taunted him into hiring Erica were shoved in a drawer where he believed they couldn't harass him anymore. He was wrong. The goading continued relentlessly.

Hiring a delivery person wasn't an extra frill for the business. It was necessity. And, hands down, the best candidate for the job was Erica Gerard.

A sliver of apprehension slid up his spine. The same feeling snaked through him during her interview. Erica didn't outright lie to him. He was certain of it. But, unless he missed his guess, she wasn't as forthcoming as she could have been.

"What's she not telling me?" He perused her application once more.

Her qualifications were undeniable. Smart, capable, and trained in the bakery business. She lacked the weakness of personality ever present in Madison. Still, she retained a personable quality that his customers would respond positively to.

What was it to him if those gray-blue eyes, brimming with confidence, held a secret in their depths? Everyone hid parts of themselves from time to time.

When Harper first left him, the bakery made him miserable. Her shadow lingered in every empty space. Did he allow his employees to see that? No. He worked with the same proficiency and professionalism he always did. Livvy and Evan were the only ones allowed a peek into his pain.

"That's it." He slapped his palm against his desk.

Why did it take him so long to put the pieces together? Erica provided her performance reviews. She freely spoke of her duties at *Cupcakes & Cookies & Cakes, Oh, My!*. The only thing she asked was that he didn't contact them personally.

It made perfect sense. A failed workplace relationship must have prompted Erica's departure. Her confidence, eyes highlighted with dark lashes, and rich brown hair with hints of red that framed full lips touched with a hint of clear gloss all begged for a man's attention. Maybe she'd even gained the attention of a supervisor with her girl-next-door beauty.

On-the-job heartbreak. Nothing trumped it for ruining the work environment. While he couldn't bring up such a sensitive subject, Will realized it must be the reason for the strange hesitance he sensed at various points in the interview.

He'd fallen prey to it. So, he couldn't rightfully hold the same against Erica, who was perfectly qualified—maybe even overly qualified. Understanding eased his doubt. Hiring Erica would work out just fine.

Chapter 4

Never, in the history of first days, had there been one so full of contention. Will was on a power trip, proving himself the alpha in a situation where his position was unquestionable.

Erica gripped the edge of the metal countertop until her knuckles turned white. One deep breath. Another. One more. Slowly release it. Let the frustration go along with the air.

Lifting her chin, she turned to her boss with a patient smile. At least, she hoped that was the expression her face reflected.

"What's your plan for announcing the new delivery service?"

Square jaw set, Will met her gaze with an unwavering one. "I thought I'd put it on the website and make printable menus for people to take as they come in. They'll have the new delivery hours and the number to call to place orders."

"That's it?"

"What do you mean, 'that's it?'" His blue eyes narrowed. If possible, his shoulders straightened even more.

Erica tilted her head to the side as she regarded him. "If

that's what you're doing to promote this new option, you might as well quit offering it now. It's going to take forever to get the word out that way."

"And what would you suggest?" The question, pushing past clenched teeth framed with a pained smile, only feigned interest.

"Something more personal." Erica ran her hand through her straight hair from her scalp to where it ended at her shoulders. "How about I put my marketing degree to work for you this morning? I can update your website with a banner announcing the new service, and I can develop your printable delivery menu. This afternoon, I'll hand them out at various businesses in town. That way, the announcement feels more personal."

"Fine. But I've only got the one computer. You'll have to work from my office."

For the first time since clocking in, Erica's smile was sincere. "That's perfect. I'm sure I'll need your input to ensure the flyers are exactly how you want them."

As much as Will hated to admit it, Erica's idea held merit. For the last hour, he'd moved around his office without reason, other than inconspicuously overseeing her work. The website updates were perfect and completed in less time than it would have taken him. Only his efforts would have resulted in less than perfection.

"Your changes will work just fine." He had to be careful not to dole out too many compliments. His new employee might not be happy with her place in the company.

Her fingers stilled on the keyboard. "If you'd like me to, I can continue updating it another day. You could increase your business by allowing online ordering."

"I do that already." Will frowned. "I get a lot of special-order requests through email."

"That's not what I'm talking about." Her hair danced along her shoulders as she shook her head. "Do you have a moment?"

She nodded to the seat across the desk. "Here, I can show you what I mean. If you're interested and have time."

Will moved the chair next to her to do as requested, though he had a feeling Erica needed to remind herself to make it a suggestion and not an order. Good. She better censor herself. Will wasn't about to be bossed by his employee, especially a new one.

The small office space left them sitting shoulder to shoulder as Erica explained everything needed to allow for online ordering of Pastry Perfect's everyday items for pick-up or delivery. It made sense as customers, busy with their workdays, didn't have time to waste sitting on hold while they waited for the only phone line to free up.

"How long would it take to implement something like this?"

"I could have it in place by Friday."

As she swung her head to look at him, Will caught a whiff of coconut, presumably from her shampoo. She smelled like summer. The thought was enough to ease some of the tension from his neck and shoulders as he allowed them to relax.

He turned to meet her gaze. Gray failed to describe the pale blue eyes scant inches from his. Gray brought to mind dark clouds and stormy skies. There was nothing stormy about Erica's eyes. They reminded him of the pale aquamarine stone he and his brothers bought their mom for Christmas one year.

He cleared his throat, turning to the computer screen.

"That sounds great. Let's put off passing out the updated delivery information until Friday, so we can make sure everything is in place and working correctly before giving customers information. We can distribute flyers on Friday afternoon. Then, delivery can start next Monday."

"Perfect."

Was Erica's voice quieter than usual?

"Perfect." He echoed her sentiment, hoping his own voice sounded sure and strong. With the details settled, Will moved the chair back to its spot and sought out his kitchen space, where everything made sense and peace was more attainable than when he was staring into those pale blue eyes.

Chapter 5

"Give me a minute to finish up here." Will didn't look up from the computer screen. "Then, we can be on our way."

Erica frowned. "Our way where?"

"To deliver the flyers around town." Still his gaze remained trained on whatever he worked on.

"Oh." Erica fought the anxiety bubbling inside her. "I can deliver them on my own. No need interrupting your work."

"It's not interrupting." Will glanced at her briefly. "That's why I said to give me a minute."

"I just meant, you don't need to rush through or anything." Erica forced her tone to remain civil. After all, Will was the boss. Her boss. She needed to remember that fact. "I know my way around town. I'm sure you have other things to do this afternoon."

Will turned off the monitor and rose from the desk. "Yes. I do."

Great. Erica allowed a small smile. Reason wasn't out of the realm of possibilities.

"I'm coming with you to deliver the flyers to local businesses."

Maybe it was further away than she thought. Her smile froze as her mind scrambled to find a way out of Will chaperoning her around town. How could she prove her worth as an employee to him or to her family if she wasn't given real responsibility?

"You almost had me." Erica tried to infuse her voice with a sing-song quality. "I believed you were serious for a moment. How dumb was I?" She widened her eyes for effect. "You wouldn't waste time and energy making a one-person job into a two-person job. You're too savvy for that."

Would he take the bait? Let her stroke his ego and give him a way out without losing face?

"You're right." Will's smile was barely tolerant. "I wouldn't. But seeing how everyone in town knows me as the face of Pastry Perfect, and you've worked for my competition for almost a decade, I believe this *is* a two-person job. Assure the town it's still the same quality product and introduce them to their new delivery person all at the same time."

"Oh." The heat filling Erica's cheeks was uncharacteristic. A lack of trust didn't inspire his decision. "That makes good sense."

"It does." Will scooped a stack of business cards off his desk. "And so do these."

She ignored the arrogance in his response in favor of curiosity over the cards. "What are those?"

"Loyalty cards." He ran his thumb up the stack, fanning one edge as he did. "One punch for every ten-dollar delivery order. Ten punches earn the customer a free drink."

"That's a great idea. Better than a coupon as it requires multiple purchases for the reward."

"I thought so. Do you have the flyers?"

She held up a manilla envelope. "Right here."

"Then let's go do this thing."

Erica's hands expressed her words as she chatted and laughed with Delores, the receptionist at Dr. Rhiner's office. The pediatrician's staff was just one of several groups he'd lost as regulars when the chain bakery opened. The way the two interacted as Erica explained the new service and loyalty program, he doubted they'd be lost to Pastry Perfect for long.

"Will?"

Both women turned to him with expectant looks. Just before an embarrassing amount of time passed, he remembered the flyers and loyalty cards in his hands.

"How many delivery menus and cards will your office need?" He opened the envelope and waited for an answer.

Delores rolled her eyes toward the ceiling and tallied on her fingers as she made a mental count. "I think two menus should be sufficient. We can post one in the break room and slip another in the business office. But would it be possible to get eight of the cards? I'm pretty sure all the girls will want to take advantage of your delivery service."

"We'd be glad to make you a regular stop." The pleasantry slipped from Will's lips as his mood buoyed at her prediction.

"Our mornings haven't quite been the same since we switched bakeries, but you know how compelling convenience can be." Delores gave a one shouldered shrug. "Quick and easy over quality and taste. Now we can have it all."

"Pastry Perfect is happy to help your mornings start off on the right foot." Erica shook Delores's hand. "Don't forget—we start first thing Monday morning, and you can even place your orders online. If more than one is ordering, just have everyone put 'multiple order' in the special requests section. We'll bring them all at once that way."

"We'll be sure to do that." Delores walked with them to the door. "Y'all have a good weekend."

Reassured with the knowledge that at least these customers left due to convenience only, Will tasted the first nibble of hope he'd enjoyed in weeks. It tasted sweet and left him with a genuine smile. He turned and waved to Delores.

"You have a great weekend too."

If someone asked him, Will would've told them while he was concerned about Pastry Perfect, he wasn't consumed with worry. But the weight hope lifted from his shoulders told a different story. While it was true only one business shared their reason for confection defection, Will assumed theirs wasn't a unique situation.

"What's that smile about?" Erica glanced his direction as they walked.

"I'm happy." Will shrugged. "Is it wrong to be happy?"

Her lips flattened along with her eyes. "Now, don't get touchy. It was an honest question. You seem more relaxed after Dr. Rhiner's office."

He was unused to sharing work details with his staff, unless it was an error on their part they needed to correct. He was the owner of Pastry Perfect. The problems were his to deal with, not those of his employees.

Harper was an exception, but she hardly counted as an employee. While she'd been paid for her work, Harper was more than staff, but she wasn't a partner either. When she left, Livvy filled the gap when he needed to vent. Even after hiring Madison, that pattern hadn't changed. It couldn't. She was so timid, Will doubted she had anything real to offer anyway.

Comparing Erica to Madison was as preposterous as considering canned frosting equal to a traditional buttercream.

It might cover a cake, but it was only suitable for a child's birthday cake and maybe even only then for a child you didn't like.

Erica's ideas, to this point, were usable and, hopefully, profitable. Should he share Pastry Perfect's troubles with her? She could be an additional source of inspiration for him. No. Not for him. For his business. Yes. Pastry Perfect needed her. Will Forrester did not.

WHAT HAD she gotten herself into with this one? She stole a quick peek at him. His square jaw was set. His blue eyes trained on the remaining businesses down the street from where they stood. His hair, longer on top and combed back, took on a just-tumbled-out-of-bed look as he ran his fingers through it.

She shook her head and jerked her gaze away. Too late. The image of Will, fuzzy with sleep, took up residence in her mind. A slight smile curved her lips. No. He was her boss, and she was here to prove herself to her family. Nothing more. Once she succeeded outside their cozy little empire, she'd be welcomed back with open arms and given the place in the business she deserved.

What was wrong about fighting for what she deserved? The thought that it might not be God's best for her, that His purpose rather than her pride should prompt her actions, buzzed in her ear like a pesky mosquito. But God wouldn't want her schooling wasted on a dead-end job. Right?

Will's voice broke into her silent debate but not quickly enough for her to grasp his words.

"I'm sorry." She met his gaze. "I didn't hear what you said. Could you repeat that?"

His shoulders fell a fraction of an inch. Had she missed an

opportunity while trapped in her own mind? Will didn't seem like the type to converse over nothing or share his thoughts freely. If she'd messed this up, would she get another chance?

"It's *Cupcakes & Cookies & Cakes, Oh, My!*."

She frowned. "What is?"

"Business at Pastry Perfect has been great. Since I opened, I've earned a good reputation and loyal customers. At least, I thought they were loyal."

"From what Delores admitted, I'd say you're right."

"But that chain bakery moved in offering delivery, and my loyal customers jumped ship. Sold out for an inferior product, just because it came with free delivery."

"Are you sure the product is really that bad compared to yours? Don't you think, maybe you're a bit biased?" She might not be on the best of terms with her family at the moment, but she wasn't ready to turn on them completely. Will made it sound like their offerings were a step above dog food. Arrogant jerk.

"Have you tried their cupcakes?" He highlighted his question with both hands open palms up in front of him and his eyes wide.

Her shoulders pushed back. "Yes. Have you?"

"Of course, I have." His voice held a sharp edge. "Do you think I'd make a statement like that without first trying the product? I don't know what impression I've given you, but I'll tell you right now, I always do my research before I state the facts." He crossed his arms over his chest and glared. "What about you? Have you given Pastry Perfect a chance or are you just in it for the paycheck?"

Guilt flared as his verbal dart hit its mark. She used the spark to ignite her anger. Was it so wrong to take the job to prove herself? After all, in accomplishing her goal, Pastry

Perfect benefited as well. Whatever her reasons, Will should be thanking her.

"Is wanting a job to pay the bills wrong?" Good sense told her raising her voice to her boss was a bad idea, but backing down was out of the question. "You're getting more than you hired me for. Maybe you should be thankful instead of judging me for not trying your precious pastries."

Waves of anger rolled off Will. A hardened look filled his eyes, and his cheek flinched as he clenched his teeth. In any other circumstance, the image of someone standing toe to toe with their boss in the middle of town like an old western shootout might make her giggle. But it wasn't so humorous when she was playing one of the leads in the production. Especially since she wasn't sure if she was the person wearing the white hat or the black.

His chin raised. Her own mirrored the action.

"We're done here."

His words, though spoken quietly, were shots fired. The abrupt exit following them condemned her to her fate. She seethed as Will stalked down the sidewalk in the direction of his bakery. At least he'd left her with the keys so she could drive back.

Anger ebbed leaving stunned shame in its wake. Erica's first experience with employment outside the family business, and she'd blown it. She couldn't prove herself, because she was a failure. A complete and total disaster.

She dragged her hands down her face with a groan. Proud, bossy, even arrogant, were words she'd grown accustomed to hearing about herself when others thought she wasn't listening and sometimes even when they knew she was. Her worst traits dogged her through life.

But one thing she'd never been accused of was recklessness. Every move was carefully planned, except this one when it mattered most. In her time with *Cupcakes & Cookies & Cakes, Oh, My!*, she'd been in several shouting matches that made this one look like a playground disagreement. Each one had been with her father or brothers.

"And there is the difference." She muttered as she got into the company van.

At Pastry Perfect, she was not the boss's daughter. Erica was an employee, like Madison—and a new one at that. If an employee talked to her father as she'd just talked to Will, they'd be sacked without apology. Pack your things, you're moving on. She'd disrespected Will, and he was within his rights to terminate her employment.

"But he didn't actually say I was fired." Her shoulders straightened. She glanced at her watch. Closing time. "He only said we were done here. Maybe I can salvage this after all."

Emotions ran too high to attempt an immediate repair. Besides, Erica needed to make sure her heart was in the right place with God before approaching Will. Dealing with her bad attitude was priority, whether it saved her job or not. She'd seek God tonight, but bright and early tomorrow morning, Erica would save her job.

Chapter 6

"What are you doing here?" Will eyed her warily as she stepped into the kitchen.

Paired with the growl in his voice, Erica proceeded with caution but detected something in him beyond anger. Since it was a Saturday without special deliveries for her to make, and since she'd possibly been fired less than twenty-four hours prior, surprise was warranted. But that wasn't it either.

When she was ten, her dog, Riley, had been attacked by a bigger dog. Erica had run to help only to have Riley growl and snap at her fingers. Her sweet Riley turned on her. It broke her heart. Her father soothed her with a simple explanation. Riley wasn't reacting in anger or meanness. The dog snapped in fear because he'd been hurt.

While Will could never be confused with a sweet, gentle beagle pup, Erica couldn't help comparing their reactions. He'd been hurt, and he lashed out to keep her from aggravating the wound.

Erica, hands behind her back, moved closer to his workspace. "I've come to apologize."

Placing the frosting bag and cupcake he was decorating onto the metal tabletop, Will said nothing. Rather his eyes narrowed, and his lips formed a straight line, committed to neither a smile nor a frown.

Erica licked her lips. "I was wrong yesterday. I was disrespectful of your position as my boss, and I'm sorry."

Still no answer, but a slight lifting of his chin. Will was listening and responding even if he didn't confirm it with his words.

"I'm not sure why your comment irritated me so much." Okay. So that wasn't true. Family pride overruled good sense. Would God forgive the little white lie in the name of peace? It wouldn't hurt anyone, since Will would never know. She pushed those thoughts aside. "You were right. I've not compared your cupcake to theirs. So, I brought a peace offering."

Erica took one hand from behind her back, revealing one of his Chocolate Obsession cupcakes. "Don't worry." She grinned. "I paid for it. But it's not for you."

His lips twitched. She brought her other hand around revealing another chocolate cupcake. The twitch stilled. Recognition of the competition's answer to his best-seller lit his eyes. If she didn't move fast, he'd have her out the door permanently.

"You've compared the competition to your baking and found them lacking. I want the opportunity to do the same." She placed both cupcakes in front of Will. Then, she pulled a headscarf from her purse. "A blind taste test. If I choose the competition's work, I lose my job. If I choose yours, you forgive me for my stupidity and give me a second chance. Deal?"

Erica wouldn't resort to begging, but hopefully Will could see the earnestness in her expression. He glanced at the cupcakes, the scarf, and finally at her. It was his call, and she wouldn't interfere. *Please, God, let him accept my apology and give me another chance.*

SHE MUST REALLY NEED this job. To humble herself enough to not only come to him with an apology but to also come up with this cockamamie attempt to win back her job. She was gutsy. Even he could admit that. And he understood what it felt like being on the other side of the table.

He'd done his apology tour for rude behavior shortly after winning *Cake That!*. It wasn't easy being vulnerable with your mistakes and hoping the one you offended showed mercy and grace. That alone might not push the scales in her favor, but Erica was also a hard worker and creative problem-solver.

Rounding the table, he slipped the scarf from her hands. "Here. I'm going to make sure this is tied properly so you can't cheat."

Careful to keep her hair from getting caught, Will draped the light fabric over her eyes and tied the ends in a knot at the back of her head. While the material was silky against his skin, it was nothing compared to the strands of her dark hair brushing up against his fingers. Her hair created an urge too strong to ignore. He gathered it in his hands under the guise of pulling the strands away from her face and let the softness slide through his palms until it hung free down the back of her neck. When the light coconut scent of her shampoo reached him, Will wished he'd missed a few wisps.

He cleared his throat and moved to the safety of the table's other side. "Wait right there. I'll cut these into manageable pieces and bring each one to you."

Spearing the bite-sized piece of his competitor's cupcake

with a fork, he lifted it to Erica's mouth. "Here's the first one. Right in front of you."

Her lips parted to accept the sweet. "Mmm. So chocolatey. Have I told you I love chocolate?"

"No." And he didn't care either. Except he did. "Are you ready for the next one?"

"I am, but it's going to be hard to beat that one. It was so full of flavor."

He repeated the process. As Erica tasted his cupcake, a low moan of delight escaped sending a shiver of pleasure through him. The previous bite hadn't elicited the same response.

"Forget what I just said." Erica licked stray frosting from her lips. "No. On second thought, I think I need another bite. I'm not quite sure."

The playful smile on her face made him wish the blindfold was gone allowing him to see her eyes. Her lips parted, drawing his attention to their fullness. He bet they'd taste sweet with a hint of the chocolate she'd just accepted from him.

Her frown drew him from his musings. What was he doing imagining kissing her? She was only waiting for another bite of cupcake. "You might as well take off the blindfold." And hopefully, end this spell in the process. "I think we both know which cupcake won."

Untying the knot, Erica removed the scarf and let it fall to the table. "It was yours, wasn't it?" She reached for the remains of the cupcake and devoured it without apology. "I've never tasted anything like it."

"You just want your job back." Will gathered the wrapper and discarded cupcake of his competition and dumped them in the trash to hide the pleasure her compliment gave him.

"Will." She waited until he faced her. "You understand how talented you are in the kitchen, don't you?"

Of course, he did. From the time he took his first food class in high school, he understood how he made magic in the kitchen, especially with baked goods. Hearing it from Erica, though, was different.

"Thank you."

He placed his hands on the table in front of him unsure what else to do. Warmth shot up his arm as her hand covered his.

"I mean it. That was the most flavorful, moist, and light cupcake I've ever eaten. And that frosting was perfect."

Afraid of what she'd see in his eyes, he peered down at their hands. Her gaze followed his. She jerked away as if only realizing what she'd done. The touch wasn't planned for effect. It wasn't scripted. However, it obviously didn't do to Erica what it did to him, and he couldn't allow it to do even that.

"I'll see you first thing Monday morning."

Her face lit up. "Monday."

She left without another word. Disappointment at her absence filled her space. It would be a long weekend.

Chapter 7

Erica smoothed her hand over her dark red sundress with tiny white, blue, and yellow flowers dotted across it. While she preferred her usual black jeans and Pastry Perfect T-shirt, today's special delivery was to a garden party. Who even hosted those anymore?

"People with more money to waste than I do."

Her reflection in the mirror didn't answer. It didn't matter who the client was. Will wanted her attire to blend with the ambiance of the occasion when she made deliveries. Baby showers and birthday parties were one thing. Weddings and, apparently, garden parties required a higher level of dress.

She stowed a change of clothes in her backpack, shoved her purse in, too, then scooped the bag off her bed clutching it in one hand. The shoulder strap was handy, but her dress might wrinkle. It would be a travesty to show up at the party in a wrinkled sundress. Erica rolled her eyes.

A quick once over and she'd be ready to head out the door. It was hard to believe a full week had already passed since her successful attempt at securing her position at Pastry Perfect.

Not once had Will brought up her horrible behavior or the creative way she won him over the next morning.

Erica had praised God for that small blessing many times through the week. When she'd taken off that blindfold, she got a glimpse behind the curtain of the great and powerful Oz. Will's mind assured him that he excelled in his baking. And he was more than happy to tell everyone who might question it. But in his heart, he doubted. It was there in his eyes, like a hunger.

The realization left her shaken. She'd placed her hand on his without thinking, offering reassurance. The change was immediate. Desire of a different sort flashed in his eyes, and she'd jerked her hand away to escape its effect.

"There's no way I can let Will know his look made me feel as wobbly as gelatin eggs at Easter dinner." Erica gave her image in the mirror a sharp nod. "He's my boss, and we're just starting to find normal."

She let her bag drop to the floor before picking up the pot of clear gloss from the dresser. She slicked some across her lips and smacked them together. Perfect. Once again, she snatched her bag from the floor and headed out the door, telling herself the last-minute addition was simply to look her best for the garden party, not to impress her boss.

WILL FROZE as Erica stepped into the kitchen. Maybe he should rethink his delivery dress code. Heeled sandals accented her shapely legs before the knee-length hem of her modest sundress drew his attention to the rest of her outfit. The sundress allowed only a glimpse of the full curves her usual jeans and T-shirt tried to hide. She'd left her hair down, framing her face. Including lips which held an extra bit of shine and quirked in a grin.

"Will?" She giggled. "You're making a mess."

"Huh?"

She nodded toward the table. Frosting oozed from the decorating bag he held over a cupcake which now sported an unappetizing glob of pink.

"Oh! How did that happen?" He set the bag aside and scraped off the misplaced frosting. Rolling his eyes as he chuckled, he sounded inane even to himself. Erica hadn't missed his appreciation of her appearance. He re-piped the frosting onto the cupcake in a more pleasing manner. "I've got the cupcakes and tarts ready for the garden party. Mrs. Silverson expects the delivery in about forty-five minutes. Is the van ready to load up?"

"Right out front."

Erica lifted three of the boxes he'd stacked earlier from their place on a nearby counter. As she did, the hemline of her dress raised. While not immodest, the sight kickstarted his pulse and the lessons his mother taught him about being a gentleman.

"Wait a minute." He hurried over to her and lifted two of the boxes out of her hands. "You take that one, and I'll get the rest."

Erica tried to snatch the boxes back, but Will shifted them out of her reach. After another unsuccessful attempt, she stood to her full height with a huff.

"I am perfectly capable of carrying these boxes. It's what you hired me for."

Will stacked another on top of the two he already carried. "I don't doubt your ability to do your job. But you shouldn't have to when I can do it for you."

"I shouldn't have to do my job because you can do my job?" Her lips twisted.

"Yes. No." Will shifted from one foot to the other. "I don't know."

"That's as clear as mud."

"Most days, I have no issue with you toting these deliveries around." He set the boxes down and ran his hand through his hair. This could get tricky. "But I've required you to dress for the occasion, and I don't want to put you in any sort of compromising position."

"How is carrying boxes going to compromise me?"

Mercy. He did not want to go there with her, but she gave him no choice. He pointed to the hem of her skirt. "Your dress. It, well, it's appropriate. You look great. Tasteful, I mean. But ... when you hoist up the boxes ... the front, sort of—"

Her eyes widened. Color drained from her face.

"Oh, no. Did I ..."

"No." He shook his head frantically. "No. You were completely covered, but I don't want to take the chance that someone might see more than you want."

Her features relaxed. "What about when I get to the garden party? Do you intend to join me on the delivery?"

The prospect of spending time in close proximity to Erica while she wore that dress was equally appealing and nerve-racking. Truth be told, he'd love nothing more than to make the delivery with her and then take her out for dinner at a nice restaurant.

Whoa. If he couldn't admit his attraction to her, a romantic dinner was completely out of the question. Besides, he had work to do at the bakery. He considered his options.

"It's at the country club, right?"

She nodded.

"I'll call ahead and tell them to have staff carry them inside for you. Once they have them on the tables, you can set them up."

"It feels silly having someone else do something I could do."

"Please." The word, not typically in his vocabulary, was heavy on his tongue. "Let me do this for you."

Without a word, Erica moved to the door and held it open. Relief released the breath he hadn't been aware of holding. They'd been on good terms lately. The last thing he wanted was to pull rank to get his way.

Will scooped up the boxes and headed through the door. Pausing just past the counter, he waited for Erica to precede him to the front door where she again held it for him. She opened the back of the van, and Will slid the boxes inside. As he grasped the door to close it, her hand on his shoulder made him pause.

"Will." The softness in her voice surprised him.

He dropped his hands and turned at the gentle pressure she applied. Her expression wavered on the border of a smile as she searched his face. What did she seek?

"Yes." When had his voice gotten hoarse?

Her hand on his shoulder slid down his arm, leaving ripples of electricity in each muscle it touched until she finally grasped his. He glanced down. This time she didn't pull away. Without thinking, he softly stroked her hand with his as he raised his gaze to hers.

This time she did smile. It was the sweetest, shyest smile Will had ever seen, and it tugged at him like a magnet pulls metal. He was a goner.

"Thank you." She squeezed his hand. "Thank you for caring enough to keep me from a potentially embarrassing situation. It might chafe a bit, but ... I just want you to know it means a lot to me."

Her words didn't sever the connection. Instead, the urge to kiss her tore through him with the force of a hurricane. They were so close already. All he had to do was lean in. She would not only accept his kiss but rise to meet him. Her eyes conveyed the message with clarity.

"I, uh ... I have to get back inside." The step back was heavy with regret. "I need to call the country club, and you've got to get on the road."

Resignation stole her smile. It was the right choice for both of them. Even in this brief moment, Will was able to see the truth. He was her boss. It would be inappropriate for him to initiate any kind of romantic gesture. No matter what her body language told him in that moment, he would always wonder if she'd accepted out of obligation or truly wanting it for herself.

"Be careful. Let me know if you run into any problems." He turned and strode away, not stopping until he'd reached the safety of his kitchen. If something didn't change, work would become a high-wire balancing act without the reassurance of a safety net.

Chapter 8

"How are things looking?" Erica took the chair across the desk from him.

Will waved toward the computer screen. "Come see for yourself."

She moved to stand behind him, resting her hand on his shoulder as she leaned over it for a better view of the report. Since the day nearly a month ago when Will almost kissed her before Mrs. Silverson's garden party, little touches and nearness had become more common place in their relationship.

The positive side of the increased interaction was the tolerance level of both rising. Every accidental touch didn't flare into the undeniable desire they had that day. She could stand close and breathe in the unusual but fitting scent of his musky cologne mixed with the sweetness of the bakery. In fact, she enjoyed it immensely and took every opportunity to do so, like this one.

"What do you think?"

That you smell nice today.

"What?"

No. No. No. Her thoughts had *not* just slipped past the guards of her lips. She stifled the groan welling up.

"I, uh, did you change colognes or shampoo or something? You smell different than usual."

Will's lips quirked to the side as one brow raised. "I smell different?"

Any other answers would only lengthen the discomfort of the situation. Erica shrugged.

"No. I've not changed colognes." He pointed to the screen. "Now, if we're done discussing my toiletry choices, what do you think about the numbers?"

Erica grimaced and focused on the report. "It's better. I think."

"But still not where they should be."

Or at the place to prove to her parents that she had more to offer their business than the paltry little tasks they always assigned her. "It's only been a month. And Pastry Perfect is in no danger of closing. You're still turning a profit."

"My margins took a hit with that chain opening up."

She glanced at the numbers again. "I think it's going to, at least a little bit. Unless you steal every customer in town away from them and run them out of business, you're not going to have the same margins you did."

"Wouldn't that be nice? Shutting the place down. One can dream."

"Yeah." Erica forced a chuckle that sounded stiff, even to her. "That would be ... something."

"I've got an idea." He stood up, forcing Erica to take a step back. "Follow me."

She followed him through the kitchen and into the front of the bakery. Madison glanced at them from the register where she handed the frazzled-looking woman in front of her a to-go cup of iced coffee and a Pastry Perfect bag.

Chocolate. The woman looked like she'd already had a difficult day, and it was only ten o'clock. Erica would bet, in addition to the infusion of caffeine, the customer needed the emotional pick-me-up of something chocolate. A Chocolate Obsession cupcake, perhaps? No. Too early for that. A dark chocolate croissant. Yeah. Definitely a chocolate croissant.

The woman took her order and headed back out into the day. As the door swung shut behind her, Erica's attention shifted to Will standing in front of the main window of the bakery. Instead of looking out, he faced inward and scanned the entire area, his features puckered in what she silently named his thinking face.

She joined him and attempted to picture what he did. Classic colors. Browns highlighted with deep cherry red and hints of a muted tropical blue. Thanks to Madison's attention, the glass display case gleamed. There was an area designed for comfort with a couple of armchairs arranged around a coffee table. High-top tables mixed with café tables throughout the rest of the space. Minimal décor created a welcoming environment without overwhelming. It allowed the customer's sense of smell to take center stage, inviting them to make their way to the counter and choose from the treats within.

"What are we looking for?" Erica didn't identify anything out of place.

"Do you think I should redecorate?" Will turned to her. "I know it's not been long, but maybe if I used that kitschy, colorful décor like everyone else uses it might seem more fun."

Erica shook her head. "Absolutely not. This place is classic, comfortable, and completely you. Bubbly and fun work for some people, but it wouldn't be *your* bakery if you did that."

"What about decorating that incorporates the town into it?"

"Still not you. I mean, I could see using local artists' work on the walls, if they had a piece that fit your theme and tone. But other than that, I wouldn't change a thing about this place."

He rested his hands on the back of a nearby chair. "I don't know. I just feel like I need to remind the town that I'm a local business, run by a local."

"I think you're on the right track with the idea." She scanned the room again. "I'm just not sure redecorating is the right option to accomplish it."

"You may be right. I hated the idea of redoing the place." Will straightened and headed for the kitchen door. "I put a lot of time into choosing the best look for Pastry Perfect."

As she walked beside him, Erica nudged Will with her shoulder. "You did a great job. We'll figure this out."

"Excuse me, Mr. Forrester?"

Will paused. "Is something wrong, Madison?"

"No, sir. Not really." She shrugged apologetically. "I just couldn't help overhearing your discussion with Erica."

Will raised his hand to stop her. "Don't worry about any of that. Pastry Perfect is doing fine. You're not in danger of losing your job."

"Yes, sir." She bit her lip. "It's just, I think ..."

"Really. There isn't any reason for concern. We're just examining ways to make this place even better."

"I understand, sir ..."

"Great. I knew you would."

The front door chimed announcing someone's presence. Will's smile was accompanied by a quick nod.

"Hello. Welcome to Pastry Perfect." He waved the man toward the counter. "Madison will be happy to help you with whatever you need today."

As the man strode to the display case, Will and Erica

walked back toward the kitchen. Madison's shoulders raised and fell with a sigh seconds before the man reached her. She schooled her features with a polite smile.

"How can I help you today?"

Erica leaned close to Will's ear as they made their way through the door to the kitchen. "She's always so sweet with the customers."

Will nodded but waited until the door closed behind them to reply. "That's the reason I hired her. I may be good in the kitchen but dealing with the customers on a regular basis is not my forte. I'm a special type of disaster during a rush."

Erica giggled. "I've seen you on a not-so-busy day. I think you should be thankful you've got Madison out front."

"Oh, I am. Believe me." Will ran his hand through his hair. "I only wish she hadn't overheard our conversation. I didn't mean to alarm her."

"I think she'll be fine now that you've explained things. We each have our strengths, don't we? You and I, we're problem-solvers. Making people feel welcome is where those like Madison shine."

"Speaking of problem-solvers, we still have one to sort out." Will opened the door to his office and waved her through.

Chapter 9

"I've got everything loaded and ready to go when you get here." Will waited for Erica's confirmation before disconnecting the call. Madison was wiping down tables from the morning rush as he made his way to his office. "I know you've got things under control here, but if something happens while we're gone, don't hesitate to call."

Madison glanced up as she continued swiping the rag over the tabletop. "Will do, Mr. Forrester. If you're not back from the wedding by closing time, do you want me to wait for you?"

"No." Will shook his head. "Go ahead and close up. I think we'll be back, but I can't make any promises."

"I understand." She motioned toward him with her rag. "If Erica's on her way, you might want to get changed."

"Right." He took in his typical workday attire. Jeans and a Pastry Perfect button up would not cut it for serving at a wedding. Good thing he'd brought a change of clothes. "I'll go take care of that."

Will changed into the black dress pants he'd ironed that morning. He planned to pair them with a more acceptable white dress shirt, his solid black tie and his special-occasions black logo apron he'd purchased when he opened the bakery.

After shedding his causal button-up, Will realized his white undershirt was a little worse for wear after packing the van. He stripped out of it and turned to the filing cabinet where his emergency stash of undershirts and bakery polos were stored.

"I'm ready when you ..."

Will spun around. Erica stood in the open doorway. In his rush, he'd forgotten to shut the door. Wide eyes took in his shirtless state as color filled her cheeks with an attractive glow. Men went without shirts all the time, so there was nothing for her to be embarrassed about. Still, he whirled back around and yanked the plain white T-shirt over his head. It fit to his form, but at least, he was covered.

"I'll be right with you." He spoke with his back still to her. He slid on his button-up and reached for his tie.

"I'll, uh, I'll wait in the van."

"WHAT IS WRONG WITH YOU?" Erica's chastisement moved from her thoughts to fill the interior of the delivery van. "You have brothers. You've seen men shirtless hundreds of times."

Her brothers. Her brother's friends. Men at the beach she didn't even know. Why had it caught her so off-guard to see Will the same way?

Will was her boss. That had to be the reason. It couldn't be that his daily attire didn't do justice to the slender strength in his chest and arms, hiding the well-defined muscles instead of showing them off.

She remembered a movie where the scrawny hero buffed up with the aid of science. Seeing his new bulk, the woman with him couldn't help herself and reached to touch his chest. Erica thought it preposterous at the time. She'd laughed at the nonsense. While Will lacked the size of the movie theater hero, Erica now appreciated the woman's response.

"Get it together." She stared out the passenger window, watching for the focus of her thoughts to exit the bakery. "You're not here for Will. Once you prove to your parents that you're worth something to their business, you'll leave and fill your rightful position in their bakery."

That goal drove her every day. It had since she walked out almost two months earlier. Erica frowned. The prospect of returning to her family as the conquering hero always ignited a flame in her heart that pushed her forward in her plans. When had that fire dimmed to nothing more than a warm ember?

She fiddled with her purse strap as she mulled over the events of the last few weeks. She and Will ended up in more stand-offs than she cared to track. However, as time progressed, he'd come to her for help with more frequency. He opened up to her. A mutual respect built between them, along with a friendship she enjoyed more than she originally believed possible.

The idea of leaving what they'd accomplished and the relationship they'd forged behind to rejoin her parents' empire doused her desire to follow through with her plan. Could she abandon her goal this close to success? If only God would tell her.

Erica straightened. "Why should He tell me anything? I ran headlong into this without asking Him if my plan was His plan for me. I just assumed it was and went for it."

God, I'm so sorry. I thought this had to be Your plan, but now, proving myself doesn't seem so important. Help me fix this. Help me find Your best for my life.

"Ready to go?"

Erica eyes flew open at the intrusion on her prayer. She'd gotten so lost in her talk with God, she failed to watch for the man she was in a quandary over.

"I better be. We've got a wedding to get to."

"AND NOW, enjoying their first dance, Mr. and Mrs. Trent Baxter."

The DJ's voice filled the room. The lights dimmed to a romantic glow with the added sparkle of a mirror ball. Erica stared, entranced, as the couple took the floor and the sound of "A Thousand Years" surrounded them. While she'd never seen, and never intended to see, the movie series the melody was written for, the song received a pass from her simply because Christina Perri was the one singing it.

Besides, the bride and groom resembled a couple out of the best romance movie ever made. He was tall, dark, and handsome. She was dressed like a princess with curls piled atop her head. She even wore a tiara that glittered in the light with every graceful spin.

"You like to dance?" Will's whisper barely reached her over the music.

Erica shrugged and rearranged the remaining plates of cake onto one small area of the table. "Other than with my father, brother, or maybe a cousin a time or two, I've never been dancing." Erica smiled watching the newlyweds. "And I can honestly say, I never danced like that with any of them."

"I'm pretty sure I'd worry about you if you had." Will chuckled.

Erica joined him. "And I'm pretty sure I wouldn't hold it against you."

While they cleaned up the cake table and packed their

supplies into boxes, Erica continued stealing glances at the pairs moving around the dance floor. Was it too much to hope one day, she would be the one leading the dance?

The image of herself in Will's arms entered her mind unannounced. She'd seen those arms earlier in the evening and could almost feel how their strength would surround her as she leaned into his chest. Realizing the direction of her thoughts, she fumbled the cake plate she held sending its contents to the floor.

"Oh. What a klutz." She tossed the now empty plate in the trash and knelt by the destroyed confection armed with the cake server to scrape up as much as she could manage in one piece. The effort left a large smear of frosting on the wood.

"Here." Will knelt beside her. "Let me. You don't need to be down here in your dress. Why don't you wheel the supplies out to the van while I wipe this up?"

She'd never heard of a knight in shining armor relinquishing his sword in favor of brandishing a wet cloth in one hand and a dry one in the other. Yet, here was Will, stepping in to clean up her mess so she wouldn't seem less than ladylike. It was the sweetest thing anyone had ever done for her.

Chapter 10

"Do not unpack this van." Erica jumped from the passenger seat as soon as Will pulled into Pastry Perfect's lot. Keying in the code he'd taught her for the kitchen door, she rushed inside and grabbed her tote bag.

Giving little thought to wrinkling her nice dress, Erica slipped out of it and into the jeans and T-shirt she favored. Stowing her dress in the bag, along with the flats she traded for a pair of Converse, Erica tossed the bundle aside and ran out the back door.

"No fair!" She glared at Will. "I told you not to unpack."

Will leaned around the boxes he carried, a smirk twisting his lips. "You're not the boss. In fact, it's quite the opposite. Now hold the door for me, if you don't mind."

Erica did as instructed, with a huff. "I wanted to do my share."

"Erica." He paused next to her as he passed. "You're one of the hardest-working people I know. You always do your share. And if I haven't told you, I appreciate every single thing you do."

The praise for a job well done warmed her middle. How

she'd hungered for that kind of praise from her family. The words weren't flowery or gushing, but their simplicity held truth she could feel inside. She could run off appreciation like that for weeks, maybe even months.

With a quick peek inside the van to make sure nothing was left, Erica shut the doors and joined Will in the kitchen. He barely glanced up as he sorted through the items needing washed and those that only needed put away.

"Can you check the front to make sure Madison got everything locked up correctly?"

"Sure." Erica's frown went unnoticed.

Madison was perfectly capable of closing the bakery. Though she or Will were always around, she completed the tasks on her own nearly every day. It was a mystery why he was suddenly worried something might have been missed.

It took only a few moments to ensure all the necessary jobs were done properly. Madison even left a reassuring note that she'd faced no problems through the day and would see them on Monday. The only task left for the day was helping Will finish the post-event cleanup.

"What can I do?" She didn't wait for the door to swing shut behind her before she asked.

Will pointed to the pile of dirty dishes on the far counter. "Start the dishwasher while I wipe down counters and prep for Monday?"

"Sure thing, boss."

As she worked, the sensation of being watched crept up Erica's spine. She turned to find Will's contemplative gaze on her.

"What?"

"I just have trouble believing it." He shrugged.

"Well, I would try assuring you, if I had any clue what we're talking about."

"You always move so gracefully."

"Okay?" She scrunched up her face.

"I can't imagine no one has ever asked you to dance."

What? It took a moment for Erica to realize his mind had wandered back to their conversation at the wedding. Once she did, she still had no clue what train of thoughts led him to the ending destination. She was only loading a dishwasher, and there wasn't even music playing in the background.

She shrugged. "I don't know what to tell you. Maybe someday." She turned back to her task to make sure she hadn't missed anything.

When the melody of an unfamiliar song filled the room, Erica stilled. She could feel Will behind her before she turned to find him standing there with his hand outstretched.

"May I have this dance?"

Even as the voice of the man sung about the way his love looked at him, tenderness reflected in the eyes regarding her. Though Erica had begun dating when she was sixteen, no one had ever regarded her with such a beautiful mixture of admiration, desire, and caring. Her breath caught as she placed her hand in his.

As Will held her close, Erica's heart beat a rhythm far faster than the ballad they moved to. It was surreal. She'd come to Pastry Perfect to find validation of her worth that her parents couldn't deny. Instead, she'd found Will.

It wasn't lost on her that he didn't ask her to dance with him at the wedding or in the parking lot or take her to any number of public places meant for that purpose. He'd invited her to be with him in this place. His kitchen. His place of safety and belonging. His sanctuary from the pains of the world.

The realization swelled her heart with her feelings for him. He was more than a boss. He was a friend. Even that descriptor didn't encompass all he was to her or begin to touch on what she wanted him to be.

She raised her eyes to his, not sure what she could say to convey what this dance meant to her, to them.

"You looked beautiful tonight." He interjected before she settled her thoughts. "I don't think I told you that earlier."

It wasn't poetry. The words lacked his usual swagger of assurance. Still, they settled in her heart and convinced her of what she should say in return. Nothing.

Erica slid one hand from where it rested on his shoulder to the back of his neck. While her fingers toyed in his soft hair, the pressure she applied drew him closer. Anticipation surged through her as his lips came within an inch of hers.

"Are you sure about this?" His whisper was hoarse.

She answered by closing the distance between them. His lips were warm and soft against hers. He slid his arms around her and pulled her tight against him. His arms around her were as secure as she imagined. His fingers threaded through her hair. Never had she experienced the contentment she found in his embrace. It spoke of home in a way her physical home never had.

Long before she was ready to relinquish the feeling, Will loosed his hold, putting distance between them. While she wanted to close the gap, a glance into his eyes revealed a desire that cried out to her and warned of caution at the same time. Restraint was necessary.

"You've had a long day." Will's smile was a caress. "You should probably head home."

As much as she hated admitting it, he was right. She brushed her lips across his cheek in a brief kiss.

"You're the boss." She grinned as she teased him. Picking up her bag from where she'd left it earlier, she made her way to the door.

Chapter 11

With an hour until opening for the week, Will and Erica decided to move their morning planning meeting to a table in the front of the bakery. While he held his coffee cup with one hand, he cradled one of Erica's under his free one on the table. His thumb traced circles on her skin.

"Good morning." Madison came through the kitchen door. She paused. The corner of her mouth tipped up before she continued with her opening tasks.

Erica's fingers tensed under his. Wanting to put her at ease, he continued rubbing her hand. After church the day before, they'd spent the afternoon talking on the phone. Before the call ended, he was confident in labeling their friendship a real relationship. If they were going to be together, there was no sense in hiding it from anyone. Holding hands was an appropriate public display of their feelings.

"Good morning, Madison." Will smiled. "I hope you had a good weekend."

She glanced back and forth between them a moment before nodding. "Yes, sir. Too short, but good nonetheless."

"Great." Will checked his watch. "I think you'll find everything in the back ready to stock the display case this morning. We're going to continue our discussion out here, but if you need anything, don't hesitate to interrupt."

"No, sir. Yes, sir." Madison rolled her eyes. "I mean, if I need anything, I'll be sure to ask."

"Good." Will turned his attention back to Erica, ignoring the sounds of Madison readying for the day. "I know we're doing well. The delivery service really seems to be helping. But I feel like there is more we could do. Something we're missing."

Erica drummed her fingers on the table. "I'm not sure. A sale won't do it. Maybe we could bring in local talent once a week."

"I don't know." Will frowned. "I'm not sure the space is large enough to support something like that. But it would remind everyone we're from the neighborhood. Maybe we should block it off and try to work something out."

Erica scanned the space. "No. You're right. I think the only way to host something like that would be to remove the comfy seating area. Even then it might be tight. And you'd have to put up and tear down each week you hosted one."

"Farmer's market?"

"Possible." Erica shrugged. "It is local, and it's another avenue for sales. But I don't think it embraces what you're looking for. Does it really say you care about the community?"

"I do give back, you know?" Will ran his hand through his hair. "I just don't care to advertise the fact that everything left at the end of the day goes to the homeless shelter. It's the whole 'don't let the right hand know what the left hand is doing' thing. I'm not going to announce that donation just to win favor with the town."

"Mr. Forrester?" Madison stood behind one of the chairs at

their table. Her fingers curled around the top of the chair as if doing so gave her strength to stand.

"Yes, Madison. Was there something you needed?"

"Not really, but ..."

"Did you need us to move to the back? Are we in the way?"

She shook her head. "No. You're fine where you are."

He frowned. Madison tucked her lip between her teeth. Her knuckles turned white on the chair. The urge to shake his head and roll his eyes almost overpowered Will's good sense. Venting his frustration with the odd conversation would be unprofessional at best, rude at worst.

"How can I help you then?" He tried to reassure her with a smile.

"I'm not worried about the bakery or my job." The strange words came out in a rush.

"Okay."

"But I had an idea that might help you with your dilemma."

"Dilemma?" Erica spoke beside him. "You mean you have an idea that might help us establish Pastry Perfect as *the* community bakery without flaunting Will's giving in other areas?"

She nodded almost frantically.

Madison needed to cut back on the caffeine. But if she had a valid idea, who was he to complain about her method of delivery?

Will gestured to the chair in her grip. "Why don't you take a seat and tell us what you're thinking."

"Yes, sir."

"And Madison?"

"Yes, sir?"

"I know you're all about respecting me as your boss, but you don't have to call me sir or Mr. Forrester. Will is fine."

Her eyes rounded as she swallowed hard. The reaction brought shame to Will. Had he unknowingly created an environment that fed Madison's unease? He would have to be more mindful of how he reacted to her in the future. Respect was one thing, but Will never wanted an employee to fear him.

"Yes, sir, um, Will." Madison crumpled into the seat.

"Go ahead." Erica prompted. "What's your idea?"

Madison's gaze bounced between them. "Have you heard of the Carrington Culinary College?"

"Of course, I had a ..." Erica stopped mid-sentence. "I had a tour there a long time ago. I always thought I would use my marketing degree in a bakery, and they have a wonderful Baking and Pastry program."

Will nodded. "I was invited as a guest speaker in one of their classes after I won *Cake That!*. They have a strong curriculum."

"Great." Madison clasped her hands together in front of her. "I've been taking classes there for a while, and ..."

"You've been learning baking and pastry?" Will felt like the wind was knocked from him.

"Yes. I wasn't sure how to tell you." Madison winced.

Will smiled, hoping to put her at ease. "It's fine. I'm just surprised."

"I admire the work you do." Madison shrugged. "I've learned so much from you. But someday, if you're willing, I'd like to spend time in the kitchen gleaning from your experience."

How could an employee of his keep something this big from him? Of course, he didn't take the time getting to know Madison like he did Erica. While he might not ever be close friends with his employees, he wanted them to know they could come to him. Later, he and Erica could brainstorm ways to make sure that happened.

"I'm glad I know now. And one day soon, we'll get you back in the kitchen." Will glanced at Erica. "I'm sure Erica could cover the front for a few days, if needed. Right?"

She nodded. "Of course. Just tell me when. But right now, we need to know how Carrington Culinary is going to solve our problem."

Will slapped his open palm on the table "Right. We need to focus. What's your idea?"

"It's two in one, actually." Madison's voice lost some of its nervous shaking. "The school hosts a yearly dinner and silent auction to raise money for their Next Step Scholarship."

Erica leaned back in her seat. "What's that? I mean, other than a scholarship, obviously."

"It's a yearly, second-chance scholarship to a non-traditional, pastry-focused student. A single parent, someone in need of a second chance after incarceration, or a person trying to reclaim their independence after hardship. It provides tuition and encouragement through mentor matching."

Will let out a low whistle. "That's impressive. I've heard of a few programs like that, headed up by big name chefs and with great success stories, but this is the first I know of that is baking-focused."

"That's why it's perfect to help establish Pastry Perfect as *the* hometown bakery." Madison's smile lit her eyes, and her hands gestured as she spoke. "First, I thought you could donate the desserts for the fundraiser. It's only two weeks away, but my instructor is frantic to find someone. The higher-level students usually make them, but a pipe burst in the kitchen. They won't have time to create desserts for three hundred people."

Will shook his head. "That's a lot to get done with only two weeks' notice and without the opportunity to alter our special-order schedule."

"We can do it. We'll all pitch in." Erica picked up her phone and swiped a finger across the screen. "There's only one special order cake that week. It looks like it's a simple sheet cake with standard decorations—roses and such."

"I can do that, no problem." Madison's expression filled with eagerness. "If you let me."

"And I'll help package and whatever else you need."

Will eyed them both. Even if Madison over-estimated her ability, he could handle one cake and the regular bakery demands along with the desserts.

"Would you both commit to being here the day and night before to help with last minute details?"

Both heads nodded.

"Then, let's do it."

Madison fished a card from her pocket. "Here's my instructor's number."

"I'll take that." Erica snatched it from her fingers. "We don't want to waste time and lose the opportunity. You guys keep talking. I'll be back in a minute."

After the door swung shut behind Erica, Will gave his attention back to Madison.

"What else did you have in mind?"

Madison licked her lips. It must not be as doable as the first part if she hesitated to broach the subject with him.

"Whatever it is, I'm sure it's a great idea."

"I think you should donate something for the auction."

Why would she be unsure about asking him for something so simple? "That sounds great. Like a gift certificate for a specialty cake or desserts for an event of the winner's choosing?"

Her lip went between her teeth as she shook her head. "No … I was thinking something more personal. Something that would really help show others your interest in the community."

Dread settled in his stomach. "This isn't a bachelor auction, is it?"

Madison laughed. "No." The laughter continued. "I would never think of suggesting something like that to you."

"Then what?"

A deep breath helped her regain control. "I thought you might auction a certificate for an internship. The winning bidder isn't buying for themselves. They're bidding on an opportunity for the student of their choice to have a two-week internship with Will Forrester of Pastry Perfect. It's a double win for the program. They receive the money from the auction, and one of their students gets the opportunity to train with and learn from you."

He couldn't have come up with a better idea if he tried, and he did. Actually, he and Erica had both attempted to and failed. Madison should have shared earlier and put them out of their misery. A thought occurred to him and brought with it a sick feeling in the pit of his stomach.

"Is this what you wanted to speak with Erica and me about last week?"

Her cheeks pinked.

Will's eyes slid shut. *I've really messed this one up, haven't I, God?*

"Madison." He waited until she gave him full eye contact. "I apologize. I've underestimated you as an employee, and I've made you feel like you couldn't come to me. Can you forgive me?"

Apprehension twisted her features.

"Yes." Her voice was breathless. "I forgive you."

Will grinned. "Thank you. Now, let's figure out the details on this amazing plan of yours."

Chapter 12

"I don't think I've had this much fun in a long time." Madison positioned the final frosting rose on the birthday cake for the special order. "We should do this all the time."

"No!"

"No!"

Erica and Will's unified answer made Madison giggle. She shook her head as she picked up the piping bag to add the flowing script to finish the cake.

"Fine. Maybe we shouldn't do it all the time. But you've got to admit, despite the work, we've had a good time tonight."

Erica surveyed the mess scattered around the kitchen. An endless array of dishes to load in the washer, tartlets cooling on racks wherever they could find space, and empty boxes waiting to receive them littered the kitchen. Her gaze fell on Madison, working with precision to finish the cake, but with a smile on her face. And across from the cake-decorating station, Will pulled another pan of his fruity desserts from the oven.

Even with scads of work left for them, Will was relaxed and confident. The kitchen was his kingdom, and he moved through it with the confidence of its rightful king. Contemporary Christian music flowed around them, mixing with their laughter at random times. Madison was right.

"It has been a good afternoon." Erica slipped her hand into a glove and began placing cooled tartlets in their boxes. "We've accomplished a lot in a relatively short amount of time. Before you know it, we'll load up the van, and I'll make the delivery."

Will's head snapped up. "No. We'll make this one."

"There's no need for that." Erica smiled, despite a sudden case of nerves. "After all, I'm the one you hired to make the deliveries. And it will save time for all of us if I do."

"That may be the case." Will slid another pan in the oven. "However, I'm making this delivery with you. I should put in an appearance."

Erica shrugged as if it didn't really matter and went back to filling boxes. Nothing could be further from the truth. Her pulse raced, and a trickle of sweat ran down her spine. Will could not be allowed to deliver the desserts, no matter what.

When Erica arranged for Pastry Perfect to provide desserts, the organizer informed her another bakery had already agreed to provide half. While Will's bakery would bring a variety of tartlets, *Cupcakes & Cookies & Cakes, Oh, My!* was scheduled to bring other sweets to the event, and they were both scheduled for delivery at the same time.

Things were going so well for Will and her, both professionally and personally. Erica had decided to scrap her plan of proving herself to her parents. She was happy at Pastry Perfect and with Will. Even in her failure to include God in her plans, He'd been faithful to place her where she needed to be.

Her family didn't understand why she left and assumed one day she would return. An honest talk was in order, but she wasn't ready for that quite yet. They didn't even know she was working for Pastry Perfect. The last thing she needed was Will standing beside her when they found out.

Besides, she still wasn't sure how to explain things to Will. He harbored serious negative feelings about her parents' business. That fact was made clear when he'd hired her. Telling him the whole truth required finesse, and this event didn't afford her the time for delicacy.

"Earth to Erica." Will stared at her. "What's up? You're off in your own little world."

She looked down at the pastry perched in her hand, hovering over its box, waiting to be placed in an empty spot. When she glanced back up, both Will and Madison had paused their work to watch her with concerned frowns.

Placing the tartlet in its place, Erica scooped up another with a pathetic giggle. "Sorry. I guess I was lost in my thoughts. Did you need something?"

"No. I just noticed you kind of freeze and was a little worried about you."

She plastered on a smile. "I'm fine. No worries."

With that reassurance, Madison resumed work on the cake. Erica continued her task as best she could with Will's gaze still honed in on her. After a couple awkward minutes, she glanced up.

He sighed. "If it means that much to you, I don't have to make the delivery with you. I trust you completely to represent Pastry Perfect with professionalism."

Could her heart hurt any worse? Will thought she was digging in her heels in response to believing he didn't trust her to do her job. At the beginning of their relationship, she might have doubted, but not now. They'd come so far in understanding each other's abilities. Will trusted her as much as he trusted himself.

He didn't think she believed that though. And she couldn't

tell him any differently without risking every hard-earned morsel of trust between them. The urge to put him at ease warred with her need to make this delivery on her own.

"Thank you, Will. That means a lot."

Self-preservation won the battle. But what was the cost?

Chapter 13

"What are you doing here, Erica?"

Nervous energy pulsed through her, hearing her father's voice. Erica finished signing the donation forms for the fundraiser. Steeling herself for her father's reaction, she turned.

Great. Her father and mother stood side by side. She hadn't anticipated them both attending to the delivery. Maybe she should have owned up to everything and brought Will along for support. No. If Will were here now, she'd probably be fired. And boyfriendless.

"Hi, Dad. Mom."

Her mother noticed first. It was unmistakable. Her eyes narrowed as her brows drew low. Considering how much her mother appreciated looking younger than her years, it took a big push to make her frown like that. Lines and wrinkles were an enemy to fight against at all costs.

"What are you wearing?"

The dismay in her tone drew her dad's attention to her attire. Another frown. Erica was two for two, but it was far from a win. He raised his gaze to hers. The questions she expected to see in the depths of his eyes, but she hadn't expected them to also show hurt.

"I thought you left us to pursue other outlets for your marketing degree."

"Excuse me." The volunteer stepped between them, keeping her from replying to his comment. Facing Erica, he handed her a slip of paper. "Here is the receipt for your donation. We really appreciate your help making this year a success." He turned to her father. "And now, if you'll step right this way, we'll get your donation taken care of."

Her father's gaze flicked to the man and back to her before he stepped to the side and motioned behind him. "Trent will take care of the details."

It didn't bode well for Erica that her dad didn't even look at the poor volunteer when speaking to him. At least, they'd brought Trent instead of one of her brothers to help with the delivery. Facing two of them frazzled her nerves. She didn't want to think about her confession being a family affair.

As Trent and the volunteer made their way to the check-in table, awkward silence fell on the trio left behind. The question her father asked remained unanswered, but Erica understood her attire wasn't the inquiry begging an answer.

"I owe you guys an explanation." Erica motioned to a currently unoccupied corner of the room. "This may take a while."

"Hey, Will." Madison entered the kitchen with an envelope in her hands. "Isn't this the certificate for the auction?"

Will dropped the scoop into the bowl of cookie dough. It couldn't be the certificate. Erica was to take it with the rest of the delivery. He strode to Madison and snatched the paper from her. Opening the flap, Will immediately recognized the border to the gift certificate he'd printed earlier that morning.

"That's not good." Madison peeked over his shoulder. "Should we call and have her come back to get it?"

Will shook his head. "I don't think so. How are things out front?"

"Locked up tight." She pointed to the envelope. "And that's the last thing I had to put away."

His gaze bounced between the dough and the envelope. "How are you with cookies?"

"I mean, I can handle scooping the already made dough and setting the oven timer, if that's what you're asking."

Will grinned at the uncharacteristic sass. Insubordination was a detriment to a business, but this time, he counted it as a positive. Madison never would've spoken like that before their earlier talk.

"Then, if you don't mind, I'll leave the cookies to you. I'll run this over to the event planners. Feel free to lock up and leave once the last cookies are out and the final dishes are in the washer."

"You've got it, boss."

Erica wouldn't like this turn of events. When Will had contemplated going along with her for the delivery, her frustration was evident. While he couldn't figure out what he'd done to make her feel like he didn't trust her to do her job, something had obviously changed.

"She's going to think I'm checking up on her." He groaned and eyed the envelope resting in the passenger seat. "Even with the forgotten certificate, somehow, she's going to take it personally."

Maybe he could sneak in and out without her seeing him. No. If she found out about it later, it would only confirm her suspicions. He would simply have to be upfront with her. The truth would eventually plant itself in her heart, erasing any doubts she harbored about him not trusting her. That she could question that was beyond him. While it happened quicker than he thought possible, there wasn't anyone in his life he trusted more.

Once at the venue, Will ambled over to one of the volunteer tables and signed in the certificate for the silent auction. His relief escaped in a sigh that relaxed his shoulders. Erica had come and gone already, and if she asked about him being there, he could honestly tell her he hadn't even checked on the delivery she made. His being there had nothing to do with her.

"I love you too."

At the familiar voice speaking such a heartfelt endearment, Will froze. A weight settled in his chest cutting off his ability to breathe. Dread weighted his limbs as he turned.

How he'd missed the trio in the corner closest to the door, he didn't know. And the sight before him scrambled his ability to contemplate possibilities. Erica stood in the embrace of a man twice her age. The man cradled the back of her head in his hand. Next to them, a woman wiped tears from her cheeks.

Did they know each other? Obviously, they had to. One didn't embrace strangers in public. The woman held a stylish computer bag with the *Cupcakes & Cookies & Cakes, Oh, My!* logo embroidered on it. Will's head spun.

Why? They were the competition. Why would she tell the man she loved him? Sure, Erica had been employed there for eight years, but this went beyond any employee relation he knew of. The questions whirled relentlessly through his mind and left him answerless.

"Why?"

All three turned as one. While the man and woman's faces both held open curiosity, Erica's reflected an unusual mixture of pain, fear, and shock.

"This isn't what it looks like." The words tumbled out in a rush.

Will snorted. "What does it look like?"

"Will." Erica stepped toward him, placing herself between him and the couple. "I'd like you to meet my dad and mom, Eric and Daphne Gerard, co-founders of *Cupcakes & Cookies & Cakes, Oh, My!*."

"You're named after your father." It was a pointless observation, but the only thing making the slightest amount of sense to Will at that moment.

Erica's smile was sad. "Yes. I am."

She stepped closer to him, reaching out to take his hand. At least, that's what his eyes told him she did. They could be playing tricks on him though. Usually, her hand on his brought warmth. Even looking down at their twined fingers, Will felt nothing.

The emptiness seeped from his hand, up his arm, and spread through the rest of him. Erica's parents. Co-founders of his greatest competition. She didn't merely work for them. Erica was one of them. Acid churned in his stomach.

"I have to go." He turned, pulling free of her grasp, and fled the building.

"Wait! Please, wait!"

He strode away, ignoring the pleading in her voice. As he reached to open his car door, Erica inserted herself between it and him. He clenched his teeth.

"Move. Now."

She crossed her arms over her chest. "No. Not until you listen to me."

Arguing would only prolong his escape. Pushing her out of

the way would speed up the process, but even as furious as he was, he would never resort to physically removing her. He'd rather walk to the bakery than cross that line.

"Fine. You have five minutes." At least he could set some boundaries for the conversation.

She huffed. "That's not fair, and you know it."

He raised his brows. "Fair? You have four and a half minutes left."

"Have it your way, then." She glared at him a moment before softening. "You're right. You don't owe me the opportunity to explain."

He refused to respond. It would only make the situation more hostile.

"I'm not even sure where to start."

"Why did you come to me for a job? Your parents are my competition. Was it a joke? Were you trying to sabotage me?"

Erica ran her fingers through her hair. "No. It wasn't an act of sabotage. My parents didn't even know about it until today. And it was about as far from a joke as you can get."

"Then, why?"

"I was completely superfluous." Erica shrugged. "It's not a good reason, but it was the one I had at the time. Officially, I'd worked for my parents for eight years. Off the record, I'd worked for them in some capacity almost my entire life."

She leaned her head back against his car. "My brothers kept rising through the ranks. My own trajectory stalled early. I believed my parents would never take me, their only girl and the baby of the family, seriously. I decided I needed to prove my worth. What better way to do that than showing them what I could do in another bakery? Pastry Perfect just happened to be hiring the day my inspiration hit."

Will ran his hand over his face. "You hired on with me to prove a point to your family? And then what? Once you showed them you were just as smart and worthy as your brothers, what was supposed to happen then?"

She swallowed hard and stared over his shoulder.

"You planned to leave all along." His quiet voice betrayed his hurt, and he hated it.

"Yes. But no."

"It can't be both. Which is it?"

"I *planned* to leave." She sighed. "But all that changed, Will. I set out to prove myself to my parents, but God showed me I was chasing a path that wasn't mine to take. I didn't need their approval. I needed to find where God wanted to use me."

"And?"

"And today, I was able to speak with my parents for the first time about all of this." Now that her confession was over, Erica resumed eye contact. "They never realized I felt that way. Part of it was my fault for not bringing it to them earlier. We're forgiving and forgetting. That's what you walked in on back there."

"I suppose they offered to take you back into the business."

"Yes."

"Good." He set his jaw. "Go be with your family."

Her mouth dropped open, and her face went pale. "But ... that's not what I want."

The pain in her voice threatened his resolve. While his hurt would give in, his anger currently held the upper hand, and he forged ahead.

"No wonder you didn't want me here today." He allowed his fury to coat each word. "You wanted to keep me in the dark. Would have kept me there had you not forgotten the gift certificate for the auction."

"No."

"Yes." He spat the word. "You had no intention of telling me. What did you think would happen as our relationship progressed and it was time to meet the folks? Were they going to become part of your sick charade? Did you think I'd fall so head over heels in love with you that I'd overlook your ongoing lies?"

"No." Her eyes begged him to understand. "I don't know what I thought. I didn't think. Telling you just became harder and harder as each day passed. I needed to, but I couldn't figure out how."

Will waved an upturned hand toward the building. "Well, this was a *great* way to break it to me. Thank you for that. Now, if you'll excuse me, your time is more than up, and I need to be on my way. Return the delivery van to the bakery. Monday morning, you can turn in the keys to it along with the rest of your things to Madison. We're done here."

Her face went completely white as he spoke. It wouldn't sway him. He couldn't let it. Trust didn't come easy, and he'd given his to a liar. He glared through her until she moved from his car. He opened the door and dropped into the seat.

"Please, Will."

He stopped with his hand on the door but didn't turn to her.

"Don't go like this." Anguish filled each word. "I love you."

What should have set off fireworks inside, chilled like a cold bucket of ice dumped over his head. He needed to leave before he said something he'd regret. Still, her pain touched a place in his heart that hadn't hardened quite as quickly as the rest.

"Find your parents. Go back to work for them. You'll be fine." He closed the door, turned the key, and drove away without so much as a glance in the rearview mirror.

Chapter 14

"We can't keep up this pace." Madison tossed the van keys onto his desk. "You have to hire someone new for deliveries."

"It's not *your* place to tell me what I need to do to run *my* bakery. I tried that. It didn't work out."

Madison sighed. They'd been down this road many times in the past month. She would overlook his attitude as she always did. He would apologize later as he always did. She would forgive, and they would move forward toward a repeat of today's conversation as they always did. Comfort lived in the texture of the now-familiar pattern, and there wasn't reason to switch it up.

"No, it's not my place."

Will's head snapped up at the fire in her voice. While Madison had grown more open with him over the last several weeks, she'd never spoken to him in that manner before. Before he could reply, she continued.

"It's *your* place to run Pastry Perfect, but you seem to have forgotten that. You put in the hours, you bake all we need, and you fill the special orders. But you're just going through the motions. Rather than hire someone, you're wallowing, and it's created a mess for both of us. You need to wake up or you're going to lose a whole lot more than Erica."

He seethed, but Madison didn't wait for an answer. Instead, she turned and strode from the room, head held high. It should have fueled his anger. However, the change was so drastic he couldn't help being impressed.

Truth was, her words scared him more than they angered him. He'd lost Erica. It hurt worse than when Harper left, and he'd never thought that would be possible. He couldn't imagine the pain he'd face if Pastry Perfect was gone as well.

Madison was right. The bakery needed another worker dedicated to deliveries. But could he trust himself to choose the right person? Madison had finally grown into a loyal and valuable employee in more ways than simply filling in his weak points. However, she didn't challenge him like Erica had, present discussion excluded.

He picked up his phone as the urge to call Livvy hit. No matter what he faced, she and Evan were there to talk it through. Their advice was always godly and wise, but the time had come for him to hash it out with God on his own. He slid the phone into his pocket. It was time for what Livvy always called a 'come to Jesus meeting.'

With a quick apology to Madison and the promise of a more heartfelt one to come, Will informed her of his plans and left the bakery in her capable hands. Being in fresh air always helped one think clearly so Will opted to walk instead of drive.

He'd barely made it to the outer edge of the park in the middle of town before the late summer warmth curbed his desire to move. He wandered to a bench hidden in the shade of an oak tree. Parents and children dotted the play area toward the far side of the park. Ducks swam in a line through the waters of the pond. Movement and life darted in the distance, but the place he sat was free of distraction. Perfect for a time of prayer and meditating on scripture.

If his attitude was top priority, those two things were a must. He pulled his phone from his pocket and opened his Bible app. The verse of the day caught his attention. Proverbs 3:5-6.

"Trust in the LORD with all your heart and do not lean on your own understanding. In all your ways acknowledge Him, and He will make your paths straight."

Funny how when he really needed it, God had a way of showing Will the exact answer to his problems.

"Thank You, God, for bringing these verses to my attention." He whispered his prayer out loud. "I know I haven't been the best at turning to You for answers. I tend to seek out the advice of others first. Even if they are Christians, they can't replace You."

"Hello. Will, isn't it?"

The feminine voice pulled his attention from the bakery window where he inspected the Help Wanted sign he'd placed to make sure it was straight. The woman couldn't deny Erica as her daughter. It was like looking into Erica's future.

Manners overrode his confusion at finding her outside Pastry Perfect. He extended his hand. She accepted the gesture.

"Yes. It is Will. And how can I help you today, Mrs. Gerard?"

Her smile was wistful. "Oh, I don't need anything. I only wanted to see the bakery that came to mean so much to my daughter."

The words hurt more than he wanted to admit. "I'm sure,

given a little bit of time, she'll settle right back into *Cupcakes & Cookies & Cakes, Oh, My!*. It'll be like she never left."

Her head tilted to the side as she frowned. "What do you mean?"

"I'm sorry." Will shrugged. "I don't mean everything will be the same. I know you worked out your differences. Erica was so pleased by that. Soon, she'll find her place, and it will be better than ever."

"I'm still not sure I understand." She ran her fingers through her hair in a move so much like Erica, it made his heart ache. "Erica isn't at the bakery."

"What? Why? Where is she?"

Mrs. Gerard laughed. "The *what* is that she never returned. The *where* is going back to school while she figures out the next step. The *why*? Well, I'm not sure I understand that one."

"What did she say?"

"Erica told us our bakery wasn't God's best for her. She said she found it, but having messed it up had to find His new best. But it didn't involve the family business."

Her intense gaze convinced Will that Mrs. Gerard knew more than her words suggested. That maybe she wasn't only speaking about Pastry Perfect.

"Is that how it works, Mr. Forrester?"

"How what works?"

"A person messes up God's best for their life, so He just gives them a new best to find? Wouldn't that make it second best?"

That was a bit of theology above his pay grade. "I'm not sure, Mrs. Gerard. But I think I'd like to find out."

Chapter 15

Erica plopped down under a tree in the courtyard of Carrington Culinary College. A fountain gurgled in the middle of the brick lined path. Voices of students walking by on their way to class mingled with the peaceful sound.

Leaning back against the tree trunk, she closed her eyes. With an hour break between her classes, the fountain provided a peaceful place to rest. While she enjoyed the courses, she was still getting used to a varied daily schedule. What she wouldn't give for the set hours she'd always known. With less than a semester completed, that dream was in a far-off horizon.

"Madison told me she saw you here from time to time."

Breathing became difficult, and her heart beat faster at the familiar voice. Still, she kept her eyes closed. As much as she longed to drink in the sight of him, it would only hurt worse when he left.

"And how is Madison?" Erica congratulated herself on sounding calm.

She could tell the moment he dropped down beside her. His presence next to her unmistakable. The urge to open her eyes, to commit every feature to memory, as if she hadn't already, intensified.

"About ready to quit, if I don't hire someone soon."

"Business has picked up, I guess?"

She could imagine his nonchalant shrug.

"Sure. But we're also shorthanded. We lost someone recently. One of the best employees I've ever had."

She opened one eye to look at him. "Is that right?"

"I'm afraid so."

"Was she really that great if you were willing to let her go?" She closed her eyes again.

He sighed. "Better than great. She did her work with amazing efficiency. And she challenged me on more than one occasion. At first, we only frustrated and aggravated each other. Then, we found our groove and made each other better."

"Sounds like a great working relationship."

"It was. But she lied to me, and I couldn't trust her anymore."

"I can see where that would make things difficult. Did she apologize?"

"She tried to, but I wouldn't listen. I was angry. And I was hurt. She made a mistake, and I didn't let her have a second chance. I regret that now."

Erica opened her eyes and stared at him. "Why? What changed?"

"I did." He smiled. "I realized I hadn't been trusting God with everything in my life. Without that, I'd let the straight path He had for me get all twisted."

The truth hit Erica in the gut. They were so alike with their strong personalities forging ahead and solving every problem that crossed their paths. It was too easy to keep the pace instead of waiting on God to show them the right roads to take.

"I get that."

"I know you do." He reached for her hand but pulled back before touching her. "And then, I had a visitor, a wise woman who, amazingly enough, resembles what I imagine you'll look like several years down the road. She was worried for her daughter. She asked me a question I'm still trying to answer."

"What was that?" Erica ignored the fact that her mother had failed to tell her about speaking with Will. Curiosity over what her mom asked Will was too strong.

"She wanted to know how God's best for someone works, because her daughter found her best but messed it up and was looking for a new best." He stared into her eyes. "Is that true?"

"That I believed Pastry Perfect to be God's best for me?"

He nodded.

"Yes."

"And is a job the only thing you found that was God's best for you?"

She shook her head.

"Can you forgive me for pushing you away?"

"Can you forgive me for lying to you?"

"Yes."

"Then, yes."

"I think I've found your mother's answer."

She smiled. "And what is it?"

"We may mess up and run ahead of God, but God's power to fix His best for us far exceeds our ability to ruin it."

She took his hand in hers, threading her fingers in his. "I'm so happy He does."

"Great." He squeezed her hand before releasing it to retrieve a folded paper from his pocket. "Then I have a delivery for you."

He unfolded the paper and set it in her lap. A giggle burst out as she realized it was the Help Wanted sign she'd answered all those weeks ago. He'd written in between the words so it now read 'Help found and most definitely Wanted.'

When she smiled up at him, he regarded her with a serious expression. He cupped her cheek with his hand, brushing his thumb back and forth over her skin and causing a shiver of excitement to race up her back. Slowly, he leaned in. Her anticipation rose with each painfully slow inch he neared until he was close enough she could feel his warm breath on her skin.

"Should I continue my search?" He whispered next to her lips.

"Absolutely not."

"I love you, Erica Gerard."

His lips touched hers and all thoughts of answering were put on hold. Will forgave her, wanted her, loved her. Despite both their failures, God brought her His best for her life, and He did so with the sweetest delivery.

Acknowledgments

I thank God every day for allowing me to encourage others through writing.

And to all the people who walk beside me in this ministry, you're blessings to me. I thank God for you each day.

About the Author

Heather Greer is a preacher's kid and pastor's wife who loves using her passion for reading and writing to encourage others in their faith. She has been a finalist for the Selah awards twice. In addition to all things book related, Heather loves baking. Christmas baking is her favorite, and each year, she makes dozens of treats to pass on to her family and friends in southern Illinois. And while it isn't her favorite, she's even been known to add gingerbread people to her cookie trays.

Also by Heather Greer

Window of Opportunity by Heather Greer

The Stained-glass Legacy Series—Book One

Faith and duty drive Evangeline Moore to protect her father's pristine image as a judge in Harrisburg, Illinois. Her resolve's biggest test? Dot, her childhood friend. With Evangeline beside her, Dot's desire for the Roaring Twenties' glitz and glamor leads the pair into questionable situations.

Born into a Chicago mob family, Brendan Dunne understands duty, but faith puts him at odds with his father's demands. Even when his brother James's propensity for trouble lands them in Harrisburg, the truth is undeniable. To their father, the lines he won't cross mean Brendan will never measure up.

When circumstances push Brendan and Evangeline together, unexpected events create opportunity to break free of family expectations. Will they be brave enough to forge their own path before the window closes on their chance to change?

Get your copy here:

https://scrivenings.link/windowofopportunity

Love in the Squared Circle

by Heather Greer

Trinity Knight is not a fan of professional wrestling. But with her husband gone, it falls to her to give their son the father-son trip they daydreamed about when he was alive. After Trinity causes them to miss a meet and greet with Jay's favorite wrestler, a random act of kindness saves the trip and starts Trinity on an unexpected path.

Universal Wrestling Organization Champion Blane Sterling hears whiny children at photo ops all the time. However, overhearing a young boy comfort his mother piques his interest. Touched by their story, Blane works with the UWO Public Relations team to give Jay the experience of a lifetime.

As they learn each other's stories, Trinity and Blane are drawn to each other. But they don't just come from different states. They live in different worlds. Trinity might learn to fit into his life, but can those in her world look beyond Blane's profession to see his heart? Or will a lack of acceptance cause Trinity and Blane to lose their shot at love?

Get your copy here:

https://scrivenings.link/loveinthesquaredcircle

Cake That!

Third-place Winner - Contemporary Romance

2022 Selah Awards

Ten bakers. Nine days. One winner.

Competing on the *Cake That* baking show is a dream come true for

Livvy Miller, but debt on her cupcake truck and an expensive repair make her question if it's one she should chase. Her best friend, Tabitha, encourages Livvy to trust God to care for The Sugar Cube, win or lose.

Family is everything to Evan Jones. His parents always gave up their dreams so their children could achieve theirs. Winning *Cake That* would let him give back some of what they've sacrificed by allowing him to give them the trip they've always talked about but could never afford.

As the contestants live and bake together, more than the competition heats up. Livvy and Evan have a spark from the start, but they're in it to win. Neither needs the distraction of romance. Unwanted attention from Will, another competitor, complicates matters. Stir in strange occurrences to the daily baking assignments, and everyone wonders if a saboteur is in the mix.

With the distractions inside and outside the *Cake That* kitchen, will Livvy or Evan rise above the rest and claim the prize? Or does God have more in store for them than they first imagined?

Get your copy here:

scrivenings.link/cakethat

Faith, Hope, and Love Series:

Faith's Journey

Faith, Hope, and Love Series - Book One

https://scrivenings.link/faithsjourney

Grasping Hope

Faith, Hope, and Love Series - Book Two

https://scrivenings.link/graspinghope

Relentless Love

Faith, Hope, and Love Series - Book Three

https://scrivenings.link/relentlesslove

A Novella

the mermaids, the ex, and
USSS

RACHEL HEROD

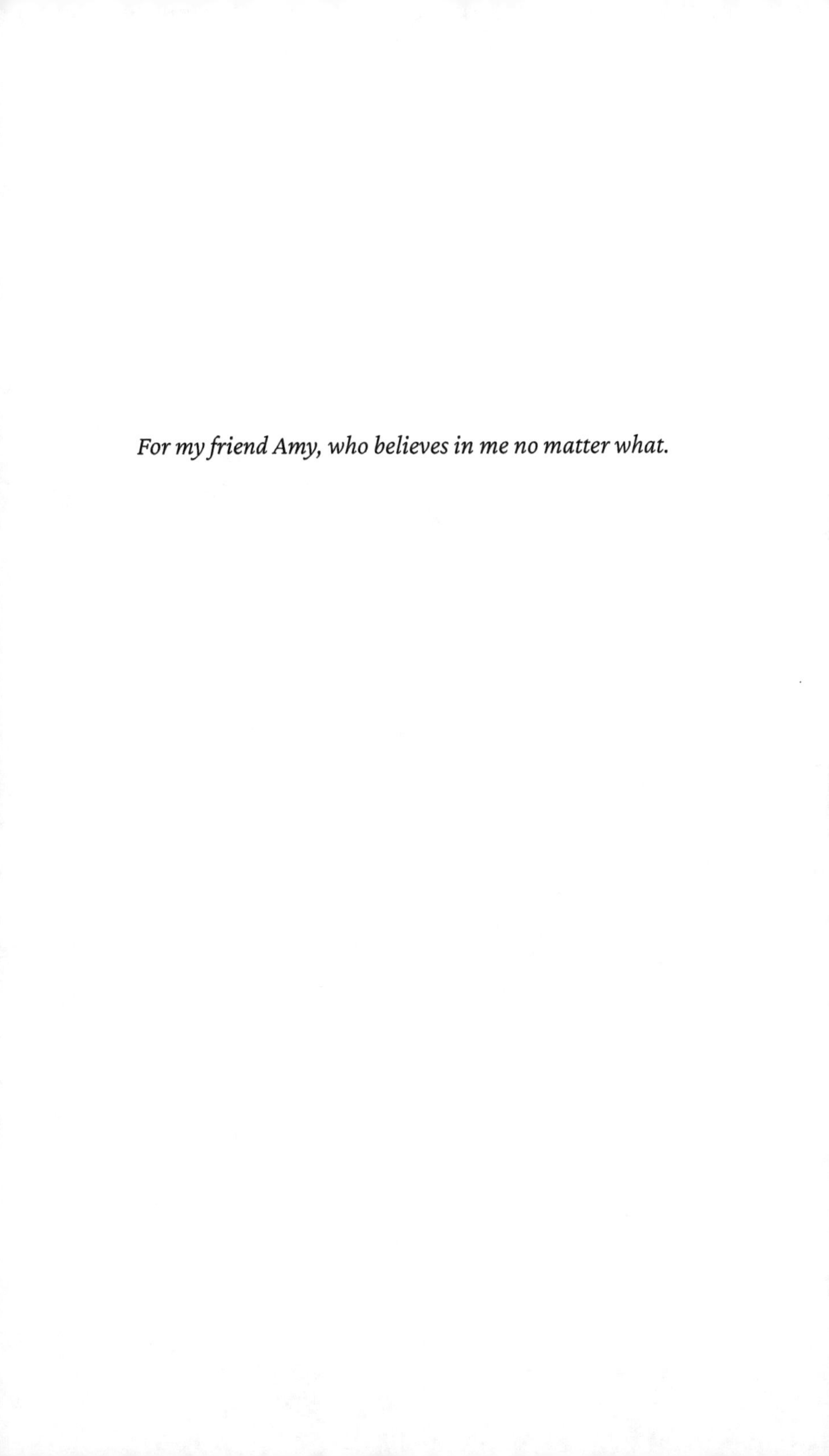

For my friend Amy, who believes in me no matter what.

Chapter 1

Who has a dog door on the *front* of their house?

All delivery drivers experience run-ins with dogs—it comes with the job. But Braig Sanborn knew a guy who was bitten once. Really bitten. And his Pidgeon, the handheld device issued to each driver, hadn't warned him either. Usually a driver's Pidge flagged houses with dangerous dogs, but this time? Nothing. So, the dude had no warning. He'd verified the address, set the package down, and stepped back to take a picture. That's when he heard the growl and got his keister chomped.

After a doctor visit, multiple shots, and being out of work for more than a week, the driver finally returned—definitely worse for the wear. And after the bandages came off, the rest of the guys at work teased that his tush was lopsided.

That's why Braig wouldn't go near the front door of number one-eleven Agapi Drive.

He leaned between the headrest and the dashboard until he had a clear sight of one-eleven's front door. The biggest dog door he'd ever seen taunted him every time he made this stop. Just because no one had reported a vicious dog didn't mean there wasn't one. This house had been on Braig's route for months now. One-eleven was his baby. It was *his* responsibility.

He crawled out of driver's seat and into the back of his delivery truck, gazing down at his Pidgeon. Still no flag on this house.

The shipments to this address had been increasing, but today was the most he'd ever seen. If he took a minute to speculate, he might believe something illegal was going on in the house protected by the largest dog known to man.

The barcode scanning could have taken half the morning, but Braig was quick and methodical. Carrying the mound of packages was not so efficient. Six trips later, the steps were covered with fifteen boxes addressed to Ella Morrison, resident of one-eleven Agapi Drive.

Standing a safe distance away, Braig peered at the stacked boxes, then glanced again at the door. He never went near the front door of number one-eleven, except that one time when it was raining. He'd tossed the delivery onto the welcome mat and raced back to the truck with high knees, screaming as quietly as he could. Later, he hoped there was nothing breakable inside that box.

That's a lot to leave so ... out in the open. He cut his eyes to the dog door. It moved, and he jumped, but nothing came out.

Maybe it hadn't really moved.

A ding sounded from his Pidge—a small, unintimidating alarm to alert him that Mr. Mann could tell this delivery was taking longer than anticipated.

"Mann, you micromanager," Braig growled as he hopped back in the truck cab. *I bet the bosses at National Express don't micromanage their drivers.* He froze and gripped the steering wheel, cutting his eyes to the left and right, face hot. What? NatEx? No way. No way it's better over there. If there was one thing Braig was sure of, it was that he would never leave the United States Shipping Service to transfer to National Express. Not ever.

Still muttering under his breath about Mann's ding, Braig swiped to the screen on his Pidge, showing his next stop. Turner Heat. Anytime a new, swanky steakhouse came to Buskerton, people were intrigued, and Turner Heat was supposed to be the swankiest.

He parked across two spaces at the back of the restaurant. Wondering if the kitchen was as upscale as everything else about the place, Braig rapped on the knobless back door, holding the small package under his other arm. "Delivery," he called.

The door swung open, Braig grabbed it with one hand, and stepped inside. A girl in a black apron stood with arms out, ready to take the box. Braig hesitated, mesmerized by the shiny tile and sleek chrome. The kitchen was definitely as upscale as Turner Heat's reputation.

"Oh, sign here, please." He handed the girl his stylus and turned his Pidge sideways.

A knock on the door he was keeping propped open drew his attention away from the fancy fixtures of the kitchen.

"NatEx," came a cheerful voice from the other side. "Would you hold this door open? Thanks."

Braig stood against the door while the NatEx driver, in his white button–up and pleated pants, strutted past, pushing a dolly. The Pidge dinged, grating in his ears, while simultaneously another sound rang through the kitchen. A lighter, almost pleasant sound—and it came from the straight, pleated pants that had just passed him. Braig glanced down at his gray polo and matching shorts as the Pidge dinged again. *This is my soundtrack, and that's theirs.* He let the door close on his way out.

Two dings. Mann was tracking his every move today. Maybe since he already had two dings, he could just chalk it up to a bad day, and drive by one-eleven one more time. Driving faster wouldn't help him make better time. If Buskerton could be famous for anything, it would be for being one big speed trap. And getting a ticket was way worse than getting dinged.

As he turned off Turner Heat's street, Braig couldn't shake the thought that the delivery at one-eleven should be farther up on the porch. Why did he have to be so afraid of getting attacked by a dog? Oh yeah, uneven cheeks.

He growled a bit as he gave into the temptation to turn onto Agapi Drive. Braig couldn't deny the worry any longer. He would count and see that all the packages were there, and the rest was out of his hands. With a delivery this large, Ella Morrison really should be home waiting for it. *Her absence is not my responsibility.* Braig said to himself. *Delivery is my responsibility.*

USSS had a tagline printed on every truck: United States Shipping Service—Your Country Courier. But around the office, there was another saying, "Delivery is our *only* responsibility." In other words, what happens after the truck leaves is out of the driver's hands.

Mann used that phrase daily, so no way would the boss approve of Braig driving back by one-eleven. Especially since his every move was tracked, always, by his Pidge. Mann observed everything at the garage.

I'm going to get it for this.

He practiced what he would say to the boss. "There's just this huge dog door on the *front* of this house, Mann, and you know what happened to Thompson ... We can't be too careful with large dogs, I mean," he said out loud what he'd been thinking all morning, "Who has a dog door on the front of their house?"

Braig pulled past one-eleven, past the black car parked on the street two houses down, and drove around the block. Positioning his vehicle where he could see through the backyards to Agapi, he slowed the truck and counted the packages quickly. Twelve. Thirteen. Fourteen. Good, they're all —wait, only fourteen?

How would he explain *this* to Mann?

Chapter 2

Ella Morrison propped her phone against a stack of patient files in the receptionists' area of Buskerton Orthodontics. "I've got the weirdest deliveryman." She picked up the phone and held the screen toward Candace. "Look."

Candace tapped away at her keyboard across their desk cluster. "Mm-hmm," but she kept her eyes on her computer. "Oh, no."

"What is it?"

"My dad emailed me. You know that week-long stomach bug that's going around upstate?"

Ella shook her head.

"It's all over the news, Ella. They closed the schools in three counties." Candace squinted at the computer screen. "My mom has it now. Dad says she should still make it to the wedding in two weeks, but she won't be coming early for the last-minute set up."

"It's really okay. I just hope she feels decent on the big day."

"Yeah. Me too." Candace sighed and clacked a response to the message.

"Oh, better get back to work. Here comes admin." Ella quipped as Sherr sauntered in.

Her mocha hair tumbled around her shoulders as she dropped a file on the desk beside Candace and leaned in close. "You think you have the right to think about getting married at a time like this?" She laughed, hard and deep, her voice echoing through the empty waiting room.

Ella glanced down at the video feed of her camera doorbell. "Seriously, you two. Check out this USSS guy. He does this every time."

Candace clicked a few times on her computer and stepped around the desk, where Sherr hovered behind Ella.

"What is he doing?" She asked her two friends.

"Why is he staring at your door like that?" Sherr laughed.

"Every time." Ella said. "That's what he does. He stares at the door for a minute, and then ..."

Candace tilted her head.

"Look." Ella continued. "He does this step back thing, then ... wait for it ..." She chuckled. They studied the screen as the man set the armful of boxes down. "There! He keeps his eyes on the door the whole time."

Sherr threw her head back, and the waiting room filled once again with her hearty laughter when the delivery guy performed exactly what Ella described.

"Look, he's going to do it again," Candace said.

He made trip after trip from his truck to the steps. They giggled and contemplated what his problem could be, until the one o'clock appointment came through the door of Buskerton Ortho.

Candace, who was the closest to reception, stepped away and greeted the mother and son pair. "Hello, Mrs. McGuire.

How are you?" She sat in the rolling chair behind the counter and opened the file that sat waiting on top. "Will you verify a few items for me?"

The other two continued the entertainment at Ella's desk. "Hey, what's in all the boxes?" Sherr asked.

"It's the stuff for Candace's wedding reception. You know that."

"Oh, yeah." Sherr lowered her voice and spoke right into her ear. "You're so nice doing this for her." She switched to the other side. "*And* for being a bridesmaid." Sherr cut her eyes to Candace and back. "*And* helping with the bachelorette party."

"Wait a minute." Ella protested, spinning in her chair.

"Oh, come on, Ella. You know you have an eye for these things. I need help. The maid of honor can't do it all by herself. You know this office administrator gig takes up so much of my time."

"Sherr." Ella gave her a serious look.

"Ella." Sherr returned the same expression.

Candace closed the folder. "Thank you, Mrs. McGuire. Please go through the door to your left, and they are ready for you in Exam Room One."

Sherr cleared her throat loudly.

"Oh, and Mrs. McGuire," Candace leaned forward on the counter and called after the woman, "Don't forget to vote for Buskerton Ortho for the local Buskie Award this year. Voting ends this week, and you can do it online."

"Thank you," Sherr crooned.

"Why do we have to do that?" Candace asked.

"Because your manager wants that banner out front."

Candace huffed as she returned to the cluster, then snatched up her phone. "Ugh," she groaned.

"Hmm?" Sherr mumbled.

"It's Aunt Ritty. She texted me a book, see?" She turned the screen toward Ella and Sherr and scrolled. And then scrolled some more.

"Looks like you weren't lying when you said your Aunt Ritty talks too much." Ella said. "What's it about?"

Candace plopped down and skimmed the text. "Oh, no. Ella."

"What?"

Candace kept reading. "Ella!"

"What?"

Candace let the phone drop. "Ella, she wants to take my mom's place and help with the reception, *and* the wedding. She has—" she cleared her throat. "*Ideas.*"

Sherr moved to the other side of the cluster. "What kinds of ideas?"

Candace scrolled back through the message. "For starters, she has a carload of tulle she's bringing."

Ella shuddered.

"And, she wants me to forward her the seating arrangement so she can approve it."

Sherr's hands flew to her hips. "Um. No, girl."

"Are you *serious* right now?" Ella leaned over the desk, almost standing.

"Then she wrapped up by saying, 'And I hope you don't plan on having any instruments other than a violin, harp, cello, bass, and flute. Anything else is not proper for a wedding.'" Candace sighed. "I don't know what to do. Ella, you're going to have to put her to work."

Sherr nodded as she swept brunette curls over her shoulder. "She's right. That's the only way. You must tell her how it's going to be. You're coordinating this event. You have to take charge."

"Easy for you to say, Sherr." Ella sat back in her chair. "You have a manager's personality. I like to sit quietly at my desk and work in peace."

Candace flushed. "Just give her things to do so she doesn't take over. Please?"

"Okay, fine. Fine. I'll have a list for Aunt Ritty by Saturday. Forward me her number."

"You could just find her on social media." Sherr sat in the chair near the counter. "Oh wait, that's right. You aren't on social media."

Candace raised her eyebrows. "Aunt Ritty is *active* on all the platforms."

"I have a phone. *And* a doorbell camera." Ella said defensively. She pulled up the app again and held the device where Sherr and Candace could view the boxes piled high on her porch steps.

They both leaned forward, staring at the screen.

"Wait," Sherr said.

Candace pointed. "Um, you guys ..."

"What is it?" She turned the phone around. The packages were still there on the porch. The delivery man was gone.

In his place, stood another figure.

A white cap cast shadows over his face. Or was it *her* face? There was no way to tell. The person wore an oversized black hoodie, baggy jeans, and reached for one of the packages. Ella had no time to react but wouldn't have been able to conjure a suitable reaction anyway. The crook didn't even look around. He picked up the package like he owned it—like it was *his* name on the address label instead of Ella's. Then, he turned and walked out of the screen.

When he was out of sight, Ella sputtered, "Hey, wait a minute!"

"You have to push the button so he can hear you." Sherr

reached down to push it for her, but Candace reached at the same time.

"No! Call the police," Candace said.

"He'll be gone by the time they get there. She needs to yell at him."

With all the hands in her way, Ella could no longer see the porch. She dropped her phone on the desk. "You guys, stop. I don't know what to do. I need a minute here, please."

Sherr and Candace stood back, still eyeing the view of Ella's porch, holding one package less than it should.

After a few seconds of silence, Sherr blurted out. "Ella, you need to go home and get all those boxes inside."

Ella shook her head. "But I have work to do."

"There's *one* patient here right now. Go." Sherr said, with Candace echoing the statement.

Ella scooted her chair back. "Okay, if you're sure. I'll come right back, promise. It'll only take a few—"

Candace gasped, interrupting Ella's long-winded assurance that she would return to work. "He's back." They all stood still, as the same figure, man or woman, clutched another one of Ella's packages.

"Ella, he's going to clean you out."

But the figure didn't exhibit the same cool behavior as he did the first time. His head jerked, he bent his knees as if to steady himself before tucking the box into his chest and spinning away from the house.

"What's he doing?" Ella asked.

Sherr's hands were in her hair. "Is he going to run?"

The figure took off in wide bounding leaps toward the street. Then, from the other side of the shot, there was another figure. "Oh!" The three friends heaved.

Gray shorts. Matching gray polo. He was faster than the thief, that was clear—perhaps he had a head start. The women held their breath, but then both the pirate and his pursuer were out of sight. There was yelling and some grunting. But the screen was still. Only the remaining packages on the porch were visible. Then, it all went quiet.

"What's happening?" Ella wailed at her phone. The friends didn't move. They stayed transfixed to the screen, determined to outwait the stillness, the silence.

"E-excuse me?"

They jumped, letting out groans of surprise. Sherr regained her composure first and walked to the counter. "Yes, may I help you?"

Ella and Candace stared at the motionless screen.

Candace inhaled through gritted teeth when someone came back in view. "Is it him?"

"It's the driver, and he has the box. He must have wrestled it away from the guy."

The driver set the box back on the stack, a glazed look in his eyes.

"I think he's in shock." Candace sat back in her own chair.

"Oh, he's writing a note, you guys. He's really good at his job." Ella laughed, not because something was funny, but because the sensation from her neck to her toes was so pleasurable. "I can't wait to see what it says," she mumbled.

Sherr finished up with the patient at the front and turned around. "You still need to step out and go put those things in your house. Go do it now, girl." Then she walked through the reception area, headed for the exam rooms.

"Oh," she said, catching herself in the doorway. "I figured out what he was staring at. That dog door you've got."

ELLA SHIELDED her eyes from the sun as she grabbed the note off the top box stacked high on the steps, rather than the porch.

"One of your deliveries was stolen today, but I was able to chase them off before they took any more. Have a nice day. —USSS"

No name. Just USSS. She flipped the note over in her hand to make sure, then sighed. Sorting through all of the items in this, the largest shipment she'd ever received, would prove to be a chore and probably take her until well past her bedtime. *I'll have to start right after work.*

What in the world was stolen? She glanced to the street, then back to the stacks. "That's it, that's it," she mumbled to herself and raced up the steps to prop the front door open. She lifted, dragged, dropped, and propped the packages inside the entry, moving as quickly as she could. When the last one was safely inside, she dialed Sherr's phone.

Sherr had barely said hello when Ella blurted out, "Hey, is there any way you can get by without me this afternoon?"

"Yeah, girl, you need to take half a sick day?"

Ella smiled and exhaled. "Yes, please. Thanks, Sherr."

"You got it. See you tomorrow. Hey Candace! Ella's ou—"

Click.

Seven and half minutes later, Ella was on the floor, her order list spread out in front of her, ripping open boxes, examining the contents, and crossing off the items. She was a true workhorse when she wanted to be, and right now moved at Triple Crown speed.

When all the boxes were open and accounted for except for one, she pointed at the two items still on the list: Party favor boxes with chocolate candies inside and personalized place cards for the dinner. Gauging the size of the box, it could have been either.

"Please be the place cards," she whispered and tore the

tape off. Inside the box were six stacks of cellophane wrapped, personalized place cards. Ella rocked backward, leaned on her hands, and prayed, "Thank you."

Spinning quickly and grabbing her phone, she immediately ordered more chocolate-filled party favor boxes from the wedding and party supply company, and on the preferred shipping page checked, *USSS-Expedited*. Then, she searched for the reservation line for Turner Heat Steakhouse.

Chapter 3

Roy Mann, district supervisor of the Buskerton branch of the United States Shipping Service, had a combover and a penchant for belittling his employees. Frosted glass obscured the view through his office door, so only shadows were visible. However, there was no mistake who occupied the room when Mann was in a bad mood.

As soon as Braig entered the office after his morning route, Jeanie, the dispatcher, turned to him, her curly blue-gray bob peeking out from underneath her USSS cap. "You okay?"

Before Braig could answer, Mann's office door flew open, but Mann himself still sat at his desk.

How does he do that?

"Greg!" Mann's voice echoed throughout the entire garage. "Get in here!"

Braig turned to Jeanie, "Do I have to?"

Jeanie turned his shoulders to face the office, and gave him a tiny nudge.

When Braig stepped through the doorway, Mann stared

directly at him, fingers pressed together in front of his face. "Have a seat, Greg."

"It's Braig," he muttered, sitting reluctantly.

"Greg, you know, I was watching your activity this morning. I was paying special attention to you. Tell me, was there an inordinate amount of traffic on the roads today?"

"No, sir."

"Did some unforeseen weather event cause you to drive more slowly or detour to avoid flooding?"

"Um, no."

"Then maybe you can help me understand, *why, oh why,* it took you an average of over four minutes per delivery today? Or why you spent a full twelve minutes on Agapi Drive this morning, *after* you had already submitted the delivery confirmation for one-eleven." He glared down his nose at Braig. "Hmm?"

Braig shifted in his seat. "Okay, Mann, here's what happened."

"That's *Mr.* Mann."

"Of course, Mr. Mann, sir. You see, there was this porch pirate, and I had to stop him, or he was going to take all the packages. Th-th-there were so many packages. This person ordered so much stuff, I couldn't just let it get stolen."

"Greg." Mann smiled, and Braig shuddered. "You see, there's this little company called Natex."

Eyelids half closed, Braig monotoned, "I know, Mr. Mann."

"I hope you do, my friend. Do you also know what Natex is capable of? Do you have any idea what Natex could do to *USSS*?" He asked, dragging out the *S* sound until droplets of spittle came spraying out from between his teeth.

"Take our business." Braig replied.

Mann stood and pounded a fist on the desk. "They could take our business, Greg! And they would do that, *how?*"

"By making faster, more efficient deliver—"

Mann's hands flew to his hips. "What is our responsibility after delivery, Greg?"

Braig took in a deep breath. "Nothing, sir."

"Delivery is our *only* responsibility. You have *none* after that, to one-eleven or any other recipient. They should be home to expect large deliveries. It's not our problem." Mann turned sideways in his chair. "You don't have a thing going on with this person on Agapi Drive, do you?"

"What?"

Mann wagged his finger at Braig. "It's a woman, isn't it? You know my policy about that, too, Greg."

"I don't know what you're talking about, Mr. Mann. There's no problem, really. I just had a bad day. It won't happen again." He stood to leave.

"No problems—that's what I like." Mann leaned onto his desk and flashed a toothy grin.

Braig took the doorknob. "You got it. No more problems."

As he closed the door behind him, Mann's voice rang out, "Mind your Pidge, Greg. And stay away from that woman!"

Braig went into the breakroom and set his Thermos on the table.

"I picked up your lunch. Here ya go," Jeanie set the tightly wrapped sandwich in front of him. "They said make sure to vote for them in the Buskies." She smiled. "What's going on, buddy?"

"Oh, you didn't hear?"

She chuckled. "I did. I just wanted to give you the chance to talk about it."

"Porch pirates were going to steal all this person's packages, so I stopped them. That's all. I stopped them, but it took too long for Mann."

"He's terrible, I know," Jeanie said, in a low voice. "A micromanager of the worst kind."

"There's more. An *Ex* was making a delivery at Turner Heat at the same time as me. He just strutted in with his perfect pleated pants and white shirt."

"I hate it when that happens."

"Me too. You know the worst part?"

"Hmm?" She asked as she ate her own sandwich.

"He was a nice guy. I didn't hate him, even though I wanted to."

Jeanie sighed. "Braig, you don't have a hate bone in your body. You've never hated any of the Exes, and you know it. And you don't have to just because Mann tells us we should. *I* don't hate them."

"You don't?"

She laughed, "No. You take what Mann says too seriously, Braig. You let it get to you. Hey, why don't you come over tonight? There's plenty."

"That's okay." He squeezed her hand. "Thanks for being my work mom. I wish you weren't retiring next month."

"Thanks for being my work son." She patted his back. "And you know the only reason I'm retiring is because Mann is transferring you to the other side of the country." Braig's face fell and he nodded. "Hey, want to hear another story about my days as a mermaid? It'll take your mind off of everything while you eat."

Braig shrugged, but held his sandwich and sat back in the chair, completely unable to refuse one of Jeanie's stories.

"There I was on the boardwalk of Aspaldiko Island. Just a twenty-two-year-old mermaid, sitting on a bench, watching the passersby, waiting for one of them to discover me for the great Hollywood beauty I would one day be. Not unlike the Buskers of Buskerton."

"You do love the Buskers, don't you, Jeanie?" Braig said, amused at her always.

"Each and every one of them." She flourished as she said, "I love the stars in their eyes. They're just like mine were, so long ago. So, there I was on the bench, when this old, feeble man, who was taking baby steps with a cane, called out. The wind had blown his hat off. It rolled down the boardwalk like a tumbleweed, and no one was doing a thing to help him. Poor guy, he could barely move, so he just stood there reaching toward the hat and calling out to it, like he could beckon it to return. Well, I would have had to run after that hat to catch it, but as you know, there is no running in a mermaid tail. So, I flipped over the back of the bench and into the water, and started swimming in the direction the hat blew. I swam as fast as I could swim, until something told me to get back up onto the boardwalk, so I hoisted myself up into the sun, and guess what."

"You caught the hat?" Braig asked.

"No," Jeanie beamed. "A child already had it and was running it over to the old man. Probably his grandkid or something. But when I glanced back down the boardwalk, there was something else. A schooner, whose navigator had fallen asleep. And that schooner came right up onto the boardwalk. It crashed into it. And it crushed the very bench I had been sitting on moments before."

Braig had forgotten his sandwich. "What happened then?"

Jeanie patted his back again. "Well, then I lay back on the boardwalk and let the sun hit my face, the happiest mermaid who ever got to live another day. That's just one of the many stories of my life being spared by the grace and mercy of God, you know."

"I *do* know, Jeanie. I do."

She laughed. "Yes, you've listened to all of them, haven't you?"

"And it's always by the grace and mercy of God."

"He is able to do *far* more abundantly than all that we ask or think, you know. His way is always better than ours."

"Ephesians 3. I do know that." Braig scooted his chair under the table and gathered their trash. "Have a great afternoon, Jeanie. Thanks again."

"May the Buskers serenade you and the sun shine upon you, sweet boy."

Braig reported to the loading dock first thing the next morning as Sam, the inventory manager, accepted a small box from a woman in a blazer.

"Hey, Braig. Add this to your morning route. It's an expedited to one-eleven Agapi. Take it ASAP."

"Thanks, Sam." Braig scanned the box in with his Pidge and hopped in his truck. The stolen box. Well, at least they reordered instead of trying to blame us for the porch pirate.

When he pulled his truck into the driveway, he decided quickly that, even after having delivered a host of packages with no dog jumping out at him, he still wasn't stepping onto the porch. So, he eyed the door as usual and leaned forward with an outstretched arm and slowly lowered the box.

Suddenly there was movement from the dog door and a shriek in Braig's ears. He dropped the box and stepped back, a little too quickly and a little too far. He was in the grass when he realized it wasn't a dog coming out of the door, but a woman.

"Hi. I didn't mean to startle you."

Braig picked himself up off the ground and moved toward

the truck. "Oh, um, it's okay. I'm just delivering your package, ma'am." He pointed at the box. The woman was dressed professionally, like she was heading to work. Her light brown hair was in a loose bun, and several strands had escaped their confines.

"I know. Thank you, and thank you for the note yesterday." She spoke fast, almost stumbling over the double thank you.

"You're welcome." He took another step toward his truck. "I'm sorry I couldn't stop them from taking the package they stole."

"Wait. What's your name?" The woman blurted.

He turned and waved as he raised a foot. "Braig. Have a nice day."

"I'm sorry, what?" She was now in the grass, closer than a customer would normally be.

"Braig," he repeated.

"Greg?"

"No." He exaggerated the sounds. "Buh. Bruh. Braig."

She furrowed her eyebrows.

"It's like *Craig*, but with a *B* instead of a *C*."

"Oh, well, thank you for your note, Braig. Oh, I already said that, didn't I?"

Braig leaned farther away from her. He waved again, hoisting himself into the driver's seat, but she spoke again. And this time she spoke with such volume and clarity, there was no possible way of mishearing her or pretending he couldn't.

"Have you been to Turner Heat Steakhouse yet?"

"Yes," he said, sitting behind the wheel. "Well, no. Not to eat. I've been there to deliver, so sort of." He waved again and shifted the truck into reverse.

"Do you want to go?"

"Do I want to go? Go where?"

She laughed. "Turner Heat. Do you want to go eat there? Tonight?"

"I-I um, I—" The Pidge dinged. A loud beep that dragged on longer than usual. He glanced down at the device, snarled at it, and clenched his fists. Then he peeked back up at her. "Yes."

"Yes? You'll go? Tonight?"

"Yes," he said again. "I'll pick you up here at six-thirty. In my car—it's blue." Then he drove away, one-eleven still standing in the grass with an adorably shocked look on her face that made him smile.

"Wait. I just violated policy," he whispered. "What was I thinking?" The Pidge dinged again, loud and long in his ear. "Oh, that's right. I was thinking, *Don't tell me what to do, Mann.*"

Chapter 4

The door was cool as Ella leaned against it after a busy day of work, sweat beading on her face and neck. *Why did I hit on the delivery man? What have I done? What am I going to wear?*

Reeling with the fear that she was a cliché at best and a desperate spinster at worst, she couldn't help but repeat in her mind, *but he did say yes.*

"He obviously was taken with something about me, too, or he wouldn't have said yes." She gasped. "Or maybe I just shocked him. Surely he's been asked out before." She squeezed her eyes shut. "Candace was right. I have to stop over-thinking this."

She grabbed her phone. 5:40. She tapped until Candace's name popped up. Before one ring had completed, Candace's voice came through, obviously on speaker phone. "Ella, I was just about to call you. Look, I'm really sorry, but I didn't have a choice—"

Ella's phone vibrated her hand. The screen displayed a number she didn't recognize. "Candace, who's calling me?"

"It's Ritty. I know she was supposed to wait for you to

contact her, but she's got more ideas, and I wasn't sure what to tell her." Candace's voice increased in both volume and speed. "Please just let her get it all out. Maybe she'll calm down after that. Maybe?"

"Okay, I'll answer, but I still haven't decided what to wear on this date with the USSS guy."

"Stop stressing. Let that jumpsuit wow him."

"Thanks, girl."

Ella clicked over to the incoming call. "Hello?"

"Ella Morrison?" Each syllable was articulated with exaggerated propriety.

"Yes, this is Ella."

"This is Candace's Aunt Ritty. You can call me Aunt Ritty, too, if you'd like," she soothed. "Candace gave me your number because she couldn't answer my questions, and I couldn't find you on social media."

"Oh, I'm not on any social media. I was just about to send you a message. Thank you for offering to help with the wedding. It's very kind of you, and I know Candace really appreciates it." Ella rolled her eyes.

"Yes, dear. She is my only niece, after all. Was always lacking in taste, however, which is why I must step in. She's too much like my little sister."

"Oh ..." Ella responded dryly.

"Now, I'm sure Candace has told you about my tulle collection, which I don't mind at all sharing with you. Also, I've hired a chamber orchestra." Her voice took a more pacifying tone. "Don't worry, dear. I'm flying them in myself. 'Twill be my wedding gift to Candace and her new husband."

Ella cringed at the way she said *new husband*. Did she just use the word 'twill? "Oh, no, Aunt Ritty. I already booked a DJ."

"Yes. Candace mentioned it, but don't worry, I called and

canceled. No DJ will be necessary. Chamber music only. And ballroom dancing."

"Chamber music—"

Aunt Ritty interrupted. "Yes. And ballroom dancing. There will be a promenade with the wedding party, followed by a waltz with the bride and groom, and then the rest of the wedding party will take the floor after that for another waltz before the other guests are invited onto the floor. Would you like me to send you the list of songs? I assure you they are all traditional for a wedding, the way it should be."

Ella's voice shook. "Okay."

"Now," Ritty continued. "What is this about pork being served at the reception? Surely Candace is mistaken. It should be a choice between poultry and fish. You agree, don't you?"

"Umm." The beads of sweat returned.

When Ella finally hung up the phone, she only had twelve minutes to get ready for her date. More reason to dislike Aunt Ritty. She threw on another outfit, sprayed her hair in place and opened the door to see if Braig's blue car was in her driveway.

"Not yet." She closed the door, still flushed and warm. She glanced at her phone.

What if he changed his mind? What if he stands me up?

She paced, shook out her arms, and took some deep breaths. She froze when the faint sound of an engine purred from the front of the house. Her mind raced as she opened the door. *Should I wait for him to come to the door? He won't come onto the porch for deliveries, so maybe he wouldn't now either. What am I doing? I'm about to get in a stranger's car.*

Ella scolded herself all the way to his passenger side door.

He glanced up from his phone, obviously stunned she was in the car already. "Hi. I wasn't sitting here waiting for you. Umm ..."

She stared back at him.

"Uh ... Ella, right?"

He doesn't know my name? "Yes, Ella. And you're 'Buh, bruh, Braig.'" She smiled.

Braig chuckled as he put the car in reverse and slowly backed out of the driveway.

Discomfort and silence hung in the air as she shifted her weight and leaned close to the window. Was his vehicle smaller than most?

This was more awkward than a blind date. Braig cleared his throat for the third time but still said nothing. He kept his eyes on the road, glancing occasionally at her outfit. He cleared his throat again. "Ahem ... um, do you call that a pantsuit?"

She peered down at the dark green one-piece, covered in large cream and pink flowers and smiled. "Actually, it's called a jumpsuit."

"Mm-hmm." He nodded and returned to staring straight ahead. It wasn't a long drive to Turner Heat Steakhouse, but Ella wondered if he had gone the wrong way, because they had been sitting in this car for what felt like hours.

She peeked side-to-side, feeling odd. "So, how long have you worked for USSS?"

"A long time. Seven years."

She cleared her throat. "Do you love it?"

"Sometimes," he said.

"Only sometimes?"

"Well, most of the time the only people I interact with are my coworkers and my boss. When I'm driving, I communicate with my boss through a device called a Pidgeon. But," Braig hesitated before continuing, "every once in a while, a person will run to the door just after I've dropped a delivery. They'll grab it and yell *'thank you'* to me. It's like Christmas morning. What's not to love about that?"

"That's so sweet," Ella said.

"What about you? What do you do, and do you love it?"

"Oh, mine's not ever exciting. I work at Buskerton Orthodontics. Hey, vote for us in the Buskies."

Braig rolled his eyes. "Yeah, you vote for USSS too."

She laughed, tired of hearing about the Buskies.

"What is the big deal, right?" He asked.

"I know! Why is it life or death who wins a Buskie around here?"

He shook his head back and forth. "Everybody wants that banner."

They both chuckled until it faded out, and then a moment of silence passed before Ella echoed, "Everybody."

A sigh escaped her that sounded contented, even though she was anything but. They were drenched in awkward silence that grew heavier by the second. She forced herself to speak. "Look, I'm so embarrassed that I asked you out. I know you don't know me. I'm sorry. You can take me home and forget this."

"It's okay," he said, and smiled like something was funny.

"What?"

"You just apologized for asking me on a date, but I said yes, remember?"

"Yeah ..." She paused again. "Yeah, why *did* you say yes?"

He laughed. "Hmm. Why *did* I say yes?"

"That's my question."

"Look, Ella, I don't want to offend you before our date even really starts."

"What would offend me? Why did you say yes?"

"Okay, okay, I'll tell you *if* you promise to have dinner with me at Turner Heat, no matter what I say."

"What? Well, now I'm scared." She cackled, whether from

nerves or actually finding something funny, she wasn't sure. "Just tell me!"

Braig grinned, but kept cool. "Do you promise?"

"Fine."

"I mean, there's no reason to ruin this evening. We both need to eat, right? Right?"

"Sure."

"Okay, the reason I said yes, is because my boss is a jerk, and he told me yesterday that I have to stay away from you."

Ella did a double take. "Wait. Why would your boss tell you to stay away from me?" She leaned in closer, eyes wide. Penn. Did Penn start rumors about her?

He laughed again. "No, no, it's not … no, just listen. When I came back to your house and tackled the porch pirate, Mann—that's my boss—accused me of having a *thing* with a delivery recipient, namely you, because I spent more time on your street than I should have. Then he wagged his finger at me and said 'Stay away from that woman' or something like that." Braig's eyes filled with tears from laughing so hard.

Ella covered her face and shouted, "That's terrible!" through nervous giggles.

Braig sighed, still quite amused. "So, I had to say yes when you asked me." He paused as they arrived at Turner Heat. "Well, that, and you're so beautiful." He threw the gear shift into park and gripped the steering wheel with both hands, staring straight ahead.

Chapter 5

Braig couldn't take his eyes off the brick wall in front of him. Several seconds of cumbersome silence passed before Braig realized someone had to speak.

"So, um," he stammered as he fumbled to get out of the car. "Uh, shall we?"

She opened her door before he could, so he grabbed the handle to help open it all the way. It was a glaringly unnecessary action. As she stood and fell in step beside him, Braig was thankful the sun had not quite set over the square. It provided light to better admire her jumpsuit.

The sound of a piano paired with a saxophone trill grew louder as they passed the pair of Buskers. Braig nodded a greeting and dropped a few dollars into their baskets. The pair acknowledged him with nods of their own.

Braig extended his elbow and Ella slipped her arm through, both intoxicated by the harmonies behind them, and they stepped in time to the music all the way to the entrance of Turner Heat Steakhouse.

He swung open the heavy glass door at the entrance of the restaurant. Once inside, Ella approached the host station, and the Maître d' smiled. "Ms. Morrison. Wonderful to see you again." He enveloped both her hands in his.

"Jorge, you work too hard. Are you full time here and at the Towers?"

"Ah, just helping to open up the place, as a favor to Mr. Turner. Now, allow me to ensure the table is ready for you both." He nodded at Braig and disappeared.

Ella turned to Braig. "I don't think I've ever seen two Buskers playing together. That was lovely."

"Sometimes they have to. Those two, Hank and Seamus, always fight over that corner. Occasionally they just give in and work together." He shrugged. "Hank's a former truck driver, and Seamus is a military man. They kind of bonded being the oldest Buskers in Buskerton. The rest are young folks trying to get discovered. Do you know who Juliana is?"

"I don't think so. How do you know so much about the Buskers?"

"Another USSS driver befriends every single one of the Buskers and keeps up with them even after they leave. She tells me everything. Did you know Seamus lugs that full-sized keyboard of his three blocks every morning and every night to and from his apartment? He calls it his baby."

Ella's eyes crinkled with amusement.

Braig nodded toward the dining room. "This place is so fancy. Fancier than the kitchen, that's for sure."

A server with a white tuxedo shirt and black slacks approached them. "This way, please."

They followed, and the melodic sounds from outside faded into the light elevator music track that was playing in the restaurant. They settled in on either side of a small two-seater booth at the edge of the room, and the server recited the drink menu and the specials. He raved on and on about their *signature steak*, but Braig said, "I'll take the chicken."

Ella ordered the shrimp, and when the server walked away, she said, "You cringed a little bit when he said steak."

"Did I? I just don't like it. I don't know why anyone eats it."

"Me, either. I can never chew it. Even when someone else says they're eating the best steak ever, I'll ask for a bite sometimes, because I think *surely* there's something I'm missing, but no. It's gross to me every time."

"Me too!"

They high-fived across the table, and when their hands were both back in their laps, they laughed at the silliness of high-fiving on a date—especially at the fanciest restaurant in town.

Ella's irises shimmered in the candlelight. He leaned closer, holding her gaze and trying to identify the color. Realizing the awkwardness, he quickly cleared his throat and repositioned in his seat. "So, what are all the packages for?"

Ella blinked. "Oh, the packages? I'm planning my friend Candace's wedding. There's so much to do. It's kind of taken over my life for the past couple of months."

"So, you're a wedding planner on the side?"

"No, just for Candace and Simon." Ella touched each fork, starting with the one closest to the place setting, straightening them to perfect alignment.

"Wait, not Simon Sanborn. The wedding the weekend after next? At Turner Towers?"

Ella glanced up from the forks. "Yes, you know them?"

Braig laughed. "Not Candace, just Simon." He stuck his hand across the table. "Braig Sanborn, nice to meet you." She shook it and laughed along. "Simon's my cousin."

"And you've never met Candace?"

"He brought her to Christmas last year, but I haven't really gotten to know her. I love my cousins, but I'm not that close with them. So ... if you're planning the wedding, you addressed the envelopes, huh?"

"Yes, but I would have remembered a Brai–" she covered her mouth and shut her eyes.

He nodded.

"I thought it was a typo, and I changed it to Craig."

"Yeah, I know."

"I'm sorry."

"I'm used to it." He smiled. It didn't matter what this girl called him. He wouldn't mind, even though when Mann called him Greg, he could spit nails. This was different. Ella was different.

Ella still flushed even as two servers swooped in, placing salads in front of them with a flourish along with a small loaf of bread.

"Thank you," Braig said in response, then to Ella, "Do you mind if I pray?"

"No, of course not," She kept her hands under the table.

After the prayer, Braig reached for his salad fork, as Ella shuffled through her buzzing purse.

"Oh, I'm sorry I have to take this." Ella held her phone to her ear. After several moments of *I see*, and *okay*, and a stressed *bye for now*, she hung up, her breathing quicker than before she answered the phone.

"Everything all right?" Braig asked setting his fork back on the table.

"I don't know. It's Aunt Ritty. She's staying with me, and she'll be at my house next Friday." She glanced down at her phone once more. "Ah, there's Candace trying to warn me." Her laugh did not sound amused.

"You don't want your aunt to stay with you?"

"She's not my aunt!" Ella blurted out then paused before continuing. "She's Candace's aunt. I—I don't even know her.

All of a sudden, she's decided she's going to help with the wedding. We're down to two weeks, and she's changing things now?"

"What is she changing?"

Ella nibbled at her salad while she prattled about the DJ, the dancing, the tulle, and how Aunt Ritty wanted to monkey around with the seating arrangement. When their entrees arrived, Ella sighed and then blushed. "I just unloaded a lot on you."

"It's okay." He meant it.

"Has anyone ever told you you're easy to talk to?"

He shook his head again, unsure.

"So, your turn to talk." She changed the subject. "Where do you go to church?"

"How do you know I go to church?"

"The prayer."

"Oh, yeah. I go to Main Street." He smiled. "Do you go?"

"I do. Southside."

They both nodded.

He tried to remain attentive but was mesmerized by her eyes. Can you stare into someone's eyes for an extended period of time on a first date and it not be weird? Braig didn't care. He continued to study her eyes *What color are they?*

After they exhausted the topic of church, discussing their preachers, congregation size, the missionaries each one supports, and how often they taught Sunday school, Braig cleared his throat. Their food was gone, and Ella had taken care of the check, much to Braig's surprise. The silence and awkwardness settled in again. He let his eyes drift to the round table nearest them. An older couple sat together, chairs close. Whereas most people would sit directly across, these two had scooted until they were side by side. *Surely I could say something about that. How romantic, perhaps? Or, would you ever sit like that in a restaurant, Ella?*

But when he opened his mouth, the words, "Ready to go?" came out.

As the large glass door was closing behind them, a voice from within shouted, "Vote for Turner Heat in the Buskies!" Ella and Braig stopped and rolled their eyes at each other.

"You know, I might be a rebel and not vote at all," he said.

"I think I'll vote for the other orthodontist in town," Ella retorted.

THE PORCH LIGHT clicked on when Braig walked Ella to her steps, illuminating the porch he had never stood on as well as the reason. "What kind of dog do you have?" He asked her, still standing on the walkway.

"I don't." There was concession in her voice, as if admitting a secret she didn't want to explain. Braig glanced from the dog door back to Ella's face and she did the same.

"Will you tell me about it?"

She nodded slowly. "I had a dog. Well, *we* had a dog."

Braig pressed his weight into his heels and crossed his arms at the sound of the word *we*.

"His name was Lloyd."

"*Whose* name was Lloyd?"

"My dog. Imagine a St. Bernard that's completely snowy white with pale blue eyes that always look pitifully sad." She chuckled. "That was Lloyd."

She moved in the direction of the door, as if discussing it drew her nearer. Braig hesitated, even though there was no more reason to worry about a dog rushing out to attack him. On the porch, she turned to face Braig as he slowly ascended as well. It was strange to be standing there, a place he had been so scared to be, so many times. And now here he was, not dropping off packages, but something much lovelier. "It was Christmas morning. I had just turned eighteen. I had begged my parents for a dog for years, and they never relented." She pushed a pillow out of the way to sit on the porch swing, and he didn't stop to ponder if that was an invitation or not. He sat at the other end. "Then, when I least expected it, there was this perfect little puppy, bouncing all over the living room, peeing on my dad's new shoes."

"So, he was a good dog, huh?"

"He was more than that. He was the last gift I ever got from my parents."

Braig folded his hands in his lap. "I'm sorry."

"Thanks," she sniffed. "My dad got shingles and they progressed fast. Then, not long after Dad passed, my mom caught a cold that turned into bronchitis, which turned into pneumonia, and so on and so forth."

"I think that's what they call dying of a broken heart."

Ella nodded. "She couldn't live without him. For a while I thought I wouldn't be able to, either. But I had Lloyd, and this house." She gestured toward the front door. "That's all that's left of them."

Braig rested his back on the swing. "When did Lloyd die?"

She scoffed. "He didn't die. He abandoned me, just like my parents did. He ran away." She shook her head. "I installed that stupid dog door after he was gone. I put it there just in case he ever decides to come home."

"Maybe one day he will." He grabbed her hand and squeezed, then let go. "Have you ever read Romans 8?"

Ella's eyebrows quirked.

"I'm sure you have. Our preacher delivered a sermon on it recently. There's a part in that chapter that talks about how we've received the spirit of adoption, and we're children of God and joint heirs with Christ. Sound familiar?"

"Sure."

"Well, he read a few of the verses from another translation. It wasn't one I was used to, but I remember a line from it. 'All who are led by God's Spirit are God's sons and daughters.'"

Ella held eye contact with him for a moment, as if pondering his meaning.

"My point is that you're still a daughter. I am sympathetic to your losing your parents. It's terrible, and I can't imagine it. But you're still someone's precious daughter."

She reached out and squeezed his hand but didn't let go as quickly this time.

After a pause and another awkward moment when he wasn't sure what to say, he stood. "Thanks for dinner, really."

"Thanks for going." She rose, too, but stayed near the swing as he moved toward the steps.

"Okay."

"Okay."

He waved, thanked her again, opened the door to his car, and before he realized what was happening, he drove away from Agapi drive. He didn't want to. He wanted to stay, but had run out of conversation topics—maybe he should make a list.

What would not be on the list, however, was the first thing he should have told her. That in three weeks, he was moving over a thousand miles away from Buskerton.

Chapter 6

After an agonizing fifteen minutes, Ella settled on her light green slick jacket, wedge pump sandals, and no umbrella. The jacket had a hood she could flip up if the drizzle escalated and threatened to mess her hair.

Main Street's church building was a different layout than Southside. Large red brick instead of small white clapboard. People filed in, tapped their shoes on the rug, shook out their umbrellas or other rain gear, and made their ways into the sanctuary. A few greeted her, and she waved at Trish, a Buskerton Ortho patient. She hesitated in the entry. Perhaps Braig was already seated, so she scanned the backs of heads. Where did he usually sit?

"Hello there." An older lady, short bluish-tinted hair, smiled with her eyes and voice at the same time. "My name is Jeanie. What's yours, dear?"

"Oh, hi. I'm Ella."

Jeanie pursed her lips as if she was trying to hide a grin. "Very nice to meet you. Can I help you find a seat?"

Ella glanced back once more. No Braig.

"Well, sure. I guess that would be fine. Thank you so much." She followed Jeanie to the front. "Oh, you sit close."

Jeanie nodded. "Here, sit by me."

Another ortho patient ran up to her and said hi. While Ella was visiting, she spied Jeanie watching the entrance too. *Who is she waiting for?* Jeanie alternated between watching the back door and gazing down at her phone as she texted furiously. Ella took one last look at the door as the congregation stood to sing.

After the first song, Ella stopped turning to look at the door, and when the preacher took the pulpit, she gave up on the idea of sitting in church with Braig.

Ella found herself engrossed and wondering why she had never made the trek across town to visit Main Street.

"As one of the most influential figures in all of human history," the preacher spoke with passion, "it is a worthwhile use of your time to learn about the life of Jesus Christ—a life lived drawing from a deep well that will never run dry. It's a focused life, church. Jesus knows why He's there and He knows what He has to do. Do we know why we're here and what we have to do? Or are we distracted day in and day out with our own entertainment?"

He paused and gave the congregation a slow, sweeping glare. "Competition?" Another glare. "Is it more important to us to carry out the will of God the Father, or to be the best among our peers? What is your focus and what *drives* you? Is it recognition here on earth? Is it a prize that you're striving to receive from man? Or is it that crown of life? Is it the hearing of the words *well done, good and faithful servant* as you stand before your Creator in the last day?" His voice rose as he asked his last question.

Convicting. Ella forgot about Braig.

"Turn to John chapter seven," The preacher continued. "I

don't know if you remember, but Jesus healed someone on the Sabbath here. Can you believe it? Those surrounding him couldn't. The Sabbath day was about peace and rest and remembrance of how God worked to make everything, but all the religious leaders of the day cared about was the imposing of the rule. Control. Not healing and peace, which is what the Sabbath was all about. Those religious leaders missed the forest for the trees. What they were doing wasn't for God's glory. What was their motivation?"

He paused flipping the Bible's page. "It was appearances. In verse twenty-four, Jesus charged them to stop. Do not judge by appearances, but judge with righteous judgment! Because appearances can be deceiving, church."

Did no one else feel the conviction and the charge this preacher laid down? She squirmed as he continued. *He's talking about the Buskies.* Those banners were the end all, be all—the world to some of these people.

"We live in a world obsessed with appearances. We're obsessed with it, church! Instead of waving a flag saying, I am the best, glorifying self and putting forth an appearance of holiness, righteousness, and even perfection, are we showing the Father, every day in our lives and letting his glory shine through us? *His* glory, church, that's what we should be seeking to show others."

Ella shivered. She had never experienced a sermon opposing the Buskies.

"And what about when our appearance, the thing that we work so hard to uphold, crumbles? What about when we don't," he paused, "win?"

Ella's mouth actually opened as her jaw became heavy.

"When we lose, church, how do we react? Do we lose our peace? If Jesus is the Lord of your life, if He's the Lord of my life, our peace is secure. We know we have eternal life! No matter what man may think of us. It's not about me. It's not about you. It's all about God and what He can do. It's how He is the best, not any human."

When the sermon was over and they stood once again, Ella found her feet heavy. She had joked about the Buskies. That banner didn't mean much to her, but what about other appearances? There could be any number of other ways she wanted to be presented as perfect to everyone on the outside—even throwing the perfect wedding, *her* way and not Ritty's.

Jeanie's voice cut through her thoughts. "I'm so glad you came today, Ella."

"Thanks so much for letting me sit with you. Is this guy such a powerhouse every Sunday?" She asked.

"He's good, right? He gets fired up around Buskie time." She chuckled. "He keeps our heads out of the clouds, that's for sure. Did you come to hear our preacher specifically?"

Ella hesitated. "Actually, I was trying to visit a ... friend. Do you know Braig Sanborn?"

"Yes, I do. He attended Southside this morning."

Ella stopped, the corners of her mouth slowly turning upward. "He's at Southside? Right now?"

"Right now. I know you're going to be in a hurry to meet up with him for lunch, but let me tell you a story before you go? Come on, I'll walk you out."

Ella turned shoulder to shoulder with Jeanie.

"I was a mermaid, long ago," she began. "On the boardwalk of Aspaldiko Island, there were about ten of us, and we fiercely protected each other. There were rules. Most people were nice, but there were some creeps who came around. We weren't supposed to date anyone who came to the boardwalk, but we all broke that rule. Then, one day, Rita, one of the girls, fell *hard* for a patron." Jeanie scoffed. "A patron. A passerby, really. He showed up one time and that was all it took. For whatever reason, call it chemical, she was hooked on him." Jeanie waved at a couple loading small children into their minivan, but stayed tuned into Ella. "None of the rest of us understood it. We saw a man who was shifty, cagey. So, we pooled our money, and we had him followed."

"Oh?" Ella was still trying to process *I was a mermaid.*

"Like I said, we protected each other out there. We had to."

"Did you find out anything about him?"

"We found out that he was in a dirty business, and he wanted Rita to work for him."

"Did you tell her before she got caught up in it?"

"We sure did, and we had the evidence to show her." She sighed. "Rita was fine, eventually. Although that girl did go through some hardships in her life. It's just like Satan to take our strengths and try to turn them into weaknesses."

Ella fell silent.

"Those of us who love the deepest and the fastest, have the greatest capacity to be hurt by those we give our hearts to." Jeanie breathed a heavy sigh. "But Rita became one of the toughest women I've ever known. Don't worry about her, though. It was the *man* who had the sad story." They reached Ella's white Toyota and stopped walking. "It's not *poor Rita.*" Jeanie turned to face her. "It's poor *creep.* You know why?"

Ella shook her head.

"He didn't have *me* standing behind him." Jeanie smirked.

"Okay ..." Ella's voice trilled nervously. "Well, thank you for letting me sit with you this morning. It was a wonderful service, and so nice to meet you." Then she smiled politely and left, head spinning.

Was that a threat or a promise?

Chapter 7

At the final amen, Braig immediately stood to leave, eager to message Ella and laugh about their blunder. He stepped into the parking lot and noted the rain had cleared. Braig punched Ella's name and held the phone to his ear. "Hi," came the greeting, obvious elation behind it.

"Hi," he repeated, too overcome with surprise and pleasure at the fact that she went to his church this morning. His turf. She sat with his friend, his work mom, his mermaid. Did Ella really make friends with *his* Jeanie?

"Um, so," she stammered. "We obviously both wanted to see each other today."

"Yeah. We did." Before Braig could suggest lunch or maybe a walk, Ella surprised him yet again.

"Well, now that you've seen my church, can I show you a few other places around town you may not be familiar with?"

"Of course. I have a few spots we could visit too. Is that okay?"

"Meet me in the park first. I'll bring lunch."

When Braig arrived, he couldn't help but whistle on the

way to the grassy knoll where Ella sat on a blanket, unpacking a picnic basket.

She showed him an array of salads—chicken, pasta, potato, and broccoli.

"Looks great. Thanks for doing this." He leaned on his arm and admired her red and white polka dotted sundress. The sky was a deep bluish gray from the rain that morning, a backdrop she fit beautifully in front of. "Hey," he said, looking from the sky to her face, and back again. "I found it."

"Found what?"

"The color of your eyes. There." He nodded toward the dusky sky behind her.

She blushed. "Oh."

He nibbled the cracker she had spread chicken salad on. Then, not wanting the awkwardness of their last date, he asked, "Why aren't you on social media?"

"Is my absence that obvious?"

He laughed. "I can't find you anywhere."

She sighed. "It's because of Mother's Day. I used to be bombarded with posts about moms on Mother's Day. And Father's Day too. All the pictures people constantly post about their parents—I don't want to see them. I found myself angry all the time. It's like I wasn't allowed to grieve. So, I deleted everything. And I'm happier now."

"I'm not going to pressure you to, but If you did ever want to get back on social media, I'd be there for you."

She huffed. "What do you mean?"

"You just need a soft place to land, that's all." He trailed the back of his forefinger down her arm.

"Thank you. I'll remember that."

"THANKS FOR GOING on this adventure with me," he said as they drove around town. "I've got a few places I want to show you, if we have time."

On the way to Jeanie's house, Braig caught sight of a blue and white truck. He made a sound of disgust and released Ella's hand to grip the steering wheel.

"What?"

"It's Natex. Just the sight of their trucks makes my stomach turn."

Ella shifted her gaze and furrowed her brow. "What's wrong with them?"

"Oh nothing," he grumbled. "Just their pleated pants and white button-ups that always stay white, and ..." He made another sick sound. "Their name." He scoffed. "Natex. It sounds like *latex*. What a dumb name."

"Yes, you're right," Ella said in mock agreement. "Ussss ..." She stuck her neck out and exaggerated a hissing noise. "That's a much better sounding name."

She stifled a laugh but failed to hold it in, and he couldn't help but join her.

Once at Jeanie's house, he parked in front so Ella would have the best view. "This is it. What do you think?"

Big, old, and lovely, the house was surrounded by mature trees. Ella was entranced. "This is the mermaid's house? She was so nice to me, although I think she may have threatened me with a story on the way out of church."

Braig chuckled. "Just wait until she gets to know you. She's the most devoted work mom and friend ever."

He considered mentioning her retirement, but then his transfer might slip out, and the day was too wonderful to ruin. Instead, he told Ella about the time Jeanie won the Biggest Loser contest at work, and how she had never been happier than when she gained the weight back.

At dusk, when they'd finished seeing Buskerton through each other's eyes, he parked on the square outside his favorite bakery. As they sat inside nibbling on muffins and fruit for dinner and finding out more about their families, their pasts, and their dreams, a mesmerizing sound filtered in.

"Oh, which Busker is that?" Ella asked.

"That's Juliana and her guitar. Wonderful, right? Want to get closer?"

"Let's go," she agreed.

Out on the sidewalk, Braig stopped in front of her. Not too close to be invasive, but the perfect distance, and he held out his hand. "May I have this dance?"

Chapter 8

Not a day passed that Ella didn't hear from Braig. Just hearing his voice brightened her days. She hummed as she pulled into her driveway after work, even though Aunt Ritty was already there, sitting in a brand new, latte-colored Jeep, three hours early. Even that couldn't dim Ella's good mood.

She extended her hand to the woman when they were both out of their cars. Aunt Ritty had a mane like Ella had never seen. Silver curls, wild, but perfectly coiled, as they hung past her shoulders. Her rectangular glasses sat on the edge of her nose as she greeted Ella in a formal way, shook her hand lightly, then walked past.

"Let's get started, then," Ritty said, waiting by the front door for Ella to unlock it. Her first stop inside were the piles of boxes in the living room. She inspected each one, not asking permission first. "Not much to see here," she said, and then, "I'll unload my car first. Then you can show me to my room."

"Sure thing, Aunt Ritty." Ella answered, stunned and striving to be gracious in the face of this brash woman. Ritty would get along great with Sherr. Ella had to remind herself she had practice with Sherr's abrupt, all-about-business personality.

After Aunt Ritty had carried in all the boxes and had proclaimed herself settled in the guest room, Ella suggested they go into the kitchen. A few bags sat on the counter. "Oh, what's this?"

Aunt Ritty began unpacking them. "Don't you worry about dinner." She pulled out some fresh produce, pasta, oils, and spices. "You'll be doing me a favor, because I love to cook in the face of stress."

Ella sat on a barstool at the kitchen island watching Ritty work. When pots bubbled, and the scents of oregano and garlic floated throughout the house, Ella could resist no longer. Was it rude to ask what color someone's hair used to be before it turned gray? Who cared? With the brazenness this woman could dole out, she should be able to take it.

"What color did your curls used to be?"

Aunt Ritty piled a plate high with saucy chicken on a bed of pasta and set it in front of Ella, with a dressed salad on the side and fruity tea in a glass, garnished with an umbrella.

"These curls?" Aunt Ritty stretched out a lock of hair and let it bounce back. "Or the hair I was born with?"

"You weren't born with curly hair?"

"Oh, heavens no."

"It's a perm?" Ella had never seen such a natural-looking perm before.

"These are mine, but they weren't always. I was born with red hair, stick straight. Then, when I had breast cancer, it all fell out, and I was bald as a newborn baby for a while. I worried it would never grow back."

"You had cancer?" Ella breathed.

"I did. Kicked its tail too. With God's help, of course. The chemo made me lose it all, and I thought my life was over, literally, when that happened."

Ella didn't touch her food.

"Finally, when the cancer was gone, my hair started to grow back, slowly at first—chestnut brown with the tightest curls I'd ever seen. Then it went gray, but the curls stayed, and I refused to cut them off and look my age."

"I don't blame you." Ella finally dug into the lovely dinner Aunt Ritty had prepared. "This is wonderful."

"It's wonderful that you're allowing me to stay here—and help with my niece's wedding." Then, after taking a few bites, Aunt Ritty sighed. "You know, being a woman is tough."

"It sure is."

"I mean, even after I had lost every single strand of hair on my head, I'll never forget, I still had to shave my legs. How unfair is that?"

Ella laughed, and Aunt Ritty joined in.

"The pictures don't do the venue justice." Aunt Ritty commented as she stacked picture frames on Ella's kitchen table. "Well done. And that Jorge is a charmer. What a treat to meet him."

"I'm glad he let you take a quick tour this morning. You're right, it's beautiful. Um ... what's all this?"

Aunt Ritty glanced around for an outlet to plug in her glue guns. "Oh, this? Well, what if, instead of the pillar candles in the hurricane lanterns, we use pebbles—I have a whole box of them—for the centerpieces. Not only that, but I have several dozen four-by-four photographs of the couple, and with these frames, we can add some tealight holders to offset them. What do you think?"

A cheerful knock drew Ella's attention away for a moment. "I'm not sure if I can picture that exactly," she said as she opened the door. Braig. Her hero.

Bidding him to follow, they returned to the kitchen. "Um, Aunt Ritty, this is Braig. He's here to help if he can."

"Lovely to meet you." Ritty's glasses slid down her nose. "Have a seat."

Ella avoided eye contact with Braig and stifled a grin. Aunt Ritty demonstrated gluing the framed photographs of Candace and Simon edge to edge, forming a square to set the tealight candle in.

"Think you two can handle this?" she said, and unloaded her boxes of tulle to compare their lengths with the measurements she had taken that morning.

After methodically following Ritty's instructions and finishing four tealight holders, Braig leaned toward Ella. "Whose church should we go to tomorrow? We don't want to make the same mistake as last week."

Blushing, wondering how he read her mind, she responded, "Let's go to yours. I like your preacher." They smiled at each other, then Ritty's voice made them jump.

"Enough with the goo-goo eyes, you two. Back to work."

They giggled and returned their focus to the frames, pictures, and glue.

Chapter 9

The whole town buzzed with excitement about the Buskies. Even the Buskers themselves, who were never included in the awards, could feel and were utilizing the energy, performing with passion on their corners. It all could have been enjoyable for Braig if his Pidge didn't ding incessantly. He tossed it in the seat next to him. He would hear about it later, but on this lovely Monday morning, he had a little white box with two muffins in it, and he was going to take a few minutes to make a pit stop.

He whistled as he turned onto Agapi Drive. When the beige siding of her house should have come into view, however, another sight did instead–a large, white and powder blue truck. Natex? What is she having delivered by Natex? The truck blocked the view of her front porch, so he slowed. When it was visible, he expected to see a delivery driver dropping a package, or the driver taking a picture with his device—the one that made a sound like an ice cream truck singing—nothing irritating or maddening like the Pidge. But it wasn't either of those. There was no package, not that Braig could detect.

Instead, standing there, on Ella's porch, was the Ex.

The same one he ran into in the Turner Heat Steakhouse kitchen. The one with the blond hair and the pleated pants and the perfectly starched white shirt. The *tall* one. Standing on the porch that Braig had only had the guts to step onto after he learned there was no dog. The porch where he hoped to kiss Ella. The Ex stood there with Ella in his arms.

Braig drove on, careful not to hit the gas and draw attention to himself. Facing front, blocking out anything that might try to invade his peripheral. The image of Ella and the Ex locked in an embrace was burned in his mind. It wasn't a friendly hug. There was something meaningful about it, that was clear. Romantic.

Braig's knuckles white-gripped the steering wheel. Were they swaying back and forth? "She's in a relationship with that guy." Braig scowled.

His lunch break would not be used to call Ella today, or text Ella, or if he could help it, think about Ella. He made his first delivery, mustering a smile when the recipient waved, then his second, and his third, but the image of his girl—obviously *not* his—in the arms of the Ex—refused to be shaken.

At ten a.m., a *good morning* text came through, and he powered down his phone.

After the morning deliveries, which were all nothing short of grueling, Braig pulled into the garage and parked the truck, not taking the time to make sure it was square between his designated lines. He made his way upstairs and into the breakroom, where Jeanie waited for him.

"I was hoping you'd be here for lunch today. I got you something special." She lifted the lid on a steaming bowl of pasta with cream sauce.

Braig plopped in the chair. "I'm here for lunch every day."

"That's not true. Friday, you spent your whole break on the

phone with Ella, remember? I guess it's too soon to do that every day, huh?"

"That's not going to happen again. Ever."

"Oh, no. What happened? You two broke up already?"

"There was nothing to break up," he said defensively. "She has a boyfriend."

"Really? Because I thought she came to the Main Street church looking for her boyfriend." When he remained quiet, she passed him a napkin and patted his back. "How'd you find out about the other guy?"

So Braig relayed to her every single detail, not touching his pasta. The compulsion to see her without plans, like a lovesick teenager, the Natex truck, the complete naivety, not suspecting for a moment that she would be making out with that guy.

"Wait a minute." Jeanie sounded confused. "Were they making out, or was it a hug? Let's keep the story straight here, okay?"

"It was more than a hug, trust me, Jeanie. It was a ... lingering embrace." He shuddered. "What was that about? And what was he doing there first thing in the morning? Did he spend the night?"

"I don't have answers about any of that, but can I tell you a story?" She twirled her own pasta on a fork.

For the first time, Braig had no desire to hear one of Jeanie's mermaid stories.

"Just relax and listen." She patted his back again. "I know I've mentioned that on Aspaldiko Island, there were some regulations we had to follow, most of which we all broke," she said out of the corner of her mouth as if it was a secret, then laughed heartily. "But there was one rule that was never to be broken. One rule we had to sign off on every year. Really, they made us sign our names on a dotted line promising we would never break this one rule."

Braig glanced at her inquisitively.

"We were to never bring in a shill."

His brow furrowed further. "A shill?"

"You know—a stooge. A con artist." She shook her head. "Well, why were we all there? All the mermaids were working the boardwalk and swimming those waters, not to be immortalized in photographs with tourists on their mantles for the rest of our lives. We were there to be discovered for other endeavors. Pictures, for example. We all wanted it, few of us got it, but *one*. Whew." Jeanie shook her head as if still in disbelief. "Bertha Higgenbotham." She shook her head some more. "Bertha was so determined, from day one, that she was going to be discovered and given a job in New York or L.A. So determined, she would do anything. She also wasn't *scared* of anyone, certainly not any of the girls telling on her. So, she brought in someone at least once a week, but especially if she thought a scout would be on the dock that day. Friends of hers, her uncle, a neighbor, her boyfriend even came through once acting like a hotshot director interested in her as the next big-screen sensation. We couldn't prove it, but we all suspected she paid a few of them too."

Ella squinted. "To do what? Did they just come around and give her attention?"

Jeanie threw her head back with laughter. "Oh, it was so much more than that, It was a spectacle. They came through with cameras around their necks—capital *F*—flirting with Bertha and Bertha alone. Taking her picture and talking to anyone who would listen about what a natural beauty she was." Jeanie focused on her food again for a moment. "I mean, it wasn't a lie. She was stunning, but it was breaking the one hard and fast, most important rule of the boardwalk, and she did it unapologetically."

Braig realized he was closer to the edge of his seat than a few minutes before. "Well? Did she get a job in pictures?"

"Are you kidding? She went on to be an absolute starlet. One of Hollywood's sweethearts. She had an unshakeable reputation as being the girl next door. Everyone loved her, and I mean everyone."

"Can you name a few movies she was in?"

"Oh, let me think. I could name them all if you give me enough time." She gazed at the ceiling. "The Chaperone's Heist, Jane and Orion, Misfit Island?"

He shook his head. "Must've been before my time."

"Oh, it undoubtedly was, but still, she was huge. She had everything we all thought we wanted."

Braig scoffed. "Unbelievable. Some people have all the luck, even when they're disgusting individuals, right?"

Jeanie chuckled. "That's not my point, Braig."

He wiped his mouth and sat back in his chair. "Here we go." He cut his eyes to her. "What's your point then, Jeanie?" He deadpanned at her.

"Appearances can be deceiving."

Chapter 10

Lloyd jumped on the bed and nuzzled Ella awake. She crooned at the St. Bernard, his fur white as snow again after the bath she gave him last night.

"Good morning, sweet boy. It's been too long." She rubbed his ears and the sides of his neck. "I wish I didn't have to go to work, but I'll play with you when I get home. You behave, and don't you go anywhere, do you hear me?"

She grabbed her phone and immediately opened the thread she had going with Penn.

She snapped a picture of Lloyd smiling and sent it to Penn. Then she navigated to Braig's name. Odd, still nothing. He never responded to her message Monday morning. Should she send another text? Was that too desperate?

Ella wanted to tell him all about Lloyd's return, but doing so would mean having to explain Penn. While her ex-boyfriend was now a brother-figure, he was a Natex driver, and therefore Braig's natural enemy. Braig was determined that USSS was so much better, even though Penn described the Natex garage like a brotherhood more than a workplace.

She hugged Lloyd around the neck and thanked him for coming home, for being found. For still loving her and never stopping. "You're all I've got," she whispered to him.

When she trudged downstairs with Lloyd at her heels, Aunt Ritty was already in the kitchen, silver curls wild and tossed over the top of her head. She bent down to Lloyd when he ran to her. "Hi there! Who's a good boy? Who's a good boy?"

"Thanks for watching him while I've been at work this week, Aunt Ritty."

"No problem at all. We love our walks every day, don't we, boy?" She scratched underneath his neck, and he melted into the tile floor. "Thanks for letting me stay with you. Which reminds me. I left some money on the counter over there to cover the expenses."

"Aunt Ritty, you've filled my house with food, checked off almost every task on my wedding to-do list, dog sat every day. You don't have to pay me."

"Nonsense. It's the least I can do. You've been more than gracious." She stood and continued to tickle Lloyd's belly with her socked toes. "Has Braig responded yet?"

Ella let her face fall into her hands on the counter. "No. I don't understand how someone can go from hot to cold so fast?"

Aunt Ritty flipped her curls to the other side and poured Ella a cup of coffee. "There's no way to know." She paused and handed her the cup. "Unless you ask him."

"How? He won't talk to me."

"When people act like this, there's always a reason." She sipped from her own cup and contemplated. "He seems like such a good Christian man. There's just got to be a reason he's ignoring you."

"I'm sorry to put this on you, Aunt Ritty. The wedding is in three days. We have to get through the rehearsal dinner tomorrow night, then I'll take care of the bachelorette party. Thank you for your help in planning that too. Sherr is just too busy with the office and getting votes for the Buskies." She sighed at the thought of the awards. "Well, I'll go get ready for work now. Thanks for taking care of everything today. You're touching base with the florist, right?"

"Yes, ma'am, and I'm calling to confirm arrival times with the caterer, minister, and photographer."

Ella struggled to pull herself into a standing position and up the stairs.

"And don't worry about Lloyd," Aunt Ritty called after her. "Don't worry about anything, sweetie."

THE GLASS DOORS of Buskerton Ortho opened and closed continuously all day. Sherr instructed the staff to fill this day as much as possible with appointments, and every client was to hear the word *vote* at least three times during their visit—arrival, during exam, and checkout.

Aunt Ritty's words rang in Ella's head as she found a moment to check her email, then her texts, hoping for a message from Braig. Nothing. She tightened her sweater and rubbed her arms. She asked Candace twice if it was cold in the office, but Candace assured her the thermostat was set to the same temperature as always.

Ella froze as a father with his children left without being reminded a third time to vote. The door between reception and the waiting area flew open as Sherr raced through the small crowd and out the front.

Oh no. She's doing my job for me. I'll never hear the end of this.

A giggle from behind Ella caught her attention away from the glass doors and her soon-to-be scolding. Candace sidled up next to her. "I've never seen Sherr move that fast."

"What's so funny?"

"Don't you know who's out there? Around the corner?"

"No. Didn't she run out there to remind that last family to vote for us in the Buskies?"

"Ella, you *have* been distracted this week. What has this guy done to you?" She lowered her voice. "Come here." Candace led her out of the reception area and to the back door of the building. She cracked it as quietly as she could and let Ella peek out. "Shhh!" she hissed and pulled Ella back in, as Ella stifled a squeal.

"Are you kidding? Sherr and Penn? When did this happen?"

"I mean, could there be a better match than the best man and the maid of honor?" Candace asked, a huge grin on her face. "Simon and I had them over to my apartment a few weeks ago, and here we are," she said proudly.

"You did this? Good girl!" Ella tapped her shoulder. "And perfect timing, right?"

"I know. At least Sherr isn't acting like a psycho about the Buskies today." They laughed and went back to reception, but even the joy of seeing two people Ella loved so happy in each other's arms, couldn't help her shake off how much Ella missed Braig.

A few minutes later, Sherr effervesced through the office, her high ponytail bouncing. "Ella, you can take your lunch now if you want."

Ella smiled, never having seen Sherr so happy. She carried her lunch bag to the bench out front, where it was warmer. Patients came and went, but her eyes glazed, not really paying attention to them, staring at a phone that was not ringing. She clicked on her recent calls and scrolled down to Braig's name, then dumped her entire lunch on the ground when the screen read, "calling." Had she bumped his name with her thumb? *Should I end the call?* She panicked and couldn't decide.

"Hello." His voice was cool and professional. It was not the warm, caring voice she was used to. It was not the voice she missed and had been dreaming about all week.

"Hi, Braig."

"Hi," he responded. Still cool. She stumbled over her words, asking how he was, receiving nothing but an *okay*. Ella was stymied, without a clue about what to say.

"Look, Ella," he said almost forcefully. "I should have told you this before, but I'm being transferred. Out of state. I leave in a couple weeks."

It took her a few minutes of stammering and staring blankly before she started crying. The conversation was short and to the point, just like their whirlwind courtship. That had reached its dead end long before she wanted it to. Long before it should have.

"Hey, wait a minute," she spoke with just as much force as he had. "You know we have to see each other at the wedding Saturday. I understand it won't be the same, but I've already had Aunt Ritty rearrange the seats so we're together."

He was silent for a moment. "You want *me* to sit beside you?"

"Of course, I still want that." She said, exasperated, but desperate to have the chance to talk face to face.

"Okay, I'll sit beside you, Ella." He sounded tired, and all Ella could do was thank him.

Chapter 11

Why was it so dreary this Friday morning? Braig had no excitement for the weekend, the wedding, or the Buskie awards. He took inventory of his fully loaded truck when Jeanie materialized at his side. "You didn't find out the full story, did you?"

Her harsh words cut Braig to the core. "What's the point? I'm leaving anyway. I should never have let this happen. There's no other explanation. She's in deep with that Ex."

"Braig, you are as bull-headed as they come, son. If something is meant to be, it will be, despite circumstances." Jeanie said as she walked away, shaking her head.

Braig went through the motions of his day, making all his deliveries and heeding the warnings issued by his Pidge, and he avoided any end-of-week scoldings from Mann.

He dropped his keys on the floor when he got home and fell on the couch. Why had he given his heart away so quickly? It wasn't the first time, and he should have learned his lesson. His stomach ached. Was it hunger or just missing Ella's presence? She would be consumed with wedding festivities and not thinking about him in the slightest. He didn't move from the couch, falling quickly into a restless sleep.

Incessant ringing roused Braig at a quarter to ten that evening. He immediately reacted as if it was the Pidgeon, screaming at him with a message from Mann. Knocking the noisemaker off his lap, he rolled onto his side, and the stiff material of his uniform shocked him awake. Finally aware of his surroundings and the time, he reached to the floor and flipped his phone over. Ella?

His voice was strained and scratchy. "Hello?"

Still in a fog, he struggled to process what Ella said. Her voice was panicked. "The band," she said. "The band is sick."

The band. What band? Why do I care if a band is sick? "Huh?"

"Braig. Aunt Ritty's chamber music band, her mini-orchestra, the guys she was flying in especially for this wedding—they all have some violent stomach bug."

He rubbed his eyes, wondering why this was his business. "So, call your DJ back."

"I tried! He's already booked. Just listen, please."

"Okay, I'm listening, but I'll be honest, I don't know why you're telling me this."

"Look, Candace and Simon don't know about it, and we don't want them to have to worry. I've got the best man here with me. He left the bachelor party, and I cut the bachelorette party short. We have an idea that may solve this problem. But we need your help."

"I'm not a musician."

"I know. It's not that. You said you have a friend at work who knows every single one of the Buskers. Right? Do you think it's possible that we could get your friend involved and convince some Buskers to work together? Maybe they can form a band to perform at the wedding tomorrow night? Ritty is willing to pay handsomely for this if we can make it happen."

"My friend?" Braig shook his head trying to wake up. "It's Jeanie. Jeanie knows all the Buskers."

"Jeanie the mermaid knows all the Buskers?" It sounded as if laughter was coming through the line, but Braig couldn't be sure. "Can you call her?"

"It's ten o'clock."

"Wouldn't you say this is an emergency? Braig, if anyone would show up for you at this time of night, trust me, it's Jeanie."

Forty minutes later, Jeanie rode shotgun in Braig's blue car. "There's something special about that girl and the way she cares about you, Braig. She didn't flinch when I told her the story about Rita. She understood my meaning—that I had your back—and she still stuck around. Not to mention, she came to find you *at church*. That's a bold move."

"I did the same thing."

"Exactly. You two may just be able to work this out. I told you not to go silent on her, didn't I? Didn't you listen? I told you that appearances are deceiving." She leaned closer to him as he drove. "You've got to find out about the Natex driver. Ask her tonight."

"We kind of have a job to do tonight, Jeanie. Don't you think we'll be too busy?"

"No. I think *I'll* be busy. I'm going to take care of this and get a few of my friends to perform at this wedding, which will give you some time to talk things out with this girl. You made a rash decision here, Braig, I know it."

"I'm moving ten hours away!"

"A minor detail," Jeanie muttered.

"The fact of the matter is I shouldn't have dated her in the first place. It's the worst time to start a relationship, and you know how fast and hard I fall for people."

Jeanie scoffed. "It's the worst time on *your* timetable. But what if it's in the perfect slot on God's timetable?"

Braig groaned.

"You very well know this could be God's mercy on your life. Your stability. Your emotions. Your well-being. Your home. Your—"

"I get it. God knows more than I do."

Braig parked in the nearly empty town square. The only other cars were a pickup truck parked around the corner, and a Natex truck across the street. He opened the car door for Jeanie and they scanned the deserted area. "Where are they?"

The side door of the Natex truck flew open and Ella emerged. "Over here, you guys."

Blood rushed to Braig's face as he marched across the street. Ella ushered Jeanie into the front where she had been and hopped in the back, beckoning Braig to join her. "What's *he* doing here?" nodding toward the Natex driver.

"I told you I was with the best man."

"*He's* Simon's best man?"

"Yes." She nodded slowly. "That's Penn. I told you about him, remember? He's like a brother to me."

"Oh, a brother you make out with?" He hissed.

"What are you talking about?"

"You and him, in each other's arms? Monday morning—I was there. If you already had a boyfriend, why didn't you just tell me, and why did you ask *me* to Turner Heat? That seems kind of twisted."

"That's why you stopped communicating cold turkey? Why say you're being transferred if Penn was the problem?"

"I *am* being transferred. I just didn't want to tell you at first. But it doesn't matter. Don't worry—I'll be out of the way in a couple weeks so you and Penn can be all over each other."

"Braig. Listen to me."

"Ahem," came a voice from the front seat. Penn and Jeanie stared at them before Jeanie said flatly, "My new friend Penn and I have been talking here, and if you two could give us a few minutes to tackle the task at hand, we think we can get it done."

Ella responded with a sheepish, "Sorry."

Braig whispered, "Okay."

Penn shook his head. "Nope. You two obviously need some time to yourselves. There's a park bench right over there." He indicated to the front of Turner Heat Steakhouse.

"Penn, you're kicking us out of the truck? But the Buskers?"

Jeanie patted her knee. "We'll be back soon. We can't have arguing in the backseat the whole time. Now go on, you two. Out."

When Penn drove away, Braig and Ella stood on the street corner, unblinking.

Ella broke the silence. "I guess we should sit on the bench like we were told."

"I guess."

Each sat on opposite ends of the bench. Ella crossed her legs and let her gaze drift down the street. Braig leaned on the arm rest, muttering about how long it would take before Jeanie and Penn came back.

"What?"

"Nothing." He mumbled.

Ella sighed. "Braig, are you ready to listen? I need to tell you something."

Braig turned to face her,

Ella squared her shoulders and met his gaze. "Penn found Lloyd."

Braig leaned forward. "What?"

"Penn found my dog. The only thing I had left of my dead parents. Remember? Penn and his work buddies found him and brought him to me Monday morning. Yes, I was emotional. Yes, I hugged him. But ... I think it was justified."

Braig eased back. "He found your dog? Well, that would explain what I saw." He shifted uncomfortably. "But why didn't you tell me he worked for Natex in the first place?"

"Because I liked you!"

Braig jumped at the sound of her shouting. "Hey, calm down."

"No, Braig. There's no one around anyway, and everything's closed. Listen." She paused. "It's too late even for Busker music. I liked you, and I didn't think you'd want to hear that I'd been so close to a Natex driver."

"You're right. I wouldn't." He paused. "Because I liked you too. It's the same reason I couldn't tell you about my transfer right away."

She pulled her knees up onto the bench. "You can tell me about it now, if you want. It's not like I can do anything else."

He chuckled. "You probably still have a million things to do. But, if you really don't mind."

Braig cracked his heart wide open and poured out all the emotions he had been holding in for weeks. The misery of working for a man who treated him so terribly, the pressure he experienced daily, Jeanie's retirement looming, how the sound of the Pidgeon haunted his dreams, and his hope that this transfer would fix everything. He let her in fully, even explaining the doubt that had blindsided him when he met her.

Braig ended with, "Thanks for listening."

Ella nodded, tears in her eyes. She scooted closer to him and nudged his shoulder with her own, so he was fully facing her. Leaning toward him slowly, she gazed into his eyes. He lowered his head. When their lips were inches apart, both of their phones vibrated at once. They jumped.

Braig asked, "Should we look?"

She sighed. "Probably."

Chapter 12

The streets were empty as Braig drove toward Turner Towers to meet Jeanie and Penn.

"You have your dog back," he said, as if that fact was just sinking in. "That's great."

"It's a dream come true," Ella agreed. "Do you want to meet him?"

"Ooh ... Meet the dog?" He grimaced.

Ella was unfazed. "Lloyd is the most docile animal. He won't chase you, Braig. Even if you're in uniform. There's nothing to be afraid of."

"Well, I don't have much time left here. I should make the most of it, right?"

Ella smiled. "You should. But I wish you wouldn't go."

Braig was silent.

"Can I convince you to stay?"

"Ella. After everything I just unloaded? You'd ask me to stay? To keep working for Mann? With Jeanie retiring, ... I-I guess I can't believe you'd even suggest it."

"That's not what I'm suggesting. People change jobs all the time."

"I'm not people." Braig said defensively. "There's nothing wrong with being loyal to a company and building a career."

Ella didn't argue further.

He peered out the windshield as the street signs silently passed, each one so familiar. He would miss this place. He glanced at Ella. He would miss her too.

The parking lot hosted a single streetlamp where Braig parked. "I guess they're not quite here yet."

"Guess again." Ella pointed as the blue and white Natex truck raced into the lot from the opposite direction, stopping next to Braig's car.

Penn and Jeanie both jumped out of the truck and were standing at the back before Braig and Ella could open their doors.

"It was all her." Penn grabbed the door handles and swung them open.

Hank's head was the first to pop out, saxophone around his neck. "You the bride? How's about a kiss?"

"No, Hank, you'll see the bride tomorrow, and only the groom gets to kiss her, buddy." Jeanie patted his back as he passed.

Juliana sat on the edge of the truck bed and gracefully lowered herself to the pavement before grabbing her guitar and smiling at Braig and Ella. "My dancers," she crooned. "Congratulations, you two."

"We're not getting married," Braig and Ella stumbled over the statement at the same time.

Another couple of Buskers hopped out of the truck, one with an accordion, and one with an oboe. Seamus stayed inside, his hand on his huge keyboard. "All right, who's helping get my baby inside?"

Penn and Braig both stood close while Seamus pushed the piano gently to the edge. Juliana threw her guitar strap over her shoulder and turned to the other musicians. "Let's get this rehearsal started. Do you guys know 'Endless Love?'" She strummed a chord and began singing. The sound of the accordion and the saxophone soon followed as they casually played, sang together, and walked toward the white reception hall.

"Wait for me." Seamus called. "We've almost got it."

Jeanie stood by the truck, smiling and calm. Ella covered her mouth with both hands and laughed, then rushed at her. "Oh Jeanie. You *are* a mermaid. A magical, magical mermaid!" She threw her arms around Jeanie's neck and squeezed for a long moment.

Then, a voice from behind made her let go. "She certainly is."

Ella turned around. "Aunt Ritty. You're still here?"

"Rita?" Jeanie's eyes were shining. She stepped away from Ella and threw herself into Aunt Ritty's arms. The women laughed and gasped when they let go of each other, seemingly in disbelief at this unlikely reunion after midnight in a parking lot just outside Buskerton, USA—so far from Aspaldiko Island where they swam and posed and smiled as mermaids in the sunshine so long ago.

"Don't tell me you live here." Aunt Ritty hooked arms with Jeanie as they walked toward the entrance, and Jeanie prattled about the past forty years. Ella lagged behind them, content.

Just before they reached the reception hall, Braig rushed around the two friends and took Ella's shoulders. "I had no idea what you were capable of."

Ella stiffened. "What are you talking about? What am I capable of?"

"The décor in there." He pointed to the reception hall. "It's something *else*."

"What? We're not decorating until tomorrow." She grabbed Braig's arm and went in.

The tablecloths were ironed on each round table, with jars of pebbles and the picture frame candle holders they'd worked so hard on last weekend in the center. The Buskers continued their melodic warming up in the corner of the room while Penn adjusted microphone stands for them. Jeanie and Aunt Ritty sat together in two covered chairs, bows carefully tied at the backs. Ella spun to take it all in.

All the tulle that caused her so much anxiety for the past two weeks now hung in thick, flowing strips all around the edges of the room. Each piece was bunched at the ceiling and cascaded to the floor, white lights glittering behind them. A ladder leaned against the corner of the room, and Sherr stood at the top, affixing the last section of tulle to the wall. She turned and smiled at Ella, then climbed down.

"What do you think?" She asked, her hair in a thick, messy bun.

Ella shook her head in disbelief.

"We never should have doubted Aunt Ritty. I'm so glad she called me tonight to come help, since you guys were dealing with the band debacle. I can't wait for Candace to see this tomorrow."

Sherr let out a small squeal, as Penn came up behind her and grabbed her around the waist. He spun her away from Braig and Ella and trapped her with a hard kiss on the lips. They walked away in rhythm to the Buskers' rehearsing, stealing a moment alone.

Braig was wide eyed, "Now *that's* a meaningful embrace."

Ella chuckled. "I forgot to mention that, didn't I? You believe me now that Penn and I aren't together?"

He nodded. "Yep. And she's right. Candace and Simon are

going to think this is beautiful tomorrow. Aunt Ritty really came through, huh?"

"She is amazing." Ella grinned and spun again to get a full three-sixty view.

"Is this what you envisioned?" He asked her.

Ella stopped spinning and whispered, "Better."

Eighteen hours later, the unconventional band deftly played a set romantic enough for a wedding atmosphere and upbeat enough to dance to.

Simon's mother touched Ella's shoulder as she walked past her table. "The ceremony was splendid, Ella. And the reception is beautiful. Thank you for everything you did." Ella thanked her in return, then scanned the room nervously.

Braig, seated next to Ella according to their agreement, leaned toward her. "Everything's perfect. What are you anxious about?"

"Don't you see what everyone is doing? They're all on their phones. The Buskies. It's terrible." She glanced at Braig's phone, set beside his plate. "You've been doing it too."

"It is embarrassing, isn't it? We're all obsessed."

"Sherr is about to give her speech, but look at her." Sherr stared intently at the device in her lap. "Even the maid of honor."

Braig's phone lit up. "We won," he whispered. "USSS won." His voice rose.

"Shh," Ella hissed. "I thought you didn't care."

Braig concentrated on the screen again. "Oh," his voice sounded disappointed. "Oh, no."

"What? Did you read it wrong?"

He sighed. "No, we actually won. Mann sent a mass text."

He turned the screen to Ella so she could read Mr. Mann's congratulations to all the USSS employees, full of disparaging slurs and insults about Natex included. "I guess I shouldn't be surprised."

She scooted the phone back to him. "Is he really encouraging you to rub their faces in it?"

Braig powered down the phone and set it aside.

The Buskers' music faded out, and Penn took the microphone, composed and smiling. "Hi, my name is Penn, and I had the absolute honor of being Simon's best man. My first memory of Simon is incidentally my first memory ever. I was five, and I distinctly remember that this new friend of mine was such a liar. We were on the back deck of his house, when he turned to me and said." Penn paused, grinning and breathing through the guffawing laughter trying to escape. "Hey, I can ride my dog. Want to see?"

Penn held the microphone closer to be heard over the chuckles in the audience. "And then, he hopped on his Doberman and made it all the way down the steps.

"People ask me if he fell off. I don't know! All I remember is being shocked and awed that he made it all the way to the yard riding that dog. I realized that day that Simon was not a liar. He was just a really funny kid. It wasn't the last time I would be in awe of my best friend.

"Simon, I've always felt inadequate next to you. *You're* the best man in the room, and the best man in my life, and I am eternally grateful that you've found the best woman. You're a light in this world, and she makes you even brighter. May you continue to allow God to work in your lives, making each other better. Even better than either of you can think or imagine."

As they raised their glasses of sparkling punch, Sherr took the microphone, tears and elation in her eyes. "When Candace asked me to be her maid of honor, I couldn't believe it. Don't get me wrong—she's my best friend, my person, my mirror in many ways. No, I couldn't believe it because Candace of all people knows how busy I am."

Braig leaned and whispered to Ella, "I remember that dog. It was huge."

"Hey, we won the Buskie, too," she whispered back, excited.

"Shouldn't you be focused on the speeches right now?" He elbowed her side.

She laughed. "I had to check. Look at Sherr. She's so emotional." Ella pointed to the stage. "She's absolutely blubbering. She loves Candace, but that's not all about her."

Sherr sighed through her tears. "Candace, you deserve a man who treats you like a princess. And today you married him."

Applause and spoons tinkling on glasses echoed through the reception hall as Simon and Candace kissed.

When the cake was cut, Ella checked the time. The Buskies would be winding down now, and everyone would have the results. The music picked back up.

"Want to dance?" Braig offered his hand.

Ella wanted to resist. This would be their last dance. But she took his hand, and he twirled her onto the dance floor. She became light-headed and forgot for a moment that he was leaving, until Penn's voice broke in.

"Hey, I just got a message from my boss. Congrats to USSS by the way." He smiled genuinely. "But I wanted to let you know." Braig nodded, inviting Penn to explain. "One of our guys just got promoted to the corporate office, so his position is open. The big man wants to know if we have any recommendations. Want me to throw your name in the ring?"

"A job at Natex?" Braig's feet stopped moving.

"It's a great place to work. Jeanie told me about what you

put up with at USSS. None of that goes on at Natex. We're like a brotherhood. They're the ones who banded together to help me find Lloyd. You would love it." Penn turned back to Sherr and started dancing again, but called over his shoulder. "Just think about it, man."

Braig was clearly in shock and stammered, "A job at Natex?"

Ella smiled at him. "What do you think?"

"I think *Natex* sounds like *latex*."

"Let's go somewhere and talk out the pros and cons, huh?" She led him down a hallway, through a metal door, and sat on the top of the stairwell, the music still drifting in from the reception hall. He sat beside her.

Ella gave him time to process Penn's offer, and after several minutes, he said, "What about my step raises?"

"Your experience would count for something," she said. "That's how jobs work."

"But it's Natex."

"Braig, what if you could get the lies Mann told you out of your mind?"

He shook his head. "Is it a lie that Natex is terrible?"

Ella took his shoulders. "Yes."

He gazed into her eyes. "I don't know what to do."

She stroked his cheek. "You don't have to decide right this second. Just breathe." Then, she leaned forward closing the gap and lightly touched her lips to his.

To her surprise, Braig laughed. Ella gasped and backed away quickly.

"Wait. Don't be offended." He caught her hand in his. "Ella, how many dates did you ask me on? And now you're the first one to lean in for a kiss?" He stopped laughing, stood, and pulled her up, as well. "You surely are a go-getter, girl. I wish I was more like you." Then, he kissed *her*, dipping her theatrically to prove he meant it.

BACK IN THE RECEPTION HALL, Aunt Ritty handed Braig and Ella a sparkler with an excited smile. "The bride and groom are heading out in just a few minutes."

They linked arms and followed the crowd outside. "Was that supposed to be you?" Braig nodded toward Aunt Ritty.

"Eh. She can be the showrunner for this production. It's fine if every single person thinks she planned it from beginning to end. I don't care. Appearances aren't everything." Then they took their place in the line of guests next to Penn and Sherr.

Penn brightened. "There you are. Sorry I didn't get your permission first, but I went ahead and told my boss about you. He said he would jump at the chance to get a USSS carrier over to the dark side." He laughed. "Can you come in and interview as a formality Monday morning?"

"Sure," Braig said, certainty in his voice. "Tell him I'm there."

Ella squeezed his hand and leaned into his ear. "You know what this means, don't you?"

"What?" He whispered back.

"You have to meet Lloyd."

He laughed. "I'll meet him for you." He spun her around again, then pulled her in for an embrace. "And what about you? Will you join a social media platform?"

"Hmm." She pondered for a moment while they lit their sparklers. "Can I post a picture of you and me and Lloyd?"

He chuckled. "Sure thing."

About Rachel Herod

Rachel Herod holds both a bachelor's and master's degree in education, which she put to good use for thirteen years as a public school teacher. When she isn't writing, you can find her spending time with her husband, caring for their two kids and three cats, and volunteering as a crisis counselor for The Crisis Text Line.

More Romance Collections
from Scrivenings Press

Love in Any Season

A novella collection

Spring Has Sprung—by Regina Rudd Merrick

Laurel Pascal, Assistant City Manager of Spring, Kentucky, is tasked with organizing the town's beloved Daffodil Festival, and she's not happy. An allergy sufferer all her life, she dreads the season from the first Daffodil bloom in the yard to the last coat of pollen on her car. Newcomer Dr. Owen Roswell volunteers to help, and soon finds that not only does Laurel need his expertise as an allergist, but help in appreciating the season she's obligated to celebrate.

What does he want more—for Laurel to fall in love with his favorite season? Or him?

The Missing Piece—by Amy R. Anguish

Beth Norton and Tommy England grew up together with best-friend moms who had a love of quilting and a business celebrating the craft. When high school ended, though, so did Beth and Tommy's friendship.

When Tommy moves back after seven years and his mother's death, he can't understand why Beth is so angry with him. Helping Beth and her mother stabilize the finances of the business, they're forced to work together. As Tommy sorts through his mother's things, he finds an unfinished quilt, and it turns into a joint project.

With each stitch taken, they work toward more than just a completed blanket.

A Sweet Dream Come True—by Sarah Anne Crouch

Isaac Campbell is living his dream of running an ice cream shop but fears he won't last past the first difficult year. Mel Wilson is a busy single mother who longs to be a chocolatier but is too afraid to turn her dreams into reality.

When Mel and Isaac meet at Bestwood, Tennessee's fall festival, it seems like divine providence. But once Mel agrees to help Isaac bring in customers by selling her chocolates at his shop, she realizes how challenging running a business can be.

Can Mel and Isaac trust in God's provision and make a leap of faith? Will their partnership end in disaster, or will it be a sweet dream come true?

Sugar and Spice—by Heather Greer

Emeline Becker, owner of Sugar and Spice Bakery, loves New Kuchenbrünn, except for the gingerbread. As the only bakery, she supplies the annual Gingerbread Festival with the one treat she can't stand. It's gingerbread everywhere.

Things get worse when Ryker Lehmann is hired as the festival photographer. He was her secret teen crush, her sister's boyfriend, and witness to her worst humiliation. Plus, he broke her sister's heart and bruised hers when he left town after graduation. Now, he's back in town, determined to fix their friendship before the festival ends.

With gingerbread and Ryker together, can Emmie make it through the festival with her mind and heart intact?

Get your copy here:

https://scrivenings.link/loveinanyseason

Candy Cane Wishes and Saltwater Dreams

A collection of Christmas beach romances

***Mistletoe Make-believe* by Amy Anguish**—Charlie Hill's family thinks his daughter Hailey needs a mom—to the point they won't get off his back until he finds her one. Desperate to be free from their nagging, he asks a stranger to pretend she's his girlfriend during the holidays. When romance author Samantha Arwine takes a working vacation to St. Simon's Island over Christmas, she never dreamed she'd be involved in a real-life romance. Are the sparks between her and Charlie real? Or is her imagination over-acting ... again?

***A Hatteras Surprise* by Hope Toler Dougherty**—Ginny Stowe spent years tending a childhood hurt that dictated her college study and work. Can time with an island visitor with ties to her past heal lingering wounds and lead her toward a happy Christmas ... and more? Ben Daniels intends to hire a new branch manager for a Hatteras Island bank, then hurry back to his promotion and Christmas in Charlotte. Spending time with a beautiful local, however, might force him to adjust his sails.

***A Pennie for Your Thoughts* by Linda Fulkerson**—When the Lakeshore Homeowner's Association threatens to condemn the cabin Pennie Vaughn inherited from her foster mother, her only hope of funding the needed repairs lies in winning a travel blog contest. Trouble is, Pennie never goes anywhere. Should she use the all-expenses paid Hawaiian vacation offered to her by her ex-fiancé? The trip that would have been their honeymoon?

***Mr. Sandman* by Regina Rudd Merrick**—Events manager Taylor Fordham's happily-ever-after was snatched from her, and she's saying no to romance and Christmas. When she meets two new friends—the cute new chef at Pilot Oaks and a contributor on a sci-fi fan fiction website who enjoys debate—her resolve begins to waver. Just when she thinks she can loosen her grip on thoughts of love, a crisis pulls her back. There's no way she's going to risk her heart again.

***Coastal Christmas* by Shannon Taylor Vannatter**—Lark Pendleton is banking on a high-society wedding to make her grandparent's inn at Surfside Beach, Texas the venue to attract buyers. Tasked with sprucing up the inn, she hires Jace Wilder, whose heart she once broke. When the bride and groom turn out to be Lark's high school nemesis and ex-boyfriend, she and Jace embark on a pretend romance to save the wedding. But when real feelings emerge, can they overcome past hurts?

Stay up-to-date on your favorite books and authors with our free e-newsletters.

ScriveningsPress.com